HE FOLLOWS ME

KATHRYN CARAWAY

ADINK.COM
AFTER DARK INK
PUBLISHING CO.

After Dark Ink Publishing Co.

www.adink.com

After Dark Ink Publishing Co. books may be purchased in bulk. For more information, please contact the publisher at info@adink.com.

Printed in USA on paper that is sustainably harvested and Forest Stewardship Council (FSC) certified.

ISBN: 979 8 9990545-5-5 (Paperback)

ISBN: 979-8-9990545-2-4 (ebook)

LCCN: 2025946219

For you—
For the love that never faded,
For finding me when I couldn't find myself,
And for showing me that I was still worth loving.

PREFACE

This book chronicles the fictional repercussions of stalking, but its roots burrow deep into my personal experience. I lived as the target of a stalker whose cruelty was matched only by his cunning. The sense of being watched, of having every movement interpreted by someone with unknown intentions, filtered into every facet of my life. I grew accustomed to the sound of my own breathing at night, the constant vigilance, the mapping of escape routes through places that should have felt safe.

After I wrote my true crime memoir, *Unfollow Me*, I was struck by the question:

What if there was a program, a lifeline, a means of escape not just from the stalker but from the psychic debris left in the wake of his obsession?

Out of this thought came the fictional blueprint for the Victim Protection Program in this story.

This book is not merely suspense or intrigue, but portrays the aftermath of stalking—the ripples that never quite dissipate. The protagonist, like many victims, is shaped as much by the bureaucracy of the judicial system as she is the cultural indifference to stalking. She is fragile yet fierce. Clever yet incapable of letting the past remain in the past. She is not me, but she carries my scars.

This fiction is liberally seasoned with truth, though often in disguise. The events herein did not happen as written, but the underlying terror, the paranoia, are all borrowed from lived experience. If the narrative sometimes veers into the surreal or the melodramatic, it is only because real life did so first.

Kathryn Caraway

CHAPTER 1

In my world, nothing is a coincidence. Especially when I'm alone, driving on a two-lane road heading back home. There's no warning, just the impact of steel against steel, a crash that crumples my car like aluminum foil. My head whips forward, and the airbag welcomes my skull with a dizzying embrace. The whole car spins, wild, out of control, heading for a ditch—the windshield blooms with fractures. I'm upside down now. Smoke drifts like a sinister ghost. It's in my eyes, stinging, clouding everything. I'm alive. Somehow.

Dizzy.

Panicking.

The other car came out of nowhere. How could I not see it?

Everything goes still. My mind goes blank—like I've forgotten how to think. I'm hanging from my seat belt. Everything is blurry. I blink rapidly. A horn blares from somewhere. Blood rushes to my skull; my hands fight the law of gravity for the seat belt. It gives way, and I fall like dead weight. My shoulder strikes the roof, causing a bolt of pain. I'm on the ceiling now —or the floor. Maybe the window. The whole world is spinning. My mouth tastes like blood. There's a voice outside: a shrill sound of panic that makes everything seem unreal. My mind won't clear.

The airbag is a limp white shroud, stinking of burned hair and chemicals. I crawl like a wounded animal; gravel and glass pierce my palms. My head throbs. I fumble at the car door handle, pushing until it gives way. The smell of burnt rubber fills the air. A bird chirps somewhere—a too-ordinary sound for a moment that feels anything but. My heart is beating fast—too fast. Someone is shouting.

"Are you okay?" A woman's voice quakes with concern. I can't see her through the haze of smoke.

Maybe I am.

Maybe I'm not.

Maybe I don't care.

I stagger from the wreckage. My head's spinning—an unbalanced top too close to the edge. The woman's shouting voice pierces my confusion.

"I called 911! Help is coming."

I cringe. There's a wicked irony in that.

"Are you alright?"

I don't know where she is. Her voice is too loud. She's close.

"You're lucky. Really lucky."

This is not luck. I am never lucky. I manage a nod; the effort is too much, too soon. She's at my side now—too close. Asking questions. I'm sure she thinks she's helping.

She's not.

"The other guy looks hurt." She points toward him, then turns back to me. "Is there anything I can do?"

The woman reaches for my arm. The touch is too personal, too invasive. I flinch away. I'm shaking like a leaf caught in a storm, untethered and terrified.

Her long, straight hair settles over her shoulder, blonde strands that look like corn silk. "Is there someone you want me to call for you?"

Cooper. Bill Cooper.

My ears are ringing, but I can still hear his voice from the meeting I just left. "If anything happens, you call me first."

Something happened. I need to make that call.

"Where's my phone?" My voice cracks as I speak, barely louder than a whisper.

"Do you want to use mine?" She extends her phone toward me.

I shake my head. "I need mine."

I don't know Bill Cooper's number, but I know I need to call him, and I know he programmed it into my phone.

"Stay here."

The lady squeezes herself into the cramped, twisted remains. Her torso disappears into the mangled metal, while her legs flail out of the passenger door. Finally, she shuffles backward, careful not to bump her head, and stands up straight. Holding my phone up, she waves her arm triumphantly.

"Must be a good mount. The screen's not even shattered."

I take the lifeline from her, forgetting to thank her. She turns her attention back to the driver of the other vehicle.

Sirens cry out in the distance. I feel the blood drain from my face. My pulse quickens. I don't have a license, nor any identification, for that matter. My mind scrambles, frantic. My fingers fumble with the phone.

I just met Bill Cooper an hour ago. He told me to call. I'm calling. My breath comes in shallow, shivering gasps.

I hold the phone with a firm grip. He'll answer. He has to answer.

Why isn't Cooper answering?

The line clicks—an endless second of static-filled silence—then his voice. I nearly collapse with relief. I imagine his expression is calm, like when he was taking my photo an hour ago for the IDs I need but don't have.

His voice cuts through my panic like a hot blade, reassuring and firm. "Bill Cooper."

He sounds calm, cool, and collected. I am not. I tell him I have been in an accident. He doesn't miss a beat.

"Ten minutes ago. You left my sight ten minutes ago."

I imagine him checking his watch. He's got it under control.

"Where are you?"

The sirens close in—closer and closer. Like they'll never stop.

I look around. "Hol—" The word catches in my throat. I draw a shaky breath before trying again. "Holden Road, just off Route 12."

"I'm on my way." He says it like it's nothing, like the police aren't about to swarm me. "Don't say anything until I get there. Hold tight." As he pauses, I let the weight of his words settle over me. "I'll handle it."

His confidence is infectious. I want to believe him. My throat tightens. "I don't have my license. I don't have anything." My voice sounds less frantic now.

"Don't talk to anyone." A quick, decisive order. I can imagine the look on his face—that hint of a smile, the one that lets me know I'm his project now. "Let me take care of it."

A police car arrives, its lights flashing—a carnival of panic. The woman waves them down, pointing to the other driver. She's shouting, but I can't make out her words—only her tone.

"How long?" I gasp into the phone. "How long until you're here?"

A second that feels like a lifetime, before his voice returns, composed and reassuring.

"Five minutes."

Less, I hope.

A policeman races toward the other vehicle. I see the driver slumped over the wheel, unmoving. There's blood. He looks seriously injured. I should feel something for him, something human, but the only thing I feel is dread. The same dread I've been feeling for years now.

It's a terrible certainty—the way my mind jumps to conclusions, connections, conspiracies. *What if this isn't a coincidence? What if he's something else? Someone else? What if it's all connected—part of some larger plan, some scheme to find me, finish me? Does he know Todd?* The thoughts gnaw at my insides, a cancer of paranoia.

Paramedics arrive. They rush to the driver from the wreckage—a tangle of limbs. I lean to the side, trying to see his face—see if I recognize him, but the movement is too much, and everything is a blur. The paranoia grows, and I convince myself it's no accident. Even though Todd Bennett is in jail, he continues to taunt me. They say inmates don't have computer access, but I know the messages I'm getting are from him. Or maybe they are from the guy on that gurney. They come from a different email address each time. Coming from hell.

The last one was specific: "On the day I kill you, I will send a dozen yellow roses to cover up the stench of your rotting corpse."

I didn't get any roses today. If someone sends those kinds of messages, maybe they will kill me for him. It's not uncommon for someone to order a hit from behind the concrete walls of a jail cell.

Fear. I can't keep it in. Can't contain it. It pulses through me in waves. *God, help me.* I am painfully aware that I am in the open and vulnerable for all to see. Maybe I'll die here. Maybe this is how Todd finally wins.

CHAPTER 2

Todd Bennett will never let me go. Never let me truly live. It's his eyes I remember most from the night he tried to kidnap me—those cold, hungry eyes. His grip on my hair as he dragged me; the memory claws at my throat, choking me.

He's a sick bastard with no regard for anyone but himself. I think about the fear, the sickening dread that floods my veins every time a shadow passes outside a window. His voice flits through my mind and hits like ice water down my spine. Todd's voice is so confident: "You are mine, and I don't share."

It's almost funny how people talk about closure like it's a door they get to slam shut. No one talks about how, sometimes, the lock is on the other side. I've become a prisoner of fear.

"He'll just move on to someone else," well-meaning friends and family tell me.

But they don't know Todd like I do. Before the trial, Todd had moved on and started dating someone else, taking her places where he knew I would be. She saw me. He moved on, but he didn't forget about me. She became a witness in my stalking case.

So, no, I don't think he will move on. I think I will suffer a death I will not see coming. And for good reason. Todd once asked if I wanted to see death coming. I answered no. Every day since, I've waited for a death I will not see coming.

Waiting.

Always waiting.

Maybe this was the death I wasn't supposed to see coming. I never saw the truck. I can't remember what happened. My knees go weak, and I grab the lady's arm. Her corn-silk strands fan out as she spins her head to me.

"Let's sit you down." She guides me to the shoulder of the road.

"What happened?" My lips move, but even I can hardly hear the sound.

"I was in the car behind you. You weren't speeding. The guy pulled out from that driveway over yonder." She turns and points.

My body is numb. I am incapable of sudden movement. I turn my head in what feels like slow motion. There's a gravel road leading up to a farmhouse.

The woman is still talking. ". . . t-boned you on the passenger side. I think that big cattle guard he has on the grille is probably what rolled your car."

Dizzy and sick, I press my hands to the ground to steady myself. There's a patch of weeds—some of them flattened, probably from the accident. Among the weeds are flowers. Not gold, not daisy, but bile, wound-pus yellow—the color of warning signs and ancient bruises. The color of Todd's promise. Yellow is a warning, a prophecy. A bloom of decay. I want to look away. I can't. The flowers multiply. Every time I blink, there are more. I wonder how many it takes to cover the smell of a rotting corpse.

Todd's sinister promise after the stalking trial hit me.

"You're going to regret this," he had said after I read my victim impact statement in court. They all said it wasn't a threat. It was just frustration. But regret is a future tense—a promise. Like the yellow roses.

After an infuriatingly short sentence, Todd racked up probation violations and was sent back to jail. That's where he is now, waiting to be released. I just left the courthouse to plan for when he gets to walk out of jail a free man.

The meeting was to plan my future. That's where I met Bill Cooper, the deputy U.S. Marshal working with the state attorney general's office on the Victim Protection Program. So many people involved; I can't keep them all straight.

But Cooper is who I need most while I wait on the side of the road.

"Ma'am," a voice in the distance calls out. "Ma'am."

I see an officer approaching me. The wreck. The driver. Todd. I want to run. But where? There's nowhere to go. The officer moves closer, his radio crackling. I wonder if he knows Todd. Todd was the IT guy for the police department. Even though he didn't wear a badge or carry a gun on his hip, he was their go-to guy for all things technical—a powerful position to hold. I've learned the hard way how far they're willing to go to protect their own.

"Ma'am, were you the driver of the other vehicle?"

It's a legitimate question, but Cooper has told me not to say anything. I swallow hard. My throat constricts with the swell of emotions threatening to overtake me. I nod.

"Are you injured?"

I touch my face. My lip is split. Fingers come away sticky and red. I shake my throbbing head.

"Okay, ma'am. Sit tight."

I watch as he rushes back to the other driver. Paramedics are crowded around him. They're trying to help, doing what I should be doing. But I don't move. I feel panic claw at me like a living thing.

"It doesn't look like that guy's airbag went off," the woman says. She gasps when he's pulled out of the truck and onto a gurney, a cervical collar already on his neck. I look at his still form as they buckle him in.

The officer is walking toward me again. "Would you like the paramedics to check you out?"

I shake my head.

"You might be in shock, miss. I'll have them look you over."

A paramedic with a bag approaches. A gloved hand probes my split lip. His voice murmurs my vital signs. He sounds distant, underwater.

The medic leans over me. "What's your name?"

I look around for Cooper. I see an officer in the middle of the road, directing traffic. There's barely any traffic on this desolate stretch. A car creeps by. The driver gapes.

"Ma'am, can you hear me?" he says louder.

I'm not hard of hearing. I don't have an answer to your simple question. Because in your simple world, a name exists. My world is not so simple.

He places an oxygen mask over my face. I catch fragments: "pupils responsive," "possible concussion," "BP and heart rate stable." The paramedic loops the stethoscope around his neck.

My eyes dart around. *Where the hell is Cooper?*

The officer approaches while the paramedic stuffs the blood pressure cuff into his bag, then looks at me. "Are you in any pain?"

I don't know. My body feels numb. I shake my head.

The officer towers over us, his hand resting on top of the gun holstered at his hip.

"She's stable. Refuses medical treatment. I'll get a form for her to sign." The paramedic grabs his bag and casually walks back to the ambulance, as though this is just another day at work for him.

"Ma'am."

My head snaps toward the officer, leaving me dizzy.

"I'll need to get some information from you. License, registration, and insurance, please."

"I . . . I don't have them," I stammer, my voice shaking. "They're . . . they're in the car." It's a lie, but it's all I have. All I can offer.

"Stay here," he orders, his tone leaving no room for argument. "I'll be right back." He turns, striding toward my overturned vehicle with purposeful steps. I watch him, my heart pounding, my breath coming in shallow gasps.

I think about the paramedic's form I need to sign. *What name do I sign? And where the hell is Cooper?*

The world is closing in, suffocating me. I cast a desperate glance over my shoulder, searching for Cooper, for salvation. There is only chaos. I am trapped. Caught between the wreckage of my car and the wreckage of my life.

CHAPTER 3

A black SUV with red and blue lights flashing from behind the grille arrives. I inhale sharply, hoping it's Bill Cooper. The vehicle jerks to a stop, and the driver's door flings open. When I see Cooper, I finally exhale. He strides toward the officer with calm assurance. Relief floods through me, a temporary reprieve. He's talking to the officer, his posture relaxed, his expression unreadable. The officer nods in my direction. I'm frozen, rooted to the spot—unable to move, breathe, or think.

Another officer approaches Cooper, and they confer, their heads bent together, their voices low. They're talking about me, I'm sure of it—deciding what to do with the woman who doesn't exist, who shouldn't be here. Time stretches like a rubber band. Seconds turn into minutes, minutes into eons. The world spins on, but I'm stuck in this moment, this nightmare.

I think back to the meeting I had before this accident. The grim-faced team from the attorney general's office regarded me with a mix of sympathy and expectation. Their offer of a new identity through the program hung in the air between us—a lifeline, they called it.

"Our proposal is protective relocation," Cooper had said. "Not as drastic as full witness protection, but sufficient to keep you safe."

He said it as if he were ordering a sandwich—no mayo. Cooper is the epitome of a seasoned federal law enforcement officer. His face bears the markings of a life of secrecy, with lines etched deeply into his skin from years of clandestine work. His right hand twitched sporadically—a slight nervous tick reminiscent of my late grandfather.

"Ms. Caraway, we understand this is an incredibly difficult decision," Deputy U.S. Marshal Akira Yamada said. Her voice was gentle but firm. "But given the imminent threat posed by Todd Bennett, we believe this is the best way to ensure your safety."

Todd Bennett. Hearing the name made my gut twist.

Yamada lowered her voice as if to imitate compassion. "Most victims of your stalker's profile do not come out unscathed. The ones that do follow our advice."

Follow our advice—like it's a one-size-fits-all T-shirt you get at a fair.

I cleared my throat, annoyed. "To clarify, he is not *my* stalker." I threw my hands up in air quotes for emphasis. "I bear no ownership in any of this, in the way I do *my* car or *my* house or *my* dog." My voice was sharp and strong. I will not allow anyone to insinuate I had responsibility for this crime—this mess that has become my life. Sure, there are things I could've, would've, should've done differently, but I didn't ask for any of this.

"It's important you understand," Cooper said, as though he were talking to a confused child. "We've seen these cases end tragically when the victim declines protection."

Yamada nodded, a neat and mechanical gesture. Her perfect black hair bobbed on the shoulder of her perfectly pressed black suit.

I think they were imagining my obituary in the newspaper. Maybe it's because I was picturing it there, too.

Papers slid across the table in a neat stack, ready for my signature. It was a sea of legal jargon, and I was in a rowboat, taking on water, like I am now. On the side of the road. Drowning in chaos, watching Cooper handle the situation.

I flicked through the pages carelessly. Tears fell. The pen moved. The room was silent, except for the faint sound of the sweeping motion of pen on paper. When I pushed the stack across the table to Cooper, my hand lingered on the top, as though my fingers were unwilling to part with it.

That's the moment when Kathryn Caraway ceased to exist. There will be no funeral, no mourners. There will only be me—nameless, on the side of the road.

The fire department is arriving. So are more officers. The blonde lady is talking to one of them—her corn-silk hair swaying in concert with her animated gestures.

Paramedics are lifting the driver of the truck into the ambulance. I don't mean to feel envious, but I do. I don't know if he will be okay. I don't know if I will be okay. Maybe I want to be on the gurney—a toe tag dangling.

Cooper breaks away from the officers and trots toward me, his eyes never leaving mine. My stomach churns, and I wonder if I'm going to throw up.

"Let's get you out of here." He gestures with a nod toward the black SUV. He opens the door and offers a hand as I climb in. I grasp it like I'm wading through molasses. Everything feels like it's happening in slow motion, but I manage to click my seatbelt into place—that's one thing I won't forget to do.

"After tomorrow, you won't need your car anyway." Cooper slides into the driver's seat.

"The other driver, is he . . ." My voice fades as I contemplate. I should ask if he is okay, but what I really want to ask is if he is connected to Todd.

"He's badly hurt, but he'll pull through."

That's not what I want to know.

"Is he connected to Todd?"

"The same thought crossed my mind. I checked. The guy lives at that little white farmhouse. Looks like he was just leaving his house."

"His airbag didn't go off?"

"Doesn't look like it. The locals will investigate."

Great. The locals—the local police who worked with Todd before he became a convicted stalker. The ones who didn't believe he was stalking me. I don't have faith in *the locals*.

Cooper reaches out and adjusts an air vent on me. "You sure you don't want to go to the hospital to at least get checked out?"

I shake my head, then realize his eyes are darting everywhere but at me. He checks the mirrors every few seconds. "No."

"Any plans for tonight?"

"Last-minute packing." I interlace my fingers to hide the tremble. The seatbelt chafes the side of my neck—I can't decide whether it's too tight or not tight enough.

My gaze drifts to the window. The black SUV makes a left turn, and I know we are not far from my house now. My nose flares with a sharp inhale. Images flood through my mind—the dead black of Todd's eyes as he watched from my backyard; the horror of finding hidden cameras in my bedroom and bathroom; the sickening realization that even my most private moments had been violated, broadcast for his twisted enjoyment. Even now, separated by prison walls, I feel the weight of his obsession bearing down on me. He is like a storm I can't outrun.

"Want me to come in with you? Just to make sure everything's okay?" Cooper turns the steering wheel as we pull into my driveway.

"Nah, I'm good."

"Alright. Just give me a call if you need anything. I'll be here at eight a.m. sharp to pick you up."

I shower. It's the last shower I'll ever have in this house—the one I've called home for nearly eighteen years. The house that belongs to a name that no longer exists. I wipe the condensation from the mirror. The woman staring back is nobody. I go to bed, which is just a mattress on the floor of my empty bedroom. I gave away all my furniture, donating what people didn't want.

Lying in my now bare bedroom, I feel the weight of what I've let go. My eyelids start to droop, but every time I get close to sleep, my brain yanks me back. I shut my eyes and count the seconds. I do this dance throughout the night—until I can't stand it anymore.

I cast a wary glance around, half expecting Todd to materialize from the shadows. It's 4:37 a.m.—too early to call it morning and too late to go back to sleep. I wrap a blanket around me and shuffle down the hallway. Every part of my body aches in protest of even the tiniest movement. But the body aches pale in comparison to the one in my chest. My eyes linger on nail holes where family photographs once hung. Memories that now sit in a box—boxes that movers will come later to retrieve and store.

The Keurig on the counter is the last remaining artifact from the array of kitchen appliances I've collected over the years. I drop a pod in and hit the button. The sound of coffee brewing echoes in the quiet kitchen. Tendrils of the rich, earthy aroma soon waft through the air, reaching me in a familiar embrace. It feels like I am moving in slow motion—maybe because this is my last morning here. In this house. In this city. In this state. In this country.

A plastic knife scrapes against toast, spreading golden butter as it melts into the crisp surface. I wipe off the excess on the edge of a paper plate, then toss the knife into a box of trash on the floor. My fingers curl around a disposable cup, and I lift it to my lips. The steam rises in lazy spirals, promising the caffeine I need to get through today. My lip is swollen—the small tear a painful reminder of the accident. I sit on a lone barstool at the kitchen counter, eating toast and tentatively drinking coffee as the sun rises. Time is not relevant. I just want to take it all in.

This is the last time I'll walk these floors, touch these doorframes, breathe this air. Boxes are stacked like tombstones—each one a piece of Kathryn Caraway buried. I am back in my bedroom, staring at the suitcase. I pack the last few items: some clothes, the novel I started last month and won't finish, toiletries, and my old teddy bear. I've hugged that little guy since I was a child. Everything I am, condensed into so little. I feel the weight of all I can't take with me—the photographs, the history, the love.

The long, flowing brown hair I once took joy in curling is tightly wound into a messy bun. Loose strands hang around my face, and I push them behind my ear, waiting for Cooper to arrive. I'm a shell of the person I was before Todd came into my life. The me that once hustled to cobble an income together to bring my house out of foreclosure now moves through life snowed by static—that's what life is like as the target of a sadistic stalker.

I stare into the mirror; an unfamiliar face glares back with sunken hazel eyes haunted by dark circles and a pale complexion drained of life. Never mind the swollen lip—the red gash where smooth pink should be. There's no need to fuss with makeup, but I manage to put on some face cream. I pull on a pair of ankle-length jeans and tuck in a white, silky blouse. Casual, comfortable for the long day ahead. I slip into ruby-red flats—the ones I once favored for late-night pub crawls with friends. Correction: the ones *Kathryn Caraway* favored.

Today is a day I am determined to face with grace.

Chapter 4

The air above the world is thinner than blood. Pressurized, stale, slow to feed the lungs. The recycled oxygen did not so much fill me as collect in the pit of my stomach, tight and stale as a plastic bag cinched over my face. A fine chill drifts from the overhead vent; it dries the skin beneath my eyes and finds the crack in my molar with a low, persistent ache. I press my head to the oval window, watch the scudding clouds, and wonder if the next inhalation will turn my insides to powder.

Cooper sits to my left, with two fingers pinched around a paper coffee cup that steams a weak offering of caffeine. The lines on his face have the hieroglyphic authority of an old stone. He wears a suit the color of a thunderstorm cloud and a tie so tight at the collar that it leaves a shelf above his Adam's apple. The small talk died at takeoff; all that remains is the polite machinery of his professional breathing and the way he watches the people in the cabin. He doesn't look at me—that's how I know I'm not the first broken thing he's had to escort.

"Drink." Cooper's voice doesn't rise above the whine of the turbines.

He shoves a bottle of water into my hand. His fingers brush mine, and they're colder than the plastic. "You look pale."

I open the bottle. The seal cracks. My throat is desert-dry, but the water tastes like pennies. Everything tastes like pennies. Drink. Gag. Drink more.

The flight attendant rattles past with a cart, distributing cellophane-wrapped nightmares passed off as food. It's always chicken or pasta.

"Chicken or pasta?"

Her cheery voice is like nails on a chalkboard to me. The pasta is safer, less likely to remind me of arteries and muscles.

"You should eat," he says. "It'll help with the jet lag."

His voice is deeper than I expected. It rolls but doesn't bark. I peel back the foil. I spear a bite and chew while the plane's engines hiccup in turbulence. He watches me eat like he's checking off a box. Hydrate the asset. Check. Feed the asset. Check.

Cooper opens his tray with the muscle memory of a thousand flights. Chicken for him. He eats without looking at the food, his eyes scanning forward and aft—left, but not right—because that's where I am. When he finishes, he wipes his mouth with a napkin, folds it into a tight square, and tucks it under his fork.

I want to ask if the program ever works, really. But that would be impolite. He eyes the flight attendant, who rattles up next to us with the cart, scraping our leftovers into a bin. When she rolls to the next row, he slides a manila folder onto my tray table.

"Here," he says. "Best to start now."

He looks away, as if he has handed me the remains of my pet.

I draw the folder to my lap. The edge nicks my cuticle, and a bead of blood rises. I don't feel it. I don't feel anything. Inside: three fresh, glossy rectangles: a passport, a driver's license, a birth certificate—imprinted with the name Tara Marie Quinn. Each letter is perfectly aligned, as if bureaucratic neatness could erase the old architecture of Kathryn Caraway. I mouth the name, but it feels fake—maybe because I know it is.

My eyes settle on the photograph. It's the same one in the passport and the driver's license, taken by Cooper yesterday. I'm torn between clinging to the memory of the woman who posed for it and accepting that she's slipping away from me. The details are correct, but none of them feel like they belong to me. Even the bogus birth date feels like a violation, as though my entire biographical record has been ransacked.

Tara Marie Quinn. On a single white sheet of paper is a lone paragraph, words spaced with surgical precision.

"Go ahead," he says. "Give it a read."

CLASSIFIED

Document Control No. VPP-750065

Warning: Exercise necessary safeguards to prevent unauthorized disclosure. Classified security regulations applicable to this document.

Tara Quinn, age 47, was born in Tupelo, Mississippi. She is recently divorced from Paul Quinn (no children). In the States, she lived in Columbus, Georgia where she worked as an administrative assistant at Greenwell Financial Group. Duties included client scheduling and data management. She has no criminal history, no prior international travel, and limited extended family. No prior medical history. Allergic to penicillin. Parents were killed in a car accident on March 13, 2016. Quinn has expressed intent to write a book, which will be closely monitored for compliance. Subject will relocate to Werneth, New Zealand.

A single paragraph is all I am now. No family. A slab of nobody from nowhere, defined by a relationship to a man who never loved her, and a job she barely tolerated. That was the whole point of graduate school, I want to tell the page.

"I have a master's degree," I say, setting the paper down with more force than necessary. The only morsel of truth is the allergy. Even that is laughable.

Cooper doesn't flinch. "We've found that degrees complicate things. Paper trail, expectations. People ask more questions. Admin assistant is easier. Safer."

"I don't even know what Greenwell is." I immediately feel the need to apologize, out of habit, out of upbringing. "Sorry. I know you didn't write it."

He shrugs, and for a moment, the armor slips. "It's always a compromise. The more generic the life, the longer you keep it."

I swallow that with the rest of my pride. I am a blank sheet, a ghost with a borrowed name.

"Never use your old name. Don't answer to it, even in your head. The most common way to get caught is by habit. Make your passwords something random. Something Tara would use, not Kathryn."

"Tara," I say, turning the syllables over like a coin. "Werneth. Is that real?"

He nods. "New Zealand. Small town, barely a blip. Pretty, though. By the sea. I picked it for you."

Cooper watches me with a sideways glance. He clears his throat. "It's important you memorize every detail—the background, the new birthdate, the town. Details matter, especially for the first month. Don't improvise. Don't embellish. It'll only trip you up."

I pry the passport open. The photo is less than twenty-four hours old, but it already feels counterfeit, as if the act of erasing myself has subtly warped my features. I recognize the shape of my jaw, the tired bags beneath my eyes, but the hair is parted on the wrong side.

"Repeat it," Cooper says, voice low and soft as the hum of the engines. "Name, date, city. Out loud."

I lick my lips and try. "Tara Quinn. Date of birth: June 27, 1975. Born in Tupelo, Mississippi." The vowels feel rubbery.

He nods. "Good. Driver's license."

"Tara M. Quinn. 331 Broad Street, Tupelo, Mississippi."

"Say it three more times. Out loud, please."

I obey. Each repetition sands away a layer of my original self. After the third, I want to throw up, but there's only a clawing burn in the back of my throat.

"You'll need to sign the passport. Practice on the paper." He hands me a small spiral-bound notepad from the inside pocket of his jacket. I scrawl the name five times. It starts tilted, then rounds off into the loops and spikes of someone unfamiliar. Tara M. Quinn.

He scrutinizes the sample, nods again. "It'll take a few weeks for the muscle memory to set. For now, just relax when you sign."

I stare at the birth certificate, baby blue and stamped with an official seal. I am an orphan built by photocopy and bad ink.

"Any questions?" Cooper keeps his voice low, but the question itself has a snap to it. Like a drill sergeant. "Speak now."

I think of a hundred questions. Where will I live? What if I need to see a doctor? Is it possible to mourn the death of a person still warm in her own skin? Instead, I ask, "Why Werneth?"

He smiles, or maybe the corners of his mouth merely consider it. "Small town. Easy to blend in. Local police are squared away, not easily bought. Population under twelve thousand, most of them retirees from all over the world. Only a third of the population is under the age of twenty-nine. Unremarkable is safest."

He leans in, conspiratorial. "I hear there's a decent café on Victoria Street where you'll find the locals friendly."

The idea of a café—sunlight, clattering cups, human voices—feels obscene.

"A lot of people like to backpack through New Zealand. Locally, they call it tramping. Most Europeans, but some Americans. Be careful that you don't end up in any selfies. I don't need to stress this, but it's worth saying."

I take the driver's license and pinch it between my thumb and forefinger. The surface is slick, like the back of a fish. I slip it into my wallet.

Cooper shifts in his seat, uncrosses and recrosses his legs. He is restless, but not with boredom. I suspect he hates this part—the handoff. The minute-by-minute slide from human to asset. The program calls it "repositioning."

He reaches across me and snaps the plastic window shade shut. "There's no going back after this," he says, softer. "You understand that?"

"Yes, sir."

He likes the "sir," I assume, though he doesn't respond.

The hum of the engine is louder now, or maybe my ears have begun to ring from the pressure. I repeat my new name in my head. I imagine the moment we land, and my last kernel of self will be burned away by the air of another hemisphere.

CHAPTER 5

A man across the aisle has dozed off, head lolling against the seatback, mouth slack. A paperback book is tented on the tray in front of him. From somewhere up the aisle, a baby cries a high, jagged pitch, the noise of protest. The mother's voice soothes it in a language I don't recognize. For a moment, I am envious of all of them; the ability to sleep, to make such noise, to be heard, to be real.

Cooper sips something pretending to be coffee, then sets it down empty. He checks the sightlines, then retrieves a paper from his breast pocket. It is so densely folded that it looks like an origami trap. "Here are the contact codes and safe phrases. You'll check in once a week for the first six months. Less frequently after. The details are inside. Memorize them. I'll be taking this back from you when we land."

My hands tremble as I take the paper. I can feel the heat from his pocket lingering on it, as if it had been incubating there all morning.

"Your handler in New Zealand will initially be Nathan Ryland. He'll meet us at the airport. Until further notice, you'll be living in short-term housing."

I manage to say, "Why an admin for a financial firm?"

He smiles—that old teacher's pet reflex. "It's close enough to your real background to minimize mistakes, but not so close you'll attract attention. If anyone asks, you're writing a book. The town's full of writers; no one will blink."

"What's the book about?" I ask, with a slight hint of defiance.

"Hopefully not about being in the program." Cooper flashes a small smile. He seems proud of himself for making a joke. I'm not laughing. "At the initial meeting, you mentioned you'd always thought about writing a book. Your undergrad is in English, so it stands to reason. Maybe use your experience and write one of those thrillers. My daughter liked to read mystery and suspense."

My mouth tastes of tin. "And I just what? Never leave? Never have a slip?"

"Mistakes happen. Most are harmless, but the program's only as good as your willingness to stay invisible. You'll want to help people. That's admirable, but risky. Best to keep a low profile, at least at first."

He glances past me.

"Ryland's a good man. He's the director of the program in New Zealand. Once you get settled, he'll assign a local handler to you."

I try to imagine this Ryland—another deputy U.S. Marshal in another funeral suit. Another stranger with a dossier thicker than my history. I hate him already.

Cooper leans in again, his voice now barely above the drone of the engines. "Listen. There will be moments when you'll want to reach out. Contact a family member or friend, even just to hear a familiar voice. Don't. It's the first thing perpetrators monitor."

I nod, each rule like a brick mortared into the new walls of my life.

The turbulence returns—a jolting up-and-down that makes my stomach tumble like wet laundry in a spin cycle. My grip tightens around the armrest. I stare at the thin gold band on Cooper's left hand, polished by years of nervous thumb-twisting. I wonder what his story is, if there is someone waiting for him in another hemisphere, if she ever wonders what mask he wears when he is at home.

He must have seen something in my face—a crack, or a sudden vacancy. He reaches across the tray table and sets his hand over mine. Not squeezing, just anchoring me to the present.

"You're not alone, Tara." He drops the bureaucratic stiffness in his tone.

The sound of my new name in his voice is so jarring it nearly undoes me. I blink hard. I want to ask him how long I have to be Tara before the echo of Kathryn fades, if it ever does.

He withdraws his hand, embarrassed by his own lapse. "It'll be strange at first. You'll feel like you're playacting. That's normal. Just let the routine settle in."

"Okay," I say, but the word has no weight. It feels like what I should say.

A long silence unspools. Hours in the air pass as I observe the etiquette of strangers.

The flight attendant returns, face frozen in the same polite mask. "Hot towel?" she offers, wielding a set of tongs.

I take one. It is warm and faintly lavender scented. I press it to my eyes, let the damp heat spread, and imagine it could melt away the old self beneath my skin.

"Anything else I need to know?" I ask, muffled by the towel.

Cooper speaks into the quiet. "I had a case, years ago, back in Maine." He doesn't look at me but at the back of the seat in front of him. "Her name was Rachel. Well, it wasn't, but you know how that goes. She was a teacher. Loved her students. The kind of person who believed in rules, but also in exceptions."

He pinches the bridge of his nose with his thumb and forefinger—the gesture intimate in its weariness. "She went into the program after a . . . bad situation. Lost everything. She was angry for a long time. At us, at herself. At whoever it was that put her there."

He stops, as if weighing the rest of the story.

"What happened to her?" I ask.

"She adapted. Found a community. Fell in love with some guy and got married." He smiles—the real kind this time, years taken off his face. "She sends a postcard to me every now and again."

He meets my eyes, and for a moment, I see the man under the armor: pale with fatigue, all the lines mapped with small, secret griefs. His steel-gray hair is caught in the overhead light—a silvery halo that makes him look older, more mortal.

"Most don't want to look back. The smart ones, anyway. But I keep every note, every message that slips through. There are worse things than starting over, Tara," he says. "The trick is not letting the old life rot you from the inside out."

The engines shift pitch. An overhead chime signals. The sleeping man snorts awake and rubs his eyes, instantly returning to the printed platitudes of the paperback. I envy his simplicity.

I hand Cooper back the origami paper I've stared at and memorized.

"You sure you have all the information down?"

"Yes."

Cooper tucks it back into his breast pocket. He glances at me one more time, and there is something almost fatherly in the way he squares his shoulders—like he wants to wish me luck, but he's been trained out of such extravagances.

"We'll be wheels down in thirty," he says instead. "You'll do fine, Tara."

This time, the name doesn't sound so foreign. Just strange enough to be survivable.

I flick open the window shade and look out. Auckland sprawls beneath us, a scatter of lights pulsing through the fog. I watch them bloom and fade, watch the world compress into a grid of lines and intersections, each promising a different life, a different story.

The descent begins with a lurch, the whole cabin tilting at an angle that makes the heart think it is falling, even as the mind knows it is only physics. The seatbelt sign dings. The man across the aisle sets aside his paperback and pulls his tray upright, his expression a small, private fear of landing.

I feel it, too—the loss of control. My jaw clicks as the pressure shifts. Cooper checks his watch. The captain announces final approach and instructs the flight attendants to be seated. I grip the armrest, feeling my pulse in my teeth.

"You'll do fine," Cooper repeats, but there is a catch in his voice—a stutter just behind the words.

The landing gear deploys with a groan. The nose pitches further down, and the city swells toward us. Cooper shifts in his seat, his eyes distant as he speaks. "There was this young woman, couldn't have been more than twenty-five. She'd gotten mixed up with some bad people, ended up witnessing things she shouldn't have. We brought her into the program, gave her a new identity, a fresh start."

He pauses, and his jaw tightens. "She was a lot like you. Smart, resilient. For a while, she was thriving. Got a job, an apartment, a few friends."

His gaze drifts to the window. "She got careless, let her guard down. Thought she was safe."

Cooper's eyes meet mine, his expression grave. "They found her. One morning, she didn't show up for work. We found her apartment trashed."

When we touch down, it is not with the violence I expect but a soft, rolling shudder.

His eyes refocus on me, the weight of his stare conveying the gravity of his words. "I tell you this because I've seen what happens when people in your position don't take the risks seriously. When they think they're invincible, or that the rules don't apply to them. I don't want to see that happen to you."

Cooper unbuckles, gathers his briefcase, and stands. We file down the jetway, side by side—no words between us.

My name is Tara Quinn now.

There is no going back.

Chapter 6

The airport is a barn of echoes: public address voices, the roll of hard-shell suitcases, the slap of shoes against tile. Cooper scans the crowd with a predator's patience. I see him triangulate—the cluster of convenience shops, marked exit doors, the throng of people heading in all directions but not really knowing where they're going.

I watch as his eyes lock onto something just beyond the gate. I glance over, and there is a man whose appearance screams "federal" and "agent"— tall and stiff, like a flagpole that learned to walk. The way his suit fits, either he lives in the gym or has a tailor with something to prove. With furrowed temples, his brows are as black and unyielding as wrought iron.

He clocks us at twenty meters, recalibrates his stance. He does not smile. Cooper and the man perform a micro-transaction of glances and nods, the territory between them mined with unsaid history.

"Ryland," Cooper intones with the warmth of a steel hinge.

"Cooper," Ryland replies, his vowels sharp and squared. He extends a hand to Cooper, who clasps it in the quick, masculine shorthand of camaraderie.

"This is Tara. She's all yours," Cooper says.

Ryland's gaze flicks to me, and for a fraction of a second, I see the audit in his eyes: height, gait, the telltale quiver at the corner of my mouth. I feel like livestock under an auctioneer's hand. He turns to me with bureaucratic courtesy—the face of a man who can assemble and disassemble you with equal fluency.

"Ms. Quinn. Welcome to Auckland."

His voice holds no warmth. He seems annoyed with me, as if he has somewhere else he'd rather be. I don't blame him. I'd rather be somewhere else, too.

"Thank you," I say, my voice sounding like it was shipped here in cold storage.

"I'm Nathan Ryland, director of the program here in New Zealand. I'm with the U.S. Marshal Service, attached to the Embassy here in Auckland. I'll be overseeing your case."

Ryland gestures down the concourse, the way a customs officer indicates a secondary inspection lane has just opened. "This way."

I look back, half-expecting to see Cooper offer some last benediction, but he is already receding into the swarm. The last remnants of him shrink until he is just another unclaimed silhouette.

Ryland walks with the calibrated rhythm of a man who's done this a thousand times. Every four steps, he checks the perimeter—eyes bouncing around. I trail half a pace behind, struggling to match his precision. My ears throb from the pressure change; my head rings. The voices on the PA system bleed into one another: English, Mandarin, something I can't place. My ears are still popping from the flight, and every announcement feels like it is addressing me—a summons to some final inquest.

We reach the baggage carousel. My suitcase is already circling. Ryland plucks it off the conveyor with two fingers, weighing it as if to estimate what pieces of myself I bothered to pack. We move through the crowd, outpacing the shuffle of lesser dramas: grandmothers in floral tunics, red-faced children clutching a parent's hand, couples with their hands locked. I look at all of them, and I want to scream: *You have no idea how precious your ordinary is!*

He leads me past a checkpoint where a uniformed woman scans our faces and waves us on with the dead eyes of the overworked. Ryland walks faster. I shuffle to keep up, dragging the suitcase that contains the last evidence of my prior existence. Sweat beads at my temples, stings in my eyes. I wipe it away, and it comes back twice as fast. I must look feverish—a liability in a place like this.

"Restroom, please," I say, but Ryland does not hear. Or he pretends not to.

"You'll need your passport," he says.

The terminal's next crucible is immigration. Ryland marches me down a corridor tiled in antiseptic blue. The air is denser here, cut with the sweat and perfume of sleepless travelers. Somewhere in the rafters, a speaker pipes in bird sounds. They're soothing, they say, to mitigate the stress of transoceanic arrival. For me, it is only more noise.

Ryland does not break stride when he shepherds me into the queue. I am aware of my posture: shoulders hunched, chin tucked, hands clutching the suitcase handle with white-knuckled devotion. I glance at the others: a Chinese woman with a knockoff Burberry scarf, a gaunt man in a Red Sox cap, two children wrestling over a stuffed animal with a price tag dangling from its ear. Their faces glow with hope. Mine doesn't. I am here only to be erased.

We reach the immigration desk. The officer greets us with a smile sharpened by training. Ryland flashes an ID. The immigration officer nods in acknowledgment. He slides my passport across the scanner, the device thrumming as it interrogates my future.

"Purpose of visit?" he asks.

Ryland answers before I can open my mouth. "Tourism. Two weeks in country."

The officer turns to me, squinting as if to decode the truth in my irises. "First time in New Zealand, Ms. Quinn?"

"Yeah, first time." The accent is all wrong—too American, too much of the South in the vowels. I feel the heat rise in my cheeks. I hope it reads as jet lag.

He nods, types something with two fingers, then slides my passport back under the glass.

"You'll love it here," the officer says.

The phrase is a knife, clean and casual. I nod, forcing a smile.

We move on. The next checkpoint is customs. There are no lines—just a scanner manned by a woman with an indifferent ponytail. She waves us through after a cursory look, not even glancing at my declaration form. I half-expect to be stopped, asked to unpack my lies, but no one seems to care what I may be carrying inside.

The arrivals hall is a theater of reunions. People erupt in embraces, laughter ricochets off the terrazzo, and cameras flash. I watch a teenage boy with a pirate's earring melt into the arms of a weeping woman. Two men bump chests, grinning, oblivious to the detonation of my private world.

Ryland doesn't stop until we reach a plain door—STAFF ONLY. He produces a card and punches in a code. The door swings open onto a service corridor lined with vending machines and wheeled bins labeled in three languages. We come to a large, open space, bustling with uniformed officers and dogs sniffing through a mountain of luggage. I watch a dog alert to a black suitcase. An officer hoists it onto a metal table with a loud thud. Piece by piece, the officer pulls items out and examines them.

The room is alive with the sounds of multiple conversations, each accompanied by the singsong pronunciation of the New Zealand accent. Their mouths form different shapes, and their words carry unique rhythms in ways I've never heard.

"There is a restroom through there." Ryland points across the room. "Leave your suitcase."

I shift the strap of my leather purse higher on my shoulder and make my way across the room. My bladder, finally relieved after a long wait, brings a fleeting sense of comfort that I wish would ripple through the rest of my body. Cold sweat prickles my skin. Anxiety sits heavy in my stomach. I look in the mirror and see how scared and uncertain I am about what lies ahead.

When I come out of the bathroom, what I see horrifies me. There's Ryland, sporting a pair of blue latex gloves, my suitcase splayed open on a cold, metal table like some kind of crime scene. I freeze, and the door gives me a little shove, forcing me to step forward and let it shut behind me. My shirts, jeans, and private undergarments lie scattered on the table like some embarrassing exhibit—bare for all to see. Ryland lingers on my cherished teddy bear, scrutinizing the seams as if I had hidden some grand secret within its plush confines. I avert my eyes, mortified, wishing I could unsee this invasion of privacy.

"Ready?" Ryland casually crams everything back into my suitcase, as if this violation is just another day at the office.

I nod, not trusting my voice.

He zips up my suitcase with a swift tug—the metal teeth snarling shut. I feel stripped naked. Ryland hands me my bag, his gloved fingers brushing mine. I recoil instinctively.

"This way," he says, clearly oblivious to my discomfort.

We weave through the labyrinth of corridors, past more uniformed officers and sniffing dogs. My heart pounds in my ears, drowning out the accents and rustling luggage.

We arrive at another door. Ryland waits for me to precede him—a small gesture of chivalry that lands somewhere between authority and pity.

"The car's outside." Ryland's hand hovers at my elbow—a warning and a leash.

We pass through a loading dock, where a security guard sits but never looks our direction. As I step out of the airport, the unfamiliar sights and sounds of this new country envelop me. The air here has teeth. It bites my cheeks—sharp and raw. I breathe in, lungs aching. The sky stretches above in a shade of blue I swear I've never seen before. People around me chatter in rapid, musical tones that I can't quite grasp. Everything feels foreign.

CHAPTER 7

The car is an unmarked sedan. You may as well mark it. It's a
government vehicle with "U.S. EMBASSY" across the top of the
license plate. Ryland places my suitcase in the trunk and
motions for me to sit in the front seat. He stops me as I head toward the
passenger side of the car.

"They drive on the other side of the road here," he remarks with mild
irritation.

I lean in slightly, wincing from the soreness where the seatbelt bruised
me during the crash. I see the steering wheel on the opposite side. I walk
around and settle into what I have always known as the driver's seat. It feels
foreign to sit there, with the steering wheel on what I always considered the
passenger side. I glare at it. It's a reminder of how everything has been
turned upside down, like my car yesterday. My mind flashes back to the
impact: sudden, jarring.

The car is moving. I grip the seatbelt so hard it presses uncomfortably
against my neck. It was a strap like this that held me in place, sparing me

from a worse fate when the car crumpled around me. The silence is so complete I can hear the click of Ryland's jaw when he swallows.

"You're doing well. Most people collapse by now."

I nod. The verdict is still out. I run my nails along my palm, digging crescents into the skin. The pain is clean—an anchor. I watch the buildings pass: glass towers, squat motels, a strip mall crowned by a neon sign. It's busier than I imagined—denser. The car makes a sharp right turn and enters a driveway. No, not a driveway. It's a barricade. A massive structure looms ahead, topped with an oversized American flag. The place must be the size of a city block. Everything about the U.S. Embassy screams overkill. Everything about the program screams overkill.

Ryland rolls down his window as we approach. A Marine standing guard looks crisp and disciplined, as if his entire life fits neatly inside his pressed uniform. He eyes Ryland's ID, then me, then a paper Ryland hands him, and finally looks at me again. I shrink back against the seat.

"Clear," the Marine calls out. A gate lifts, and we drive through.

The sedan glides to a stop in an underground lot. I stare at my hands—pale and raw in the dashboard light—trying to remember if I've always had these veins, this knuckle shape. Ryland opens his door with a motion so controlled it might be rehearsed, and I follow. The air reeks of fumes and brake dust. We cut through a concrete tunnel, empty but for the sound of our footsteps. Up a flight of service stairs, past an unmarked door, and into the building. The walls are the color of old teeth, and the floor is tiled in a pattern that makes me feel I'm walking in place.

Ryland punches a code into a keypad. The door opens into a small, windowless room that looks like a conference cell built for confessions. A steel table bisects the space, and two plastic chairs face each other with the adversarial symmetry of a chessboard.

"Sit." He gestures. Not a suggestion.

I obey.

A young woman enters and hands Ryland a manila folder.

"Thanks, Maddie."

He places the folder in the exact center of the table, sits across from me, folds his hands, and meets my eyes with an administrative stare. "This will be brief."

The first page is a checklist—like one favored by coroners and people who catalog lost children.

"Item one: No contact, direct or indirect, with previous associates. That includes email, social media, and so-called burner accounts. Understood?"

"Yes," I say, but it comes out sounding like a question.

"Item two: Mandatory weekly check-ins, Monday morning, oh nine hundred. Failure to do so will trigger escalation. Understood?"

I nod, biting my tongue.

"Item three: In the event of an emergency, use the red flag protocol on your mobile device. The phone will guide you. Confirmed?"

"What is a red flag protocol?"

"We'll get to that in a minute, when I give you the device." He flips the page. "Item four: You are not to leave the metropolitan area without permission. If travel is required, notify the handler seventy-two hours in advance. Consequences for deviation are immediate and nonnegotiable."

I exhale, slow and deliberate, and focus on the hum of the fluorescent panel above us. It flickers at irregular intervals—a Morse code I will never crack.

"Item five: There is no tolerance for improvisation. We expect full adherence to protocol. Any deviation, no matter how well-intentioned, is grounds for termination from the program." He lets this hang in the air— the threat coiled and absolute.

He produces a small blue rectangle from his jacket. It's a phone, but not any model I recognize. He slides it across the table, screen down.

"This is your lifeline. All calls are encrypted. Do not install applications, do not use it for personal browsing. Destroy the device if you believe it's been compromised. The six-digit password is your new date of birth. Questions?"

I reach for the phone. It's quite heavy, as if it contains more than circuits and glass.

"Here is a debit card and cash, in local currency. Enough to get started. You will receive a monthly stipend to cover basics, not extravagances. Use it sparingly, and do not attempt to transfer funds. Every transaction is monitored."

The debit card looks normal. It bears the name of a New Zealand bank. Below the logo is the name Tara Quinn—the name I will have to get used to.

"Please read and sign this." Ryland pushes a document across the table.

I read through it quickly, barely taking in the words on the page. I recognize this document: an acknowledgment that I will inform the program of my residential address, employment, any breach of the contract, and any incidents of concern.

"I already signed this."

"Correction. Kathryn Caraway signed it in the States. Tara Quinn needs to sign it in New Zealand." He offers me a pen.

I take it, hold it in my hand, and hesitate. I scribble Tara Quinn's name on the line and push it back across to Ryland. He shuffles the page in with the rest, tucking them neatly into the folder.

"You'll spend tonight in a hotel near the waterfront. I'll escort you there myself. Tomorrow, you'll fly to your final destination."

"What if I need—what if something isn't working?"

"You can contact me directly. The number's programmed in. Or use the protocol. But understand, this isn't a democracy. We don't debate best practices. You follow, or you're out."

He stands, pushing the chair back without a sound. "Come on. Let's get you to the hotel. If the jet lag hasn't already set in, it will. Trust me."

I rise on unsteady legs. The room feels smaller than when we entered.

Every interaction with Ryland feels colder—he's all business, with a serious expression that barely shifts. I can't blame him. This work must be tough. It's a stark contrast to my interactions with Bill Cooper. I appreciated the stories he shared about his other cases. It almost makes me wish he'd stayed here with me.

The route to the hotel is short. Ryland walks me to the lobby and handles the check-in. The clerk slides over a plastic keycard—no questions. The elevator ride is silent except for the elevator's voice: "Floor two. Floor three. Floor four."

At the door to my room, Ryland pauses.

"Tomorrow, oh nine hundred. I'll collect you. Order room service for anything you need. Don't venture out on your own. Try to rest."

Hearing the phrase "I'll collect you" hits me in the stomach. I remind myself that, to him, I'm merely an asset he has to handle.

I fumble with the keycard. He waits until I'm inside, then disappears— the sound of his shoes receding into the carpeted hush. The room is a box. White walls, blue bedding, and a window that doesn't open. I set the phone on the nightstand, stare at it, waiting for it to ring, explode, or confess my sins back to me.

In the mirror, I look like a woman assembled from spare parts: hair limp from recycled air, face too thin for this world.

Somewhere in the city, Ryland is probably briefing someone, telling them how compliant I am—how unlikely I am to cause trouble.

Sleep comes gradually, but at least it comes. In the morning, I will follow the rules. I will answer to the name Tara Quinn. I will be what they need: a compliant mechanism.

CHAPTER 8

The hotel lobby is a terrarium—sealed, self-regulating, humid with the breath of transients and air coming off the sea. I sit closest to the elevator, one ankle knotted over the other, my suitcase anchored by both hands as if it might otherwise walk off. The carpet is patterned in navy and oyster, a tidepool of stains and ground-in neglect. My room key, bank card, and the blue phone all occupy the same pocket—a holy trinity of survival. I check the time: 8:31 a.m. In Ryland's dialect, I'm sure nine a.m. means 8:45.

A man's cane clicks with every other step; the woman's perfume advances several seconds ahead of her. The man sits with a noise that could be pain or relief, or both. They consult a laminated map, parsing the city's attractions: the Sky Tower, Mount Eden, the zoo, and the art galleries of Devonport. The woman insists on visiting the casino.

The man shakes his head. "Maybe we should just go back to Werneth. I liked it there."

A tiny, traitorous current of excitement snaps through me. Werneth—not a code or a string of coordinates—is an actual place someone likes.

"But we've already seen Werneth." Their accents are English—London, maybe.

"Excuse me," I say politely. "I'm heading out to see Werneth today. Any sites you recommend?"

He laughs—a cough-gargle hybrid. "Phoenix Bay, they used to call it." He raps the map with a nicotine-stained nail. "Where all the ships came in, back in the day. Make sure you visit the harbor and the museum."

I bend over my phone, thumbs moving with urgency as I type "Werneth, New Zealand" into a browser. This isn't personal; it's research related to the program. Results bloom in a grid of images: the harbor, a church, streets lined with cottages. I click on the Wikipedia link: "Founded 1869, population 11,800, primary industries shipping and agriculture." My fingers scroll. The next link is to the local paper. I click on it to read the headlines and come across an article about the museum. The story is dated three years ago: "Town Marks Fire Centennial with Parade, New Museum."

I read the first two paragraphs and learn more than Cooper offered. In 1872, a fire swept the town to the waterfront, reducing it to a blackened ribcage in a matter of hours. "They rebuilt," says the article, "stone by stone, sometimes using the char as mortar."

There is a grainy, undated photo of women in floor-length skirts forming a bucket line across the street. The mayor stands at the center, arms folded, jaw set like a municipal bulldog.

"They didn't think we'd survive. They didn't think we'd do more than bury the dead and get the hell out. But people are still people. And these people rebuilt. They know what it means to rise from the ashes, how to take root in what was charred and scarred."

I scroll faster, clicking through a gallery of then-and-now shots: a church in ruins, then painted white; a row of shops as a burnt husk, then the same row, signs hand-lettered, awnings freshly laundered. The faces in the new photos are proud—almost defiant—like they've won an old grudge against the elements and plan to keep the trophy in plain sight.

Without warning, I think of my own old house—how I painted over water stains every spring, layering white latex over the creeping brown, as if it would buy another season of respectability. It always bled through by July.

The elderly couple is now bickering over the best way to get to Devonport. The woman says, "We'll take the ferry, it's more romantic."

The man replies, "Ferries make you sick, Gladys. You remember the Cook Strait Ferry?"

I check the time: 8:47. My eyes flick back to the page on the phone, and I study the facts again. I'm halfway through a list of restaurants: three Italian, two sushi, one "authentic American BBQ"—when a voice at my elbow, flat and undeceived, says, "Ms. Quinn."

I look up. Ryland is less formal than yesterday, but no less imposing. He wears a slate-gray windbreaker over an equally gray shirt. His shoes, despite the rain, are spotless.

"Ready?" he asks.

I slide the blue phone into my pocket. "Yes," I say, and to my surprise, I mean it.

He gestures toward the revolving door. After a short drive, we arrive at a small airport, not the international one I flew into yesterday. The terminal, if I can call it that, is a prefab shed on a strip of asphalt, flanked by the carcasses of decommissioned vehicles. A Cessna waits on the tarmac, its tail number partly obscured by a seagull's blessing.

"The weather has passed, and you've got clear skies ahead. Your pilot's finishing the preflight," Ryland says. "You'll be on the ground in Werneth around eleven."

"What about you?" I ask, before I can stop myself.

He smiles—the ghost of a real one. "You'll make the flight alone. A local member of the program will meet you when you land. I'm your primary contact, so call if you need anything."

Ryland stands beside me as the pilot finishes with the clipboard. He seems about to say something, but instead, he surveys the horizon. I follow his gaze. Somewhere out there—beyond the cloud line—is the town that rebuilt itself from ash, that turned disaster into a permanent identity. I feel a twitch of genuine anticipation.

The airplane is small. It's less a vessel of flight than a toy scaled up to fit two adults and a suitcase. The pilot is in place, headset angled askew over a bald, sun-stippled dome. He nods at my approach, then steps down, offers a perfunctory handshake, and stows my suitcase in the aft compartment. The smell of the plane is mineral and old vinyl baked by generations of sunlight, oil, coffee, and the dry, spectral scent of aviation fuel.

I climb into the copilot's seat. The leather is cracked at the seams, peeling like a bad sunburn. The pilot mumbles something into the radio, voice blurred by static, then turns and gives me a thumbs-up. I try to reciprocate, but my hands are slick with adrenaline. He grins, as if terror is the most natural reaction to a machine like this.

The engine coughs to life, a throaty, uneven growl. The plane shudders. Screws vibrate in sympathy. I watch the drops of condensation spiral off the propeller. I taste the sour penny of nerves on my tongue. The wheels clatter over seams in the tarmac, the horizon cants, and then there is air underneath. Takeoff is less a launch than an insistent refusal of gravity. The city snaps to a miniature, each car and building a child's toy. I see the blue fracture of the harbor, the green-brown patchwork of outer suburbs, and beyond that, the dark swells of ocean, indifferent and total.

The turbulence comes without warning—a dip and roll that nearly empties my stomach and tightens every muscle in my neck. The pilot doesn't react. I breathe through my nose, counting each inhalation. The land below shifts from geometry to topography. The hills rise, dense with conifer and native brush, cut by narrow, meandering roads. I spot a river, silver in the sun, and finally, a sprawl of buildings pressed against a semi-circular bay: Phoenix Bay. Werneth.

The wheels touch with a double thump, the fuselage shivers along its length, and then we're taxiing at an almost comic slowness. The pilot gives me a sideways look—silent, assessing. I unbuckle and follow his lead down the small metal ladder.

The air here is cooler, sharper. Salt rides the wind. It stings, but also wakes me from the transit. The sun, magnified by its southern angle, paints the grass in impossible clarity.

I cross the tarmac, suitcase bumping behind me, when a woman appears. Her eyes are hidden behind oversized, tortoise-shell sunglasses, making her pink lipstick more prominent. She's wearing a garishly pink sheath dress with a bright blue belt and matching shoes. If it weren't for her brown hair, she'd be a dead ringer for a Barbie doll.

"It's so great to meet you, Tara," she chirps, stretching out the vowels like taffy. "I'm Maddie. I'll be working with you here in Werneth."

"Oh, for the love of all that's holy," I mutter under my breath.

"My car's out front. I'll drive you to the hostel where you can check in. Ryland gave you a bank card, right?"

"Yeah," I manage, trying not to let my exasperation seep through.

Maddie has all the traits of a sorority girl fresh out of college, with a title that is probably more important than the work she does. I trail behind her to the car, and she chats with more energy than I can handle. I bite my lip, only to remember it's scabbed over from the accident. A pain shoots through, and I tap it with my finger to see if it's bleeding. It's not.

Phoenix Bay is postcard-perfect. The water is a muted jade, and the boats are in trembling rows at their berths. The houses nearest the shore are a mix of painted wood and raw stone, roofs clustered at odd angles to the sun. I watch a pair of children chase each other along a pier, their laughter faint through the glass.

Up the hill, the architecture shifts. It's Victorian, then deco, then an interlude of dull, practical cement. The main road, Victoria Street, is a single block of commerce: a bakery, a post office, a liquor shop, a café, and a chemist.

"Oh, yeah. I learned the hard way that the chemist," she points to the building, "is what they call the pharmacy here."

Maddie slows the car as we approach the old church at the town center —its bell tower rebuilt in a paler shade of stone, the seams of the restoration visible but not ashamed. It's beautiful and magnificent in its patchwork way.

"Look at that. We're nearly there."

We turn onto a street lined with hedges and trash bins at the curb. Finally, we pull up to a weathered hostel, two stories of clean windows framed by flaking paint at the door.

I look at the sign over the door: "The Phoenix House."

"This is where I leave you. Ryland wanted me to remind you to do the weekly check-ins on the phone. Call him if you need anything." She pulls her sunglasses down and looks at me. "He means it. Like, anything."

I nod.

Satisfied, she pushes her sunglasses back up. I walk inside, my suitcase in tow. I don't look back. The place smells of lemon cleaner and the tangy rot that collects in old buildings. I ring the bell on the counter. The sound echoes through the building, as if announcing not just a guest, but a resurrection.

A young woman with the no-nonsense posture of a former athlete, emerges from the back office. She greets me by my new name, and I nod, amazed at how quickly it's become both mask and anchor.

She shows me to my room, where the walls are painted a shade of blue I instantly despise but will learn to live with. The window shows the harbor in the distance.

"You'll love it here. Everyone's nosy, but in a good way." The woman turns and walks away.

I sit on the narrow bed, hands shaking, the suitcase at my feet. The silence is immense but not empty. I look down at my phone, at the unmarked key to my new door. Through the window, a bird glides against the sky. The tide is out, and the harbor reveals its stones, its wounds, its history. I take a breath, and this time, it's not just survival. It's arrival. I think about the bucket brigade, about the way a town survives by refusing to admit the end.

I pocket my key and step out onto the street. The air has a wet edge, but the sky is clear enough for the sun to cast hard shadows against the stone. I pass by a seamstress shop advertising "Alterations While You Wait." The street curves down to the harbor, blue and bright as a new bruise.

A man with arms like driftwood stacks fish crates onto a handcart. He looks up as I pass, gives a half-nod, then returns to his work.

Further up, a woman in cycling gear calls to a neighbor across the street. "Did you see the sunrise this morning?"

The neighbor walks a dog smaller than most cats. "It was magnificent. Enjoy your ride."

Every few steps, someone makes eye contact, nods, or says "G'mornin'," like it's a password. The first time it happens, I mumble a reply. The second time, I get it right. By the third, it's almost natural.

I drift past the bookstore, reading the window display: "Local Authors, New Voices." The covers are all unfamiliar names. I feel the urge to go in—to ask about jobs or events—but the idea of conversation turns my hands cold, so I keep walking.

I walk toward the square and see a market. My steps are careful, and the cobbles feel alien under my feet. Each "G'mornin'" and "G'day" from a passerby is a small reminder that even in a place rebuilt from ashes, the work of fitting in is never finished.

CHAPTER 9

The first sensation is wet cotton—drool on my cheek and a heartbeat in my throat. For a few seconds, I don't know where I am. Then the ceiling comes into focus: plaster, pocked with faint stains, a hairline crack stitched like a surgical suture. Above me, a single fly orbits a bare bulb. The room is cold but smells faintly of the off-brand laundry powder from the hostel vending machine.

I roll over, hear the creak of unfamiliar bedsprings, and try to inventory the situation. The blue phone sits on the nightstand, with its LED pulsing every seven seconds to let me know it's transmitting something. I find this strangely comforting.

The sound of voices filters up from below. Someone is arguing about toast. I force myself upright. I dress quickly and avoid the shared bathroom. I use the sink in my room to brush my teeth, cold water making my gums flare with protest. I study my face in the mirror and repeat my new name: *Tara. Tara. Tara.* It never sounds right, but it's all I have.

Outside, the day is not yet awake. There's a fog blanketing the harbor, softening the edges of the world. I hug my jacket tight and walk the block to Victoria Street, shoes clicking against the ancient brick. The shops crowd the street at uneven intervals, their windows showing hopeful slogans in English and Māori.

A truck idles in front of a bakery, the driver behind the wheel. A man with a push broom attacks the pavement outside the fishmonger's, cigarette glued to his lower lip. I amble up the street and try to memorize the geography. The chemist is already open, an old woman inside dusting shelves with a peacock feather. I round the corner and see The Cottage Café. The sign is hand-painted, chipped at the corners, the letters looping in a style that belongs to another century. Under the windowsill, a pair of blue planters are overrun with bright, perky flowers.

The bell above the door announces my arrival. Inside, the café is a living organism of steam and noise, warmth and light. The air is dense with espresso, vanilla, and the faint vegetal scent of the day's soup, already simmering. There's a shock of color and quick movement at the counter— a woman in a bright green apron, her head wrapped in a red bandana, arms stacked with to-go cups like she's building a pyramid for a pharaoh. Her hair escapes the bandana in wild curls, eyes big and brown as river pebbles. She sees me, and I am immediately categorized.

"Morning, love!" The accent is local, vowels soft around the edges but quick. She wipes her hands on her apron, leaving a streak of white.

"Good morning." I drift to the counter, eyes flicking over the handwritten menu.

She sets down the cups and leans in, conspiratorial. "Let me guess: flat white, extra strong. That, or you want filter coffee that tastes like regret?"

A laugh bubbles up before I can suppress it. "You're not far off."

"Called it," she crows in triumph, snapping her fingers. "What happened to your lip?"

"Oh, that." I touch it slightly with the pad of my fingertip. "My face collided with an airbag."

"Ouch! Name's Kass, by the way." She spells it out, two S's—like a hiss. "You new in town, or just laying low?"

"Just moved here. I'm Tara." I offer my hand, bracing for the handshake.

Kass takes it with both of hers—warm and a little damp. "Welcome to the armpit of the South Pacific, Tara. Do you want a loyalty card? We give a free drink after your tenth existential crisis."

I can't help smiling. "Just a flat white, thanks."

Kass winks and spins to the espresso machine. As she pulls the shot, she keeps up a running commentary about the weather being shy, like a possum, but it'll bite if you ignore it. The café is empty except for an old man reading a newspaper in the corner, but Kass acts like it's standing room only. She gestures grandly to the pastry case, where a battalion of scones and muffins wait for judgment.

I buy a cranberry scone, mostly as a prop. I carry both to a small table by the window and arrange myself with the studied awkwardness of a transplant. I watch Kass ferry milk to the old man, complimenting his choice of tie and recommending the carrot cake. Her gestures are precise, dramatic, but never insincere.

I sip the coffee. It's hot, bitter, and, as promised, strong. I relax a fraction. Outside, the sun is still rising. The milk truck has moved on; the fishmonger's is open, its sign swinging in the breeze. I feel the town waking up around me, the rhythms of small business and smaller talk.

When the bell shrieks again, I snap my head toward the door. A woman in a smart skirt, carrying a laptop and an air of casual authority, strides to the counter. She exchanges pleasantries with Kass, the kind of jokes only regulars can manage. The woman orders her coffee without looking at the menu. I watch, taking mental notes. Already, I am plotting how to fit in.

I nurse the scone and my cup for half an hour, cataloguing every customer. When the café fills, I cede my table and drift to the counter, tucking my hair behind my ear in what I hope is a nervous, harmless gesture.

"Hey, Kass?" I say, voice pitched low.

She slides a stack of plates onto a shelf, then glances up. "Yeah?"

"Do you . . . is there any work here? I mean, part-time. I don't need much. Just enough to keep from going feral."

For a second, I think I've crossed some invisible line. Then Kass lights up—energy and eyebrows all at once. "Oh my God, you're an answer to prayer. Our girl bailed last week. Said she was going for a walk and just never came back. Miss Sue's been frantic." She leans in, lowers her voice. "You need to meet her. She's the owner. Bit of a legend. Can I tell her you're interested?"

I nod before I can talk myself out of it. The normalcy of the situation is both terrifying and deeply comforting. I'm so used to being the wild card, the statistical outlier, that the thought of having a job reference and a regular schedule makes my bones tingle with anticipation.

Kass's eyes are bright—the color of weak tea. "Sit tight. I'll get her."

She scurries to the back, leaving me at the counter, exposed and waiting. I take a deep breath and exhale slowly. *I can do this*, I tell myself.

Above the register is a framed photo of the café staff. Kass's hair is longer, her smile even wider. An older woman stands beside her—a tower of composure in a buttoned blouse and tartan skirt. I study her face, prepping for the next performance.

I stand at the counter, pretending to study the array of syrups, teas, and flavor extracts, but I'm measuring the angles—the door to the register, the register to the back kitchen, the distance to the pass-through. The safety calculus is simple: nothing blocks a straight path out. If the owner dislikes me, I can leave in twelve steps. If she wants to keep me, I'll have to learn to love the constraints.

An older woman emerges from the rear with the careful, clockwork gait of someone who manages pain and time with equal severity. Her hair is shot through with silver, braided tight, and pinned behind her head. She wears a crisp white shirt under a navy cardigan, and her face is unreadable except for the crow's feet that deepen when she spots a dirty teacup left on the counter.

She clocks me, then the teacup, then me again. In five seconds, she has already decided if I am fit for duty.

"I'm Sue, the owner. And you are?"

"Tara." The name comes out perfect, not even the ghost of a question.

"You're looking for work?'

"Yes, ma'am." The "ma'am" is a slip. It tastes like an artifact from my prior life.

She doesn't flinch. "Ah, an American. Kass tells me you've just moved. How long do you intend to stay?"

"Forever, if my residency comes through."

Miss Sue's eyebrow ticks up.

Kass, hovering in the pass-through like a poltergeist, supplies a glowing review. "She's quick. Picked up on the menu before I even finished my pitch."

Miss Sue gestures to the register. "We'll start you on the counter. If you can work the till and not steal from me, you'll last longer. Wages are paid weekly."

She moves to the espresso machine, her hands in constant motion—checking the hopper, the milk carafe, the drip tray. She narrates as she works, her tone brisk. "This one's a Rancilio, bought it from the old bank after they went under. She's moody. Sometimes the shot pulls too quick, sometimes she sulks and chokes the crema. Treat her gentle, and she'll surprise you."

She grinds a double, tamps it with a surgeon's touch, and slides the portafilter home with a flourish. Miss Sue is the kind of woman who could have run a shipyard if she'd been born into a different life. Tall, hands pale but fierce. Every gesture is deliberate—no wasted movement, no softness except the perpetual smile lines bracketing her mouth. She smells of soap and sweet pastries.

Kass reappears and begins coaching me on the point-of-sale system. It's a slab of ancient iPad grafted to a cash drawer with duct tape and despair.

"Press this for 'flat white.'" Kass stabs at the screen while I tie on an apron. "Long black here. If anyone asks for 'American coffee,' I just double the water and charge extra for the trauma."

I run through the buttons, pretending it's the cockpit of a small plane. There's a rhythm to the work: greet, log order, scribble name on cup, swipe card, pour shot, steam milk, assemble, call name, repeat. After half an hour, I've memorized the placement of everything within arm's reach.

Customers trickle in—first the old men in hi-vis jackets, then a trio of teachers, then two mothers with strollers and expressions of terminal fatigue. The mothers are louder than the babies.

"Did you see what Sheila wore to the last school meeting? I mean, that's a choice."

"I saw her talking to the manager at the grocery," an eyebrow shot up, "I think something might be going on there."

Kass treats them with the same theatrical kindness she grants everyone.

By ten o'clock in the morning, I'm solo on the register while Kass preps sandwiches and hums a foreign tune. Miss Sue is in the back, fielding delivery calls and, I suspect, secretly grading my performance. I keep my head down, my voice low and friendly but not memorable. I avoid eye contact unless necessary. I am almost comfortable.

At 10:15 sharp, the bell shrieks. The woman in the doorway is small, less than five feet. She wears a bright purple blazer, a brooch shaped like a bluebird, and her hair is a lattice of white hairspray, enough to stop a bullet. She carries a satchel and a sheaf of folded paper. As she enters, she scans the café as though each object might be an entry on a ledger.

Kass materializes at my elbow, voice a conspiratorial whisper. "That's

Peggy Whitfield. Town Chronicle. She knows everything about everyone—and will want to know what side you butter your toast on."

I glance back. "Should I be worried?"

"Just stick to the facts, or invent new ones. She's more interested in the performance than the truth."

I square my shoulders. "Showtime."

Peggy approaches the counter with the air of a school principal greeting a truant. "Morning, dear." Her eyes laser-locked on my handwritten name tag. "You must be new."

I manage a smile. "Morning. What may I get for you?"

Her mouth twists into a feline approximation of a smile. "Flat white, extra hot. And a scone with clotted cream, if you please. You're from the States?"

"Yes, ma'am. Georgia." The words feel like they're melting as they leave my tongue.

"Werneth's a far cry from Georgia. What brought you here?"

Out of the corner of my eye, I see Kass lean in. "A divorce." I deliver the line with gravitas, just as I'd practiced.

Miss Sue appears at my side. "I see you've already met our resident Shakespearean, Ms. Whitfield."

"Oh, now, Sue." She chuckles. "She says that because I like to write short stories. I'm Margaret Whitfield."

"I'm Tara. Nice to meet you."

Ms. Whitfield levels her gaze back at me. "And where are you staying?"

"At the hostel. For now. Might find a flat if I don't scare off my employer."

She purses her lips, as if weighing my suitability. Ms. Whitfield pays cash, then takes her bounty to the corner table and produces a tiny notepad, scribbling with a practiced claw.

Kass leans in. "You survived! She likes you."

"Is it always like this?" I ask, keeping my voice low.

Kass laughs. "It's worse if she doesn't like you. She'll send food back just to test you. Be glad she only asked for the basics. If you really want to impress her, volunteer at the museum. That's her fiefdom."

The rush dies down, and I wipe the counter with a borrowed vigor. A restless energy pools in my chest, a sense that every new interaction is a test I can't afford to fail.

At noon, Miss Sue returns. She inspects the café with a glance, notes the lack of spills or casualties, and pronounces the shift "acceptable." She gives Kass a list of tomorrow's specials, then turns to me.

"You've got a good manner with customers. I'll keep you on for the week. Try not to run off with a boy or join a cult."

I nod, heart skidding sideways.

Kass sticks her head out from the kitchen, face smudged with flour. "You're in! Don't let the weirdos scare you off."

I want to tell her it's not the weirdos that frighten me. It's the routine. The comfort, the possibility of being seen and known.

CHAPTER 10

It only takes me a month to memorize every imperfection of the espresso machine. I know the way its portafilter sticks if you twist too hard, the shuddering death rattle when it's overdue for descaling, and the subtle whine when the grind is off by a millimeter. By six weeks, I've memorized the habits of our regulars: the fisherman who drinks his first coffee of the day black and his third with three sugars; the pair of hairdressers who speak in coded insults about every other customer; the trio of retirees who meet at the corner table to swap rumors.

By now, I know to roll the scone dough with a light touch. I know that if Miss Sue is in before six, she's testing us; and if she's in after opening, it means something in the kitchen has gone to hell. I know Kass will start humming at 10 a.m.—and that she will never, not once, get through a day without trying to make me laugh.

Most days, I let her. The laughter is welcome. I find myself inventing stories—where I lived before, my work as a secretary at a financial firm, the time I got lost in Atlanta and ended up at a wedding for people I'd never met. The stories are half-true, but no one here questions them.

I keep up my check-ins with Ryland, as agreed. Every Monday. He never answers with more than a word, but I picture him reading the messages, making a new note in his file:

Week one: Found a job. Adjusting.

Week two: Nothing to report. All clear.

Week three: Settling in. Added contact: Kassandra Mitchell. Background clear.

There are still days, hours, moments when the muscles behind my eyes seize up and the world tilts. Once, a man came in just after opening. He was tall, lean, and wore a hooded jacket with the hood up. He ordered a black coffee and never removed his hood, even inside. When he paid, his hand brushed mine, and I dropped the cup.

Afterward, Kass cornered me by the pastry fridge and said, "You okay? You looked like you'd seen a ghost. And I do not do exorcisms before lunch."

I shrugged it off, but my hands shook for the next hour.

Another time, a car backfired outside, and I was under the counter before I could think. Kass made a joke about earthquakes. "They happen here, too, just smaller. Like everything in New Zealand." She fetched me a glass of water. She never mentioned it again.

Today, there is a man at the window. It's almost closing time, and the café is empty except for Kass's playlist softly humming through the overhead speakers. She's wiping down tables, singing quietly—the lyrics right but the tune completely wrong. I'm restocking sugar caddies when I feel a prickling at the base of my skull, like the first warning of a migraine.

I look up. A man is outside, standing perfectly still. He stares at the door with the patience of someone waiting for a train that's always late. He doesn't move—not even when a pair of kids on scooters shoot past, shouting. He doesn't necessarily look out of place, but he feels out of place. Maybe it's because he's staring into the café. Maybe it's because I'm paranoid.

Dark skin. Dark hair cropped neat. Hands tucked into his pockets. I don't even realize I'm cataloguing everything about him.

Kass sets her rag down, crosses to the coffee machine, and begins pulling a shot.

"You see him?" I ask, voice so thin I hardly recognize it.

She nods, tamping the grounds, keeping her eyes on the machine. "I saw someone. Could be an accountant. Could be a debt collector. Could be a man with a passion for watching small-town coffee shop drama from the street."

She finishes the shot, pours it into a mug, and pushes it toward me across the counter. "Here. Caffeine is the universal antidote to paranoia."

I sip. It burns, but the pain is grounding.

Kass leans against the counter, folding her arms. "You get a lot of weirdos working in a café. People who want to be seen. People who want to be invisible. People who show up just to prove they still exist. You're not the first person to hide in here, Tara. You probably won't be the last."

I look up. "Is it that obvious?"

She grins, then softens. "No. But sometimes, when you space out, you look like you're trying to memorize an escape plan."

I shake my head, embarrassed. "It's nothing."

Kass shrugs. "It's always something." She taps the counter twice, then goes back to cleaning.

The man lingers a little longer but moves on down the street toward the church. Kass and I walk out together, and I wait while she locks the door. My head swivels—left, right, then left again.

"Are you still freaked out about that guy?"

I try to laugh, but my lungs are tight.

"Wanna come back to my place?"

"No, thanks. I'm heading back to the hostel to get some rest."

"I can't wait for tomorrow!" Kass says enthusiastically.

"Oh, yeah?"

"Don't pretend you don't know. I've got something planned."

Whatever Kass has planned might be my only chance to find some semblance of peace—a reset of sorts. But only if I don't encounter that man again.

The café is already pulsing when I arrive, condensation silvering the glass. Kass is orchestrating a dough ritual on the counter—forearms dusted with flour, bandana tied in defiance of food safety rules. She kneads with the wild energy of a third-act solo, hips swaying to the bass line of her playlist.

"Birthday!" she shrieks as I enter, pitching the word over the espresso machine's scream.

At first, I think she's talking to the dough. Then I see a party hat on the counter—bright neon cardboard in a style only desperation can justify. Before I can protest, she's around the counter, pressing the hat onto my head.

"Happy, happy day, mate! Surprise!" The word explodes into a cloud of rainbow confetti from a popper I didn't see her set off. Shreds land on my nose, in my hair, on the pastry case.

I freeze, my mind lurching for the correct response. *Is today my birthday?* I try to scroll through the mental file labeled "Cover Story," but the page is blank. The new documents gave me a birthdate, but it was just numbers, not a lived experience. Then I remember—the passcode for the phone is my new birthday. It's today.

"Wow. How'd you know?" My voice is steady, almost convincing.

Kass grins. "A little birdie."

She snags a lighter from the register and produces a blueberry muffin with a single white candle protruding from the top—like a flag of surrender. She lights it, cupping her hand against the updraft from the steamer, then pushes it toward me.

"Make a wish, Tara!"

The flame is a dot, dancing in the draft. I stare at it, wondering what someone in my position would wish for—longevity? An uneventful day? The piecing-together of a life that never was?

I blow it out. The smoke curls up and vanishes.

Kass beams, then launches into a rendition of "Happy Birthday" that pivots through three different keys and at least two time signatures. By the second line, Kass cuts the muffin in half. She plops one chunk onto a saucer, sliding it across the counter with a flourish.

"First slice is yours."

She shoves the other half into her mouth—a colossal bite.

I take the plate, balancing it as if it were a sacred object. The muffin is still warm at the core, blueberries bleeding into the crumb. I eat with the slow deliberation of someone on their last meal. The taste is familiar and alien at once. It's not the flavor of home, but it could be.

Kass leans in, elbows on the counter. "So, big plans? You gonna rage?" She winks, daring me to admit to anything fun.

"I think I'll keep it low-key, but thanks. This is . . . this is great."

She seems pleased. "You say that now. Wait 'til you see the lunchtime crowd. Word's out."

"Word?"

She cackles, delighted by my horror. "Relax. Just the regulars. And I might have ordered a cake because I'm an enabler. No clowns, no strippers —unless you want them. I can get them here."

"I really don't." I mean it.

The door jangles, and it's Miss Sue. She always arrives just before we open. She enters, brisk and starched, her hair in a no-nonsense twist. She sees the hat, sees the confetti clinging to the pastry case, and her eyes narrow, lips pinched. For a moment, I'm sixteen again, and my mother is scanning for infractions—the ledger in her head ready to tally every small rebellion.

"Kass," she says, voice velvet over steel. "Have you started festivities without me?"

Kass wipes her hands on her apron, smears of flour turning to paste on her wrists. "We're celebrating all day, Miss Sue. This one's worth it." She throws an arm around my shoulders and squeezes until my bones grind.

I smile, ducking my head so the hat stays put. Miss Sue approaches with a small, pearly gift bag, ribboned at the top with blue satin.

She sets it on the counter, directly in front of me. "For you." Her tone is warm, but there's a formality to it—like she's reciting a blessing.

Wrapped in a sea of tissue paper is a seashell. It's as large as my palm, glazed in stripes of ultramarine, white, and crimson. The spiral is flawless—no chips or barnacles—and the inside shimmers with mother-of-pearl. Along the convex ridge, a miniature scene has been painted: the café, with its blue planters and window, set against a field of foaming surf. The detail is obsessive, even as the size is small. Even the letters on the sign are legible: COTTAGE CAFÉ, in hand-inked block letters.

I stare at it, not sure what to say. Miss Sue doesn't give me the chance to fumble.

"I found it down at Rabbit Island Beach," she says, almost shyly. "Took ages to paint. That brushwork is murder on the wrists." She rotates her hand as if recalling an old injury.

"It's beautiful," I say, and the words stick in my teeth. "Thank you."

Kass leans in, studying the shell like a jewel thief. "She paints one for all the staff. You're the first to get one this soon—probably because she likes you better than me."

Miss Sue's mouth curves into a smile so small it could be mistaken for a tick. "Don't fish for compliments, Kass."

She turns back to me, gentler now. "You're a good fit, Tara. People notice when someone works hard."

Kass pipes up. "Wait, does she know the legend?"

Miss Sue rolls her eyes. "There's no legend, Kass. It's just a shell."

Kass ignores her. "Okay, so, legend says that if you find a shell this perfect, it's because it's traveled the whole world—been in the gut of a whale, encased in ice near Antarctica, carried north by the currents. It takes thousands of years to get here. And if you put it to your ear . . ." She mimics the gesture, tilting her head, eyes wide and theatrical, ". . . you can hear the voices of everyone who ever held it."

I pick up the shell, careful as if it's still alive, and set it against my ear. There's the expected rush of ocean, the pulsed air trapped in the spiral, but underneath that, a faint echo, a syllable I can't parse. It's probably just blood, but I close my eyes and pretend it's a message.

"What's it saying?" Kass asks, winking at me over the rim of a mug.

I let the silence stretch, then say, "It wants cake."

Kass whoops. Miss Sue shakes her head, but I see the smile lurking there, deep and private.

The day rolls forward in increments: orders, pickups, refills. I'm behind the register, with "Birthday Girl" perched above my head—the elastic biting into my chin. The hat is so light I barely feel it, but its presence is psychic, radiating an aura of embarrassment visible from orbit. Every other customer offers a birthday greeting. I lose myself in the comfort of routine —the muscle memory of tamping, steaming, pouring, wiping down milk spatter, restocking the biscotti.

By three, the sugar high is waning, and so am I. I retreat to the corner, slip off the party hat, and let the relief wash over me. The café is a skeleton of coffee rings and crumbs. Kass wipes down the counter, humming an unrecognizable tune, and finally corners me by the sink.

"We're going to Harry's, and don't try to weasel out—birthday clause is binding."

The thought of returning to the flat holds no appeal. I protest anyway.

"I have—"

Kass animatedly shakes her head. "You have a rare and precious obligation—to drink beer and humiliate yourself at pinball. Even Miss Sue can't override a birthday clause."

Miss Sue emerges from the back at that moment, pointing a rolled-up ledger at me like a gavel. "Go. If she keeps you out past midnight, Kass is fired."

"Eleven-thirty," Kass says. "Tops."

We leave the café. Harry's is a bar in the way old wounds are scars: dark, a little raised, but functional. The only lighting comes from neon beer signs and a flickering flatscreen mounted above the bar, looping muted rugby highlights. There are exactly four other customers: two in the throes of darts, one with his face buried in the racing results, and a woman at the end, a glass of white wine untouched, eyes sharp and predatory.

We claim a booth by the window. The seats are sticky, but we have a prime view of both pinball machines and the entire dartboard trajectory.

Kass orders a round, and when the first pint arrives, she insists on a toast. "To birthdays," she says, "to new starts, and to the best damn café staff south of the equator." She clinks her glass against mine, splashing beer onto the table. "And I only say that because I've never been north."

She gestures to the far corner, where two battered machines wait: one themed for a long-forgotten sci-fi show, the other a relic covered in faded rockabilly stars. "Pick your poison."

I pick the one with more intact lights. It's called "Galaxy High Noon," and the back glass art is all cowboy hats and green tentacles. I approach with calculated caution, but the ball drops straight down the middle—no resistance. Kass howls with glee, and the regulars at the bar turn to see what the fuss is about.

By the third round, I've adapted. My hands learn the timing, my wrists the angles. I score a series of jackpots, and Kass feigns a tantrum, collapsing into the booth in mock defeat.

"You're a shark!" she accuses, but there's pride in her voice. "You sandbagged me."

"Beginner's luck," I say, but inside, I'm grinning. The high score flashes "TARA," all caps—anointed by the machine's chirping approval.

I imagine myself staying. Not just here, in this town, but in this skin, this life. The old anxieties are there—circling like sharks in deep water—but tonight, they keep their distance. On the walk home, the sky is crisp, stars pinpricked through the clouds.

Inside, I unwrap the shell and set it on the nightstand next to my phone. I think of the story Kass told—about the shell drifting through oceans, battered and aged but still, somehow, arriving. I remember the places I've been, the parts of me I left behind or tried to, and how every day here is a small exercise in not breaking.

The shell is a reminder that things can, against all odds, survive the journey. It's as if the shell and I share a secret: what it means to be reborn in a strange place, painted over and made new by the hands of someone else.

I run my thumb along the ridge, tracing the brushstrokes. The painting is crude but true: the café, the window, the blue planters. And if I look closely, I swear I see two figures in the painted version of the café. It could be anyone. It could be me and Kass. I hold the shell to my ear. I hear the echo of laughter, a pinball hitting a bumper, bottles of beer clinking together.

CHAPTER 11

After the morning rush, the night catches up with me. My feet throb with every step as I dart between the cash register and the espresso machine. The repetition soothes me—the hiss and rattle, the heavy thud of dough on the counter. I'm learning the regulars by the grain of their voices before their faces: the mechanic's wife, always a long black—nothing else; the gangly twins who run the marina, they eat together but never speak to each other; the old stonemason who smells of moss, who asks every week if we've heard about his daughter in Sydney—as if repetition might summon her home. I fit myself between their habits.

Kass runs the counter like a stage director, her voice bright even in the early morning hours. "You've got the touch, love." I take the compliment and file it away. I'm good at blending in, not rocking the boat.

Making my way to the tables, cloth in hand, I scrub the sticky surfaces, feeling each movement radiate up my legs. Kass is in the back, on sandwiches for the lunch rush, singing a snatch of "Good Morning Starshine" in a key known only to people born without fear of shame. I work the floor, ferrying plates and dodging elbows.

At 1:38 p.m., the bell above the door gives a jingle. I don't look up right away—the first rule of survival is not to make a pattern out of the wrong moments. But there's a shift in the room that makes me check the door.

He's here. The man from the window.

He stands just inside the entry, scanning the room. His suit is thread-perfect gray, every seam unyielding. He moves with an old-school economy of someone raised on parades—every motion squared off and perfectly measured. He could be forty or fifty, depending on how the light hits his dark features.

He doesn't come to the counter for service. Instead, he selects a table at the far end, in direct line with the register. Sits, left hand on the table, the right resting at the exact midpoint on his thigh. He surveys the café again—not as a man would, but as a drone would.

Kass comes out of the kitchen, sees him, and gives a half-wave. "Customer at table seven," she mouths, then disappears again.

I take the order pad and approach, aiming for casual. My hands are already damp.

"Good afternoon." My words seem to paste together with glue and caffeine. "Can I get you something?"

He looks at me, and for a second, I think maybe he's waiting for someone. His eyes are sepia—nearly translucent. They scan my face with a slowness reserved for morgues and dental X-rays.

"Americano, black. No sugar." His voice is flatter than the horizon outside—every syllable held at the same altitude.

I turn to go.

"You're the new girl."

It isn't a question, and I almost don't answer. "Yes. Tara."

He nods. "You haven't been here long."

I detect a hint of the Midwest in his dialect. "You're American?"

He smiles, but only on one side.

I nod, tell him I'll bring his coffee right over, and retreat to the machine. As I load the portafilter, I realize I'm trembling—tiny, microscopic spasms from wrist to elbow. I fix the problem by focusing on the work: purge, dose, tamp, pull. By the time the cup is full, my hands are steady again.

When I deliver the coffee, he is exactly as I left him. His body squared to the table, eyes fixed on me. He thanks me with a nod but doesn't drink right away. Instead, he traces the rim of the cup with one finger—methodical.

"Do you like it here?"

"It's quiet."

He tilts his head, measuring the words. "You're from the States?"

"Yeah." I instantly regret it.

He nods again. "That's a long way from here."

He regards me for a second longer, then finally sips the coffee.

"Did you want to order anything else? Lunch?"

"No, thank you. I'll just have coffee."

I leave him with the check, but he doesn't move to pay. He sits, his hands now folded on the table, watching the room. Every time I look up from the counter, his gaze is on me, never quite resting.

The normal smattering of customers comes and goes. The door jingles again, and another man in a suit enters. He's younger—mid-thirties maybe—with close-cropped hair and a twitchy demeanor that sets off warning bells in my head. He scans the room with the same calculated efficiency as the first man, then selects a table near the window, his back to the wall.

I feel a knot form in my stomach. One man in a suit is an anomaly. Two is a pattern.

There's something about the new guy's posture, the way his hand keeps drifting to his coat pocket, that sets me on edge. I glance at the man with his Americano. He's watching the newcomer, too—his expression unreadable.

The door opens again, and a woman enters. She's dressed in a sleek black dress. Her hair pulled into a bun speaks business. She heads straight to the table by the window where the man is sitting. He greets her with a scowl. Her expression is taut with anger, her hands making sharp gestures. The man shakes his head.

I pick up a bin and a rag and move toward the table near the couple to clean. While I scrape a plate into the bin, their voices rise.

"Just go find another house. I'm paying you plenty."

"She is not moving into *my* house. I'm keeping it, Joe!"

With my back turned to them, I can't help but smirk. Someone else's life is falling apart.

The day dissolves into the slow sediment of crumbs and loose coins. The retirees migrate in for scones; the students arrive in a tangle of power cords. But the man in the suit remains. His cup untouched past the occasional sip, eyes tracking every movement as if building a case for or against the universe's continuity.

I wipe down the counter, then sidle up to Kass at the register. "Hey," I say softly. "You know anything about the guy in the suit? He's giving me the creeps."

"Mr. Mysterious? Must have an iron bladder."

"Seriously, though, what's his deal?" I keep my back turned, resisting the urge to check if he's still watching.

Kass shrugs. "Could be anything. Lawyer, accountant, undercover health inspector. We get suits through here sometimes." She leans in. "But you're right—he doesn't quite . . . fit. Like he's on the wrong movie set, you know?"

I nod, relieved it's not just my paranoia. "Should we say something to him?"

Kass snorts. "And risk a potentially scathing Google review? No thanks. As long as he pays, he can be as weird as he wants."

At 3:21 p.m., he stands, straightens his jacket, and approaches the counter.

"I'll pay cash." He produces a bill, perfectly flat—as if it just came off the press.

I ring it up, hands numb. "Thank you. Have a good day," I say, with the professional cheer of someone who will never have a truly good day again.

He smiles, this time with both sides of his mouth. "I always do."

I watch him walk down Victoria Street—posture unchanged, pace unhurried. He does not look back.

After closing, I clean the tables with extra care to delay my departure. By the time I leave, the sky is the blue of frozen glass, and the wind coming off the bay is sharp. I shower off the day, letting the hot water peel away the residue of coffee grounds. But I can't get the coffee out of my nose, or the man's eyes out of my skull.

With my hair wrapped in a towel, I check the blue phone that never rings. There's a missed call and a message. I drop onto the bed and read it:

> RYLAND
>
> Call me when you have a minute. No emergency.

There is no preamble, not even a please.

My hands tremble. Did the man in the suit recognize me? Did a message get intercepted? Or did someone from the past finally decide to buy a plane ticket?

My stomach flips, then sours. I try to remember the emergency protocols, but all I get is a tangle of rules and half-remembered code phrases. I dial and press the phone to my ear, counting the rings. He answers before the third.

"Ryland," he says. Not even a hello.

"Ryland." I mimic his tone. I let the silence stretch until he breaks.

"You're well?"

"As well as I can be." I pick at the splintered edge of a crate with my free hand. "You said to call."

"The reason for my call is procedural. I'll be transferring oversight of your case to a local contact at the consulate there in Werneth. It's standard practice after the initial period. They're better resourced for long-term integration."

I'm not sure if he means less paperwork for him or less scrutiny for me. Maybe both.

"Deputy U.S. Marshal Wes Kade will be your contact. He'll be discreet. Unless you prefer I handle the handoff in person?"

"I'll survive unless you think I need babysitting."

Another long pause. "You seem stable," he finally says, as if reading from a checklist. "If you notice anything out of the ordinary—surveillance, strange vehicles, unfamiliar faces—report it immediately. Understood?"

"Understood."

"Be at the consulate office in Werneth at nine a.m. You still have my number if you need anything."

I nod, then realize he can't see it. "Okay."

"Then we're good."

He hangs up. No goodbye.

I feel like a debt being sold to a new collector—the terms rewritten, the balance never quite zero. I lie back, stare at the ceiling, and listen to the sounds of the hostel: foreign voices, the clanking of pans from the kitchen, and somewhere—water running. The shower, maybe.

I send a quick text to Kass:

ME

I've got something to do in the morning. Can you cover for me?

KASS

K

I type another message to Miss Sue:

ME

Unfortunately, I won't be in early. I checked with Kass, and she'll cover for me. I'll be in before the lunch rush.

MISS SUE

Thx

I clutch the phone, hold it against my chest, and wait for morning. I wonder if this is how it feels when the old life catches up—when the web finally goes taut and the spider comes to collect.

I tell myself it's nothing. That tomorrow, I'll go back to the comfort of coffee, scone dough, and the small-town life I've made for myself. But as the hours burn on and the darkness outside thickens, I convince myself the man in the suit is not a glitch. He is a message.

CHAPTER 12

City Center, a block off the main drag, is a nondescript office. It is surrounded by squat, sun-bleached buildings that advertise the tax office, the council, and an insurance branch with mirrored windows. The U.S. Consulate building is a blank white face with glass doors. A placard beside them is stamped in both English and Māori, as if that might make it less foreign.

The air smells of the sweetness of flowers, but I don't see any around. There's a waiting area to the left, consisting of four chairs and a low table stacked with copies of *National Geographic* and a single, recent issue of *Home & Garden*. The walls display large, framed photos: the U.S. Capitol building in Washington, DC, Times Square at night, an oil derrick somewhere in Texas, the Hollywood sign in Los Angeles, and a color photo of the current U.S. president. Every little trinket in the lobby feels like a postcard from a memory lane I'd rather not stroll down.

A woman looks up from a desk and smiles. I recognize her. She was the woman who picked me up at the airport.

"Hey, Tara." Her big, brown eyes light up, which immediately annoys me. "How's the hostel?"

"It's fine. I have an appointment with Deputy U.S. Marshal Kade."

"You're a bit early," she says cheerfully. "Kade is wrapping up his previous meeting. Why don't you have a seat, and we can chat while you wait?" She gestures to the cozy waiting area. "You have to spill the tea on Werneth. I got here two weeks before you did, and it's totally boring."

I smile politely. "What do you do?"

"I'm a program analyst, but really, anything that needs doing. It's just the two of us in this office. Small town. You know."

I nod noncommittally, unsure how to respond to her exuberance. I inventory the space the way Ryland would: two exits—one up, one back; a camera dome in the corner, angled good for the front door but not for the chairs. I pick up a dog-eared magazine, open it at random, and flip through it, hoping Maddie will stop talking. She doesn't.

"You like working at the café, huh? I bet you get to meet so many people there. Anyone caught your eye?" Maddie's eyes are bright with genuine interest.

I set the magazine down without reading a single word. "It's just a job."

"I'm just so excited to have you here. It gets a bit sleepy sometimes, you know? But I have a feeling things are about to get a lot more interesting." She winks conspiratorially.

I shift in my seat, unsure of how to respond to that. Luckily, Maddie's attention is briefly diverted by something on her computer screen.

"You can follow me to the conference room." She stands. We walk across a carpet runner down a corridor. I stare at the back of her head, watching the blonde streaks from an old highlight job swish side to side. We pass a kitchenette, an empty room with glass walls, then a pair of locked doors marked with scanners. Maddie stops at the last and holds the door open for me.

The conference room is colder than the hallway, and the air is dry enough to sting. There's an oblong table, polished to a reflective gloss, with chairs. My eyes land on the man in the room, and I am immediately annoyed.

Maddie closes the door, and I am left with the man I assume is Kade. He stands with his back to the window, posture perfect. The suit is the same shade as his hair—black. His face is rawboned, mouth set in a straight line, eyes so translucent they seem colorless. He does not smile. He just wants it to be clear he's in charge.

"Wes Kade," he says, extending a hand. His palm is perfectly dry—skin like high-grade paper. Mine is clammy.

He releases the handshake and gestures to the chair opposite the window. "Have a seat, please."

I sit and inventory the items on the table: a file folder and three stapled packets.

Kade takes a seat, spine ramrod straight, then leans forward slightly. He pulls the folder toward him and opens it.

"Thanks for coming in. You met Maddie?"

"Yeah."

"So, you've been here about a month?"

"Forty-eight days."

He nods. "And you've found work, established a routine. Any problems?"

The question is loaded. I let it hang. "You mean besides a creepy man in a suit staring at me while I'm working?"

"I needed to observe you in your natural environment, Ms. Quinn." A smile lingers on his face. "You notice things. That's good. Most people don't."

Kade doesn't break eye contact as we sit in silence. "You say 'a creepy man in a suit,' but you didn't call it in?"

I'm caught. According to the protocol, I should have called it in.

"Well," I tuck my hair behind my ear, "it's not like I thought you were threatening. Just creepy."

Kade's eyes never blink. "You don't trust your gut, Ms. Quinn. Any other unusual contacts? Approaches? Odd behavior?"

"No."

He makes a note on a pad—old-school, not digital. "No one has followed you? Made you uncomfortable?"

"No."

Kade sets his pen down, then leans in just enough to make it clear the next question matters. "How are you sleeping?"

This surprises me. "Not great."

He nods, as if this confirms a hypothesis. "That's normal. New identity, new place—the brain needs time to catch up. If you need something to help, let us know."

He says "us," but it's clear he means "me."

Kade stands, moves to the credenza, and pours himself a glass of water. He offers one to me. I decline. He circles the table, stopping close enough that I can see his cuticles need pushing back. I catch the scent of his cologne —dry, not sweet, with a faint hint of aftershave and spice. He props one hip on the table's edge and looks down at me.

"There's a question I always ask," he says, voice pitched even lower. "Do you trust your own judgment?"

I know it's a trap, but I step into it. "Sometimes."

He smiles, genuine but not soft. "Good. Because sometimes, our minds play tricks, especially after trauma. You're going to see things, feel things that aren't always there. The question isn't whether it's real. It's whether you react."

He straightens as he stands, then walks around my chair to the other side of the table. The movement is smooth, but there's a sharpness to the turn—like he's used to pacing interrogation rooms.

"I know this is stressful. You're doing better than most at this stage. You recognized me from the café."

It isn't a question. I swallow, my throat dry. "Yes."

He nods, satisfied. "Good. It's important you notice things. That's how you stay alive."

I watch his hands. They are perfectly still on the table. He waits, giving me space to react. When I don't, he continues.

"I'm here to protect you. That means sometimes I watch from a distance. Sometimes I test boundaries."

I let that sink in. There's a logic to it, but not a comfort.

He opens a folder, pages fanned out like the feathers of a bird not meant for flight.

"You're settling into routine. That's good. Routine is security. But routine can also be exploited. We need to talk about your patterns."

He lifts a page. I recognize my schedule at the café. "Every morning, at six oh five you leave your apartment. You work six-thirty to three-thirty, Tuesdays through Saturdays. You go to Harry's on Wednesdays with Kass. Library on Mondays. He snaps the folder shut. "No deviation in two weeks."

"Is that a problem?" I ask.

"It's a vulnerability." He leans forward, eyes leveled. "Predictability makes you easier to target. You need to randomize. Change routes. Shop at different places. Sometimes skip work or show up late."

He watches my reaction, and I wonder if he's waiting for me to resist— or hoping I will.

"I can do that," I say, but I can feel the lie in my throat.

"Good." He runs a hand over his chin. "Per our program, you're eligible for sponsored housing for six months. We've short-listed three one-bedroom units—furnished. The program covers the deposit." He slides the first packet toward me.

"What happens after six months?"

"You pay."

I nod as I study the first packet. It's an upstairs flat above a butcher shop—definitely not the place I'd bring a date, not that I'd have to worry about that. The second is a block closer to the water—long windows, grim old carpet, but clean. The third is a ten-minute walk to work, above a frame shop. Small, but with the most decent kitchen.

"Which would you pick?" I ask.

Kade doesn't hesitate. "The last one. It's not much, but no shared walls. Quieter. If you want to see them first, that's fine. But the market's tight, so I recommend deciding today."

I sign for the third flat, sight unseen. "I'll take your word for it."

He smiles, but there's nothing soft in it. "Practical. I like that."

He pushes a rental application and a ballpoint pen across the table. "You'll need to fill this out and take it to the address at the top of the page. We'll transfer the deposit to the bank card Ryland gave you. After that, rent will be posted to this card at the end of each month, payable at the start of the following month."

We sit in silence as I fill out the paperwork.

"I can arrange local labor to transport your things. Or, if you prefer, you can move yourself."

"Light packer. One suitcase. I think I can handle it on my own."

He studies me a moment longer, then relaxes. "Good. Pass me your phone."

I slide the blue phone across the table. He takes it, fixated on the screen as his thumbs tap buttons.

"People always forget the basic features," he says softly. "This is more than a phone—GPS, dead-man switch, all the toys. But it only works if you carry it."

He walks me through the emergency notification screen, the "hold for five seconds" distress button, and the secondary code for lower-level alerts. When he's finished, he slides it back to me.

"Sometimes, people are afraid to use it, worried they'll look crazy. You're not one of those people, are you?"

I hesitate. His proximity has drained the room of oxygen.

He cocks his head. "If you're not sure, trigger the protocol. The worst that happens is we waste a few hours."

He waits, scanning my face for dissent. When I nod, he exhales slowly, frustrated.

"My number is programmed. Use it for anything, any time. No filters, no judgment." He nods, then stands. "You're adjusting well, Ms. Quinn. If you need anything—anything at all—you call me. Understood?"

"Understood." I take the application and head straight to the address listed. It's just off Victoria Street, not far out of the way.

Outside, the air is cold and sharp. I stop, glance back at the building before I turn the corner. The windows reflect the light, but behind them, I see the silhouette of Kade standing, arms crossed. Only then do I realize my hands are shaking—a micro-tremor from wrist to fingertip.

The application feels promising as I head to the rental office. There's a familiar warmth in the hostel, being among so many others. I know I can't stay there forever. I remind myself to breathe deeply. This apartment will be a doorway to this new life I am building. I must not let the fear of solitude overpower me—not this time.

I turn the corner, then the next, and do not slow down until I reach the rental office. Somewhere in the bones of the town, Kade will be mapping my every move, waiting for the next deviation. I wonder if I'll notice it before he does.

CHAPTER 13

KADE

That backward glance is a tell, in my experience. I've seen it countless times. That look. That momentary hesitation that suggests unfinished business, lingering questions, doubts she can't quite shake. I have seen that look before in assets wavering on the edge of trust. It's a look I have learned to track, to measure, to use. Because in my line of work, doubt is a vulnerability. And vulnerabilities can be exploited.

I watch Tara—Kathryn, as noted on her real birth certificate—until she disappears around the corner. Then I turn away from the window. I make the slow, unhurried walk back to my office. The air here tastes faintly of sea salt and disinfectant, a blend that only ever makes sense in old government buildings. I loosen my tie and head to my office as I make notes in my head:

The asset exits Conference Room B with her hands folded so tightly her knuckles are white. She keeps her eyes fixed on the fire exit sign. Her posture is tense, calcifying in the set of her shoulders. Trust will have to be earned.

Maddie peeks her head into the hallway. "Kade, you're not on the schedule for any—"

"I'll be in my office, Maddie." I cut her off with a small, careful smile, keeping the muscles around my eyes perfectly still. "No disturbances. I have a protocol review."

She dips her chin with exaggerated solemnity, a move I suspect worked for her as a child. Her presence irritates me. From the moment I landed and met Ryland, he couldn't stop praising her. He insists she is a rising star in the analyst world. Something about his enthusiasm seems calculated, as if there's more to her role than meets the eye. An affair, maybe. That would explain why he wants her in Werneth—close but not too close.

I keep walking. My door closes with a hush. I flick on the overheads and let the dim blue from the monitor spill across the desk. The ugly prints on the wall become featureless voids. That's how I like them.

It's always like this in the beginning. They tell you she's adjusted, she's compliant, she's grateful for the protection. But you see it—the blink rate, the hairline tremor, the way her steps hesitate at thresholds or when rounding a corner. She's bracing for the next trap.

There are days when I can almost believe Werneth is safe. That's the promise, after all. But promises are nothing if not calibrated lies, and I have been running this protocol long enough to know that the only thing harder than keeping someone safe is convincing them they are. It's almost elegant, the way a little paranoia can keep someone alive just long enough to regret it.

I settle into my office to pull up Tara Quinn's case. Inside the portal, it's all folders with cryptic codenames. The Marshal Service assigns codenames, which double as the asset's safe word in the program. Click on the wrong one, and alarms I'll never see go off. I go straight to Wildfire. The folder is orange to signal threat level status. I open it from the digital recesses of our computer system, overly burdened with multiple layers of authentication. I submit my required credentials and wait. I stare at the official seal. The case files load.

It's a biography told through bureaucracy: driver's license photo of

Kathryn Caraway, followed by college transcripts, and eventually, the mugshot-quality passport photo of Tara Quinn. The two faces hardly resemble each other. The woman in the driver's license has open, guileless eyes and a mouth caught smiling. The later version, Tara Quinn, shows a woman who has forgotten how to find joy, every muscle drawn tight around the absence of expression.

Buried in a subfolder are captures of Caraway's old social media profiles, now dead links scraped and archived by the Marshal Service before deletion. I scroll through them, pausing at a snapshot from a parade. Red, white, and blue bunting, with a crowd dense enough that nobody stands alone. Caraway is with her known associate, Lauren, holding up red plastic cups. Her eyes are not scanning the crowd for threats the way they do now.

I linger over a police report from the day after Bennett's stalking conviction. He was wearing an ankle monitor digitally tethered to Caraway's cell phone. An alarm notified her that Bennett was near her house. From the police report, I'm pleased to see she had a gun.

If she owned one, it suggests she is comfortable with firearms and possibly adept at using them. This is valuable information. I make a mental note of it.

In the folder is a report that an analyst prepared before Caraway entered the program. It sits near the bottom of the long list of PDFs. The report mentions an anonymous email Caraway suspected was from Bennett, stating he would send her yellow roses on the day he plans to kill her. The analyst notes, "Ms. Caraway understandably associates yellow roses with fear and finds them triggering."

The analyst also notes that Caraway's experiences have understandably made her wary of relying on others for protection. "Her faith in the justice system and those tasked with ensuring her safety has been shaken. Patience and consistency will be key in building a productive working relationship."

This report tells me everything I need to know. Trust will have to be earned, as her demeanor today demonstrates. I've handled assets like this before. She'll need to see me as a person, but respect me as her handler. I think about another case I had. I went too personal too early, and she balked. With this case, I have to choose just the right moment.

I navigate to the "Court Mandated" section, seeking the perpetrator's psychological evaluation, but it's just a blank tile with a spinning hourglass. I read the case notes: "Pending review from jurisdictional authority," which means the evaluation either never arrived or, more likely, someone upstream buried it, given that this perpetrator worked for the police department.

Ryland will facilitate this. I shoot him a quick message on our internal instant messaging system. His avatar, assigned at random by the system, beams next to his name. Before I click send, I lean back in my chair. I could just call Bill Cooper for it. He runs point on the case in the United States. I met him for lunch before I came to New Zealand, and that was the first time I had a conversation with him. We've known each other, working for the same service, but we've never run an operation together.

He cares about the work he does. He doesn't see the files as Ryland or I do. He sees the faces behind the files. Despite the agency's stern warnings about maintaining professional distance from assets, I think he finds it hard to suppress his empathy. It's deeply rooted in his psyche. His tendency to get attached probably intensified after the tragic loss of his daughter to a fentanyl overdose.

I glance at the time: 11:12 a.m., which means it is just past eight o'clock in the evening in the United States. Not so late that I'll catch him at home, not so early that he'll ignore a call from overseas. That would be breaking the chain of command, though.

I know Ryland does not take kindly to those who break the chain. I went through the academy before Ryland did, but he's pulled ahead of me in rank. He cares about those things in ways I don't.

I delete the message on my screen and pick up the phone. I dial Ryland's number from the consulate's secure line. I enter the required six-digit PIN. It rings so long I nearly hang up, but at the last second, a click and a drawn-out sigh announce his presence.

"Ryland." His voice is as clipped and cold as the day he forced me into this posting. Ryland. Not "Nathan," never "Nate." Always the surname.

"Kade. Quick update."

He makes a grunting sound that doubles as acknowledgment. "Go."

"Met asset this morning. Initial consult suggests high compliance but elevated sensitivity. Case file lacks the court-mandated psych eval on the perp. Can you get with Cooper stateside and track it down?"

Another pause, filled with keyboard clicks as Ryland, I assume, enters the update into whatever system they make him use now. "Sure. Do you like her chances?"

"If the system works, yes." I keep any hint of doubt out of my voice.

Ryland hums, almost a chuckle but not quite.

"When I left DC, I thought this transfer would be like early retirement," he says. "I picture him in his office—sour coffee and a stack of policies taller than him."

"They say New Zealand's like a vacation, but I don't see the appeal." He pauses, voice lowering an octave as if what he's about to say is meant for a smaller room. "I've been here two years, and my wife is already bored. How are you handling it, Kade? Any second thoughts on the transfer?"

I let the silence stretch long enough for him to imagine a dozen answers. "It's a slower pace. It suits me for now."

Ryland sniffs, either unimpressed or mildly pleased. "How many years you got left?"

"Enough to see this asset get settled, maybe a couple more."

"All right. Keep me posted."

"Always." The call drops.

I stare at the phone for a moment before returning to the file, turning the pages as if touching them might produce some deeper understanding. Each document builds a picture of what Kathryn Caraway once was and what she has become. I want to know her, not just the highlight reel. How she moves when she thinks no one is watching, how she picks up a cup or signs her name. The tells are in the hands, always.

I read everything: the formality of the intake statements, court transcripts, police reports, and a private investigator's report. Clever girl. With Bennett's background in law enforcement, I bet she had to. I know from experience how the blue brotherhood protects its own.

Lunch is a little more than a protein bar and a bottle of water. The building is even quieter after midday, the only sound a far-off printer shrieking to life and dying again. A wind picks up outside, rattling the office window in its metal frame. I check the sightlines, an old habit, and scan for anything out of place. There is nothing. This town is essentially dead. No action. My job now is to keep it that way.

I return to the file on my monitor. It's a ritual as old as the job itself, the illusion that if you know enough, you can get ahead of the threat. I know it's not true, but rituals don't require belief. Only repetition.

When I log out, the day has turned to that blue-gray dusk particular to this coast—a sky too overcast to promise anything but more of the same. I leave the desk lamp on as I go.

I'm not sure what I expect from the next meeting with the asset, but I know exactly how it will begin. I'll shake her hand, look her in the eye, and tell her, "You're safe here. Nothing's going to happen to you on my watch."

And I'll mean it, right up to the moment I have to prove it.

CHAPTER 14

TARA

The flat is a leisurely walk from the café. The rhythm of my steps on the uneven sidewalk reminds me of the small freedom I don't take for granted. The local paper calls this part of town "historical," which means the paving stones are all at odd angles and the curbs are worn to rounded nubs, slick with moss and the memory of centuries of wet feet. The houses stagger up the hill with their ancient, inward faces, but my building is a bland gray cube, maybe forty years old.

A picture framing shop sits directly beneath my apartment. It's closed three days a week and open only for the precise hours between the owner's breakfast and his mid-afternoon nap. The sign on the window, hand-painted with a flourish, reads "Werneth Fine Frames," although a closer look shows the 'r' in "Frames" droops, as if it's tired from being so upright all these years. I have no real use for frames, but I suppose it's better than a laundromat or a hair salon. Less foot traffic, less noise. Less to remind me of the comings and goings of other people's lives.

The stairs are on the side of my building. My door is a battered brown slab with a tarnished brass knocker shaped like a seahorse. I fish the key from my pocket and unlock the door, bracing myself for the interior. I let my suitcase fall with a thud just inside the door. Even with sundown and a brisk wind coming in off the hills, the air inside is thick and sour—the scent of aged milk and bleach pressed flat by a month's worth of closed windows. The paint on the walls is some shade between hospital jaundice and two-day-old custard. The realtor called it "eggshell," but only if you imagine the egg belonged to a very sick chicken.

The interior is a single open room pretending to be three. There is a slab of kitchen counter to the left, a chipped laminate rectangle with a stainless-steel sink and a two-burner stove. Above it, cabinets the color of cigarette ash—and the smell to match—hang at a slight angle. The window above the sink is filmed over with some kind of privacy coating, but still, the light seeps in. A refrigerator sits off to the side as though it were an afterthought during construction.

The middle of the room functions as a living area: a squat beige sofa and a low coffee table scarred by mug rings and what looks suspiciously like cigarette burns. An armchair with a deep crater in the seat completes the arrangement. The carpet underfoot is industrial blue, coarse and flat. The bedroom is a half-hearted alcove to the left, separated from the main room by a sliding door with a cracked pane of frosted glass. The bed is a double, with a mattress that looks as though it once served time in a county jail. There is one closet, and it is mercifully empty. Opposite the closet is a small bathroom. No tub, just a shower, which is fine with me.

The whole place is barely larger than the living room of my house in the States, but it has the singular virtue of being anonymous. No photos on the walls, no hint of its occupant beyond the battered suitcase. It is, in the truest sense, a safe house.

It could be a tomb if I let it, and I am determined not to let that happen. I throw open all four windows, small and stiff, and stand in the center of the room. The wind pours in, dragging with it the sound of the harbor in the distance. I breathe in and try not to think about how easy it would be for someone to watch from the street, to trace the fugitive outline of my silhouette against the jaundiced walls.

The kitchen is stocked with exactly three plates, three bowls, and three mismatched mugs. The drawers yield a single dull paring knife, a warped wooden spoon, and a bottle opener. I run the faucet until the water runs clear, then fill one of the mugs and drink it in one long, uninterrupted pull. The taste is strange—chlorinated, but not unpleasant. Better than any water I had back home and leagues ahead of what came out of the taps in the hostel.

There is a note on the counter, written in the realtor's precise and slanted handwriting:

Welcome, Miss Quinn.

Let us know if you need anything. The rubbish is collected Wednesdays. Bins out by 7 a.m. Shops are down Victoria, left at the bakery.

Regards,
Werneth Realty

Below the note is a business card with a number I'm to call if there are maintenance issues. I make a mental note to call and complain about the smell. It probably won't help, but it's good practice for being assertive in this new life.

I move to the bedroom and test the mattress. It sighs under my weight but holds. I sit for a long while, letting the wind rattle through the flat and push out the stale air. I am truly alone, and it feels both exquisite and terrifying. The walls are thin, but there are no neighbors, just the empty echo of the frame shop below and, somewhere far off, the low drone of a cargo ship pulling out of port.

I unzip my suitcase, fold the shirts, and tuck them into a drawer with a missing handle. I grab the other two pairs of shoes I have, including the ruby red flats I wore on the flight, and line them up in the closet. When I am done, the room looks less like a holding cell and more like a temporary refuge. I move to the kitchen and arrange the mugs by size, feeling a strange surge of pride at their orderly alignment.

The wind picks up again, battering the windows. I lie back on the bed and let it lull me, eyes on the cracked ceiling, listening for any hint of someone at the door or someone moving on the stairwell. There is nothing. Just the safe, sterile silence of a new beginning painted in the color of bad milk and sour memories.

The morning does not arrive so much as ooze through the gaps in the curtains, bringing with it a dull, damp gray that settles in my lungs. I wake to the sound of nothing, which is so unfamiliar I almost miss the chatter of the hostel. I stretch, yawn, and stare at the ceiling until I remember why I am here and who I am supposed to be.

I dress in neutral clothes: dark jeans, a faded blue pullover, and scuffed sneakers. My wardrobe has a thrift shop quality. I've selected every item for maximum forgettability. I pull my hair back in a low ponytail. I amble past Werneth Fine Frames, but I catch movement inside. A man at the counter, watching me with the curiosity of someone who has seen every face in town at least once and knows mine is new. I hesitate, then push open the door.

He looks up, pencil poised mid-air. "G'mornin', miss," he says, the words brisk and shaped by a local accent I am still learning. "You just move in up top?"

I nod, summoning a bashful smile. "Yesterday, actually. I'm Tara."

"Nice to meet you, Tara." He stands, smoothing the front of his brown button-down shirt. "I'm Stan. Stan Holloway." He pronounces it "Sten." "You from the States? New York, maybe?"

I blink. "Is it that obvious?"

He grins, showing slightly crooked teeth yellowed by age. "You'd be surprised. I'm good with voices." His eyes crinkle at the corners. "Always wanted to see New York, myself, but I suppose Werneth will have to do. What brings you to our little corner of the world?"

The question is expected, and I have a canned answer ready. "Needed a change of scenery. Kind of a fresh start, you know?"

Stan makes a sympathetic noise. "Lot of folks pass through for the same reason."

I nod, wandering to the far wall, feigning interest in a display of rustic driftwood frames. They are all slight variations of the same weathered gray, the kind of thing my mother would have found charming. I run a finger along the edge of one, feeling the fine grit of sand still embedded in the wood.

"Flat's not bad, is it? Had a young couple in there before, but she got pregnant. Moved out in less than a year. Hope you'll stay longer."

"It's fine." I let my hand fall back to my side. "Quiet. I like it."

"Should be. We're only open a few days, and I keep the noise down. But if you ever need anything fixed or, you know, framed . . ." He shrugs, a salesman's gesture more than a neighbor's. "Just holler."

"Thank you," I say, meaning it. I mumble a goodbye and slip out.

Outside, the wind has picked up, and the sky over the harbor pulses with a blue so deep it looks manufactured.

The department store is a low, flat-roofed building that looks unchanged since the 1980s, its windows plastered with posters advertising sales on men's shoes and garden tools. I grab a red plastic basket and move through the aisles, ticking off the mental list I made last night.

Dish soap, sponge, bleach wipes, toilet paper, paper towels, and a lavender-scented candle. I select sheets from a sale bin. One is white with pink flowers, and the other is a smooth purple. I stroll around the store and find the duvets. I pick out a nice floral pattern that will give the bedroom some color. A kettle, the cheapest they have, and a four-pack of mugs in cheerful primary colors. I pick up a set of flatware, a few towels, and hand towels. I look at my cart and realize I'll never get all this back to the apartment by myself. I'll need to get a taxi.

I head over to the register, my basket overflowing. The cashier, a young woman with dyed red hair and a nose ring, starts scanning my items. She looks up at me with a raised eyebrow as she bags the bleach wipes and sponges.

"Doing some deep cleaning, huh?" There's a hint of amusement in her voice.

I force a smile. "Something like that."

She shrugs and continues ringing me up. I watch the total climb higher on the display. I have to be careful with money for a while. The cashier hands me my receipt, and I gather up the bags, straining under their weight as I head for the exit. Outside, I spot a taxi idling by the curb and flag it down.

"Where to?" the driver asks as I load my bags into the trunk.

I give him the address and settle into the worn leather seat as he pulls away from the curb. Within minutes, I rattle through the front door and dump my haul on the sofa. I dart down to the grocery store, eyeing unfamiliar brands, trying to match their contents with what I'm accustomed to in the States. The bread is soft and gummy, the cheese pale, but it will do. I splurge on a jar of locally made peanut butter. Werneth's peanut butter factory sits just outside of town, and tourists seem to love it. I've been told there's a museum there, a gift shop, and a small café where you can get a peanut butter and jelly bagel sandwich. I add a small bag of apples and, in a burst of optimism, bananas. The total is more than I hoped, but I pay in cash.

The cashier, a woman about my age with bleached hair and a tattoo of a crescent moon on her wrist, barely looks up as she rings me through. She bags my things with bored efficiency.

"Thank you," I say, but she is already looking over her shoulder at the next customer.

The walk back is uphill, and I feel the weight of the shopping bags in my arms. My hands ache, knuckles whitening against the plastic. I keep my head down, eyes on the sidewalk, trying to blend into the rhythm of the street. A dog barks in the distance, then falls silent. A single car passes, music pulsing. At the top of the hill, the wind gusts, pushing me sideways as I stumble on the bottom step. I can feel Stan's gaze from behind the shop window, but when I glance back, the store is dim, and he's not there.

Inside, I sit the bags on the kitchen counter and take stock, arranging each item in its proper place. The process is slow and deliberate. When I am finished, the cupboards look less empty, the shelves less bleak. I boil water in the new kettle while washing my new mugs with my new dish soap and sponge. I make tea, watching the steam curl up toward the ceiling. The mug is warm in my hands, a small anchor.

From the window, I see the harbor, gray and restless, and the thin road that leads out of town and into the hills. It is the edge of the world, and surprisingly reassuring in its remoteness. I sip the tea. It's bitter, with a hint of lemon. The warmth spreads through me. The flat smells less of sour milk and more of possibility. For now, that is enough.

Dinner is a peanut butter sandwich, sliced apples, and a mug of sweet black tea. I arrange my meal with the reverence of a banquet on the coffee table. The bread is soft, yielding beneath the knife, and the peanut butter is gritty—nothing like the Skippy I grew up on. I take a bite, the taste unfamiliar but oddly satisfying.

I eat slowly and think about nothing, or maybe just the clatter of the spoon against the mug, the gentle ticking of the heater as it cycles on and off. I finish the sandwich, sweep the crumbs into a neat pile, and carry my dishes to the sink. When everything is squared away, I stand at the window, looking out at the clouds.

I close the curtains, turn off the lights, and sit on the edge of the bed. I stretch out, feeling the weight of the day settle into the synthetic duvet. For a while, I lie still, listening to the wind moan through the cracks. I imagine a future in this place where I cook dinner, learn the names of every street, maybe even invite Kass over. But tonight, the tea is warm in my belly, the air is free of threats, and I am not afraid to be alone.

CHAPTER 15

KADE

There's a taste in my mouth like metal filings. I fish through a box marked KITCHEN that sits among all the others shipped over from the States. I come up with a bottle of Aberlour scotch, three-quarters full, and a glass that will pass for clean. I pour two fingers, then set the bottle down with a thud, savoring the controlled violence of the motion.

I drink. The scotch is raw, like a solvent on the back of my tongue. I let it burn. I am aware, too aware of the clock in the next room. It's 21:36. There's no reason to sleep, and every reason to avoid it.

The second drink goes down easier. I drop into the lone armchair, ignoring the groan of the frame as my weight settles in. Five medals on a line of cardboard shims pass for decoration in my rental. I stare at them propped up on the mantle, standing guard over a fireplace I'll never use. Three Army Commendations: the Meritorious Service Medal, the Soldier's Medal, and the one I gaze at the longest is the U.S. Army Commendation Medal for a mission that never made the news. The citation reads "exceptional conduct in the face of operational adversity." The summary might as well have been written in invisible ink. In the end, I got the medal and six months of classified testimony. The rest is going to the grave.

I've managed harder cases than Wildfire—real threats, not just scared civilians. Once, in the Green Zone, I broke a Tier 2 operative with nothing but a deck of cards and a lie about his mother. He cried for two hours, then gave up a list of names I still have memorized.

The Wildfire case is different. It's a knife stuck in my ribs. Every time I turn, it twists. It should be routine. Victim protection is a process, not chess. Relocate the asset, isolate, observe, and report. But this asset is a tangle of nervous energy and barbed wire. The way she looks at me sometimes, like a rabbit measuring the distance of a hawk. The way she fakes calm so poorly. I admire her stubbornness, her refusal to be stifled by protocol or paperwork.

With her, I need a new approach. She's not an adversary. She's not a partner. She's—what? Something to protect, something to fix, something I could break if I'm not careful.

I set the glass down, refill, and toast the medals. I toast the empty room. I toast the girl who would rather die than submit to capture.

Tonight, the world is quiet. Tomorrow, I'll make it quieter.

The office break room is a relic. It has old linoleum, appliances that predate the century, and a vending machine locked on "exact change only." The coffeepot in the afternoon is a war zone: scorched remnants in the carafe, an inch of black water pooled at the bottom that's thick as molasses. I resist the urge to smash it against the sink.

The Cottage Café will be closing soon. I grab my coat and head out, leaving the lights on in my office. I slip out without Maddie noticing. Wildfire is the only case we're working on, and Maddie seems too invested in it for an analyst. Every analyst I've collaborated with dreams of a case that will propel their career and gain recognition. Her ambition isn't new to me, but it's still annoying.

The walk to Victoria Street is all headwinds. The town is built for secrets, not for comfort—every block a blind corner, every alley a funnel for the sea's salt ache. At the corner, I pass a trio of teenage boys in hoodies, all eyes and elbows, and they go silent when I approach. I like that. I take the main road, letting my pace stretch out, then cut down the side street to the bakery. The bell above the café door gives a single jingle.

Inside, the place is almost empty. An elderly couple nurse cups of tea, arguing over a crossword. A woman in a blazer clicks at her laptop, mouthing something to herself. The counter is clean and freshly wiped, the pastry case down to the dregs, including one scone, a trio of muffins, and a loaf of sourdough scored so perfectly I want to shake the hand of the maniac who baked it.

Miss Sue notices me the second I enter, her eyes shrewd above the half-moon readers on her nose.

I order a long black, no sugar, and she pours it herself. "You've been in town, what, a couple of weeks now?" she says, more statement than question.

I nod. "Starting to feel like home."

She leans in, lowering her voice. "They say you work at the consulate. That true?"

"It depends. Who are 'they'?" I match her volume.

She gives a sly smile. "Bet you see all the best bits. Not like this lot," she jerks her chin at the customers, "who never have a secret between them."

"I do help U.S. citizens handle passport or visa issues. Mostly paper pushing."

She glances over my shoulder, then back to the register. "Speaking of which. You know Tara, my new girl? She's American, too. Just came here."

I keep my face neutral. "I've met her. I'm helping her with her visa."

Miss Sue slides a cup of coffee to me. "Let me know if she needs a sponsor. She's a good employee. I'd hate to lose her."

"Thanks, I'll keep that in mind."

Tara is at the far end, restocking the sugar caddies, her hands moving in quick, defensive bursts. She senses me before she looks up, and when she does, her face closes like a fist. I approach slowly, letting the distance shrink in a series of neutral steps.

"You want something, or just here to observe?"

"Needed a caffeine fix." I take a sip for good measure.

Behind us, the couple raises their voices over a disputed clue. "What's a seven-letter word for 'delusion'?" one shouts.

I answer without turning. "Fantasy."

The room goes quiet, and I hear a pencil scratch the answer down.

Tara rolls her eyes, but a flicker of something flares before she kills it. Amusement, maybe. She stacks the sugar caddies, then steps aside. She begins to restock napkins in the tabletop dispensers. I reach out and help. Our hands brush once, and she snatches hers back as if I'd burned her. I immediately retreat and return to drinking my coffee.

She gives me a cold, clinical look, like she's dissecting a frog she already knows is dead. "You always on the clock?"

"Only when I need to be." I smile and make an effort to show some teeth. When my cup is empty, I set it on the counter and tap twice—a habit from a life I don't talk about. Tara glances at the motion.

I scan the room again. No threats, no tails, just the rhythm of a shop getting ready to sleep. Miss Sue kills the front lights, then rattles the coin drawer in the till, a code to the regulars that nothing free will be dispensed tonight. The last customers shuffle out wrapped in scarves.

"Closing in five, if you want bread for home," Miss Sue says for my benefit.

I take the sourdough loaf, pay cash, and thank her. As I leave, I catch Tara watching me, her face half-shadowed by the lights. The bell jingles, announcing my departure. I stand outside, tearing off small chunks of the bread and eating them. There's a texture to fresh, homemade bread that reminds me of my grandmother. My eyes drift down the street, absorbing the details I am trained to notice. People bustle past, a blur of diverse faces. Some chat animatedly on their phones, others huddle in groups, and a few simply enjoy the afternoon sun. A couple that looks like they're from out of town is snapping photos while a busker strums a gentle chord on his guitar. In front of him, an open case holding a sprinkling of coins. I stroll over, take a few bills out, and toss them into his case. He nods, a gesture of grateful acknowledgment.

Tara emerges from the café and stops, crossing her arms over her chest defensively. "I can walk myself."

"Indulge me."

I'm sure she's considering telling me to bugger off, but something in her posture relents.

"Fine."

I move to the curbside, body angling her toward the safety of the shopfronts. She rolls her eyes at the maneuver but doesn't step out of range. We walk in silence past the liquor shop, then the hardware store with its window displays of power tools and rat poison. I scan the rooftops, the alleys, the parked cars. Old habits die hard. She notices.

"You ever turn it off?" she asks, not bothering to specify what.

"Not in this line of work." I keep my voice light.

She grunts.

I decide to let her in on the trade secret. "If you want to survive, you assume everyone is lying. Even the good ones."

She laughs. "Is that in the handbook?"

"Page one."

We cross the street. Werneth is a small town. News travels on foot, then by rumor, then by text. I feel the weight of observation, but it's friendly.

She hugs her bag tighter, her gaze fixed ahead.

I try to draw her out. "What do you miss most about your old life?"

She blinks, clearly thrown by my question. "What?"

"In the States. What do you miss?"

She shrugs. "Decent coffee."

"That all?"

She walks another ten steps before answering. "That's the price, right? I get to . . . not die."

I watch her for signs of a break, but she's solid—at least on the outside. "Do you ever think about home?"

She shivers, either from the cold or from memory. "I think about it all the time, but I'm not stupid."

The words hang in the air, loud as a siren.

I change the subject. "Have you taken any self-defense classes?"

"Not since I left the States. Do you think I should take a refresher?"

"Couldn't hurt."

We reach her street, Victoria Terrace. I follow her to the frame shop, then pause at the steps leading up to her apartment.

She fishes for her key and then goes up the stairs while I watch from below. The door clicks behind her, and I wait, listening for the lock.

On my way back to the office, I tear off a piece of bread and eat it dry, chewing slowly, thinking of the way her voice cuts even when she tries to keep it level. She's going to be more work than I thought. Whatever Bennett did, I pity any man who tries to get close to her now.

I pull out my phone and check for messages.

> RYLAND
>
> Confirm Friday 09:00 for polygraph calibration.

> ME
>
> Affirmative

I've done baseline polygraphs at every duty station. It's routine. The polygraph needle will twitch at my half-truths, but Ryland won't push. I feel an itch between my shoulders. It is a warning I've learned to trust. I pace the block once, twice, watching for tails, listening for the echo of steps that aren't mine. I finish the loop. Satisfied there is no tail, I continue to the office. When I arrive, Maddie has left for the day. Remnants of her presence remain at her desk—a lipstick-stained mug and a candy wrapper.

In my office, there is an old school gunmetal gray four-drawer filing cabinet—ancient enough to predate every operation I've worked. From the bottom drawer, I retrieve my briefcase. Inside, underneath the week's expense report and an unopened goodbye card from my previous staff, is the flip phone. Most people refer to this as a "burner" because it's hard to trace, the kind favored by hitmen. It's also standard for deniable ops by the agency.

I slot a new SIM card in. I have an entire arsenal of these tiny cards. These aren't like the extras at the office. I acquired these personally, ensuring they are untraceable. The phone powers up, and I watch the tiny welcome screen flicker through its death throes.

The number is stored in muscle memory, not the phone itself. I let it ring once, twice, and on the third, a click. Not a voice, not even a static shuffle, just the implicit acknowledgment that someone is there.

"Status update," I say, keeping my tone bland and matter of fact. "Contact established. First impression within margin. Asset presents as an average risk for flight, but nothing outside expected variance."

I listen carefully to the question.

"Negative," I continue. "No deviation detected. She's hypervigilant, yes, but not suspicious. It's classic textbook. She wants to believe this is a sanctuary. I'll work to help her believe that."

I listen, imprinting an invisible note in my head. My mind does this of its own accord, a vestige of the years I spent interrogating field assets, always with an eye on the twitch and tell.

"No, not yet. I need her pliable, not adrenalized. Give it time."

The connection ends with the simple vanishing of a presence. I snap the phone shut, remove the SIM, and break it with a pair of nail clippers kept in the desk drawer for just this purpose. The phone goes back in the briefcase, the spent SIM into an old pill bottle, nondescript and generic.

I pull up the file and start a new entry:

SUBJECT: QUINN, TARA (FKA KATHRYN CARAWAY)

ASSESSMENT: Asset continues to exhibit expected surges of anticipatory anxiety. Observed marked increase in shoulder tension, repeated self-soothing gestures, and two incidents of environmental scanning while in transit. Notably, asset performs redundant security checks when unobserved. Hypervigilance exceeds baseline estimates, possibly comorbid with stress-induced dissociative episodes.

ADVISED: Escalate to enhanced direct and indirect contact.

I reread the lines, feeling an odd, low-grade empathy for the person in the file. The urge to revise comes. I do not indulge it. I save the file and close the database.

The world falls away beneath me, and I feel the slow, sure click of the trap closing.

CHAPTER 16

TARA

The morning sun pokes through the filthy windowpane. I watch Mr. Holloway's son spray the sidewalk with a hose. This is one of the few days the frame shop will be open. He never looks up. I pace the length of my bedroom—seven steps from door to bed, six steps back. I'm also counting the seconds until Kade's arrival. My phone says 8:18 a.m. He's due at half past.

When the knock comes, it screams Kade: three hard raps, spaced with military symmetry. My spine snaps to attention, and I nearly drop the mug I've been pretending to sip from. I sit it down and wipe my palms on my shirt. I force my shoulders back before I open the door.

Kade is standing there as if he's been waiting for hours. His hair is neat, and the tie is knotted like a tourniquet. He is wearing the same charcoal suit from yesterday, with a sharper blue shirt. His shoes are the color of a saddle I once rode on a horse.

"Ms. Quinn," he says, with the faintest of bows. He closes the door himself and gestures for me to follow. "Let's walk through the basics, room by room." His tone is easy, but there's a wire behind it—something coiled.

With a clipboard in one hand, a pencil in the other, he steps past me, scanning the air as if it may contain contraband or a stowaway. I'm still standing by the door, and when he looks over his shoulder at me, I'm sure he senses my reluctance.

"This is standard protocol," he says, voice pitched to fill the small space. "Just a walk-through. Shouldn't take more than twenty minutes." The vowels flatten out to a Midwestern, maybe Wisconsin, accent—or perhaps it's just generic.

Kade walks the perimeter and pauses at the window, fingers brushing the lock. He toggles it once, twice, then makes a note on his clipboard. His gaze sweeps the street below, then up to the row of flats across the alley. He studies the angles, the sight lines, the shadows. I wonder what he sees that I don't.

He turns to me, all business. "Any visitors? Maintenance, delivery, unexpected knocks?"

I shake my head. "Just the landlord once, to check the fridge. And a stray cat."

His mouth twitches like he's holding back a smile. "Best to assume all cats report to someone."

I have no idea if that's a joke.

Kade moves to the balcony door. It's a thin slider that opens onto a strip of concrete and a view of the alley. He unlocks it, slides it open, then closes it, his hands mapping the frame as if memorizing every imperfection. "The catch on this is worn. I'll get a bar installed."

He walks to the kitchen, which is just a countertop barely wide enough for a kettle and the world's loneliest microwave. He opens and closes the cabinet doors, inspects the inside of the fridge, and makes more notes. I watch in horror at the intrusion and can only imagine what he has in store for my bedroom and bathroom.

"This window needs a second lock," he says, voice clinical. "The fire escape access is visible from the alley. If you're concerned, I can have the department send someone to fit a bar. Takes five minutes."

He moves to the bedroom before I can respond and opens the door without asking.

"Bedroom's just the bed, a nightstand, and the dresser, correct?"

"Yep."

He circles the room and inspects the window latch above the bed. The blue phone on the nightstand catches his eye, and he checks the cord that leads to a nearby outlet. "You keep it charged?"

"Always." It's not a lie.

With the tip of his pencil, he pushes the bathroom door open. I catch the shape of my damp towel on the rack, the half-spent toothpaste tube, and the hairbrush that needs a haircut on the sink. After looking at the showerhead, checking the vent, and closing the door softly behind him, he jots something on his clipboard and heads back to the kitchen.

He sits in the chair, back perfectly straight, and lays the clipboard flat on the small, scuffed-up table. The pencil remains angled in his hand as if he's about to write.

"I know this feels invasive." He looks directly at me. His eyes are intense, but then again, so is he. "But it's for your safety. We've found that most lapses in protocol happen at home. People get comfortable, and that's when the old life catches up."

"What's with the floor plan you drew?"

"For my knowledge. In case I need to get to you."

His tone is earnest, almost fatherly. It makes me want to confess to things I haven't even done. He flips the page and puts pencil to paper.

"We'll need to rearrange the bed. Push it to the opposite wall. That way, if someone tries to break in, you'll have time to react." He draws a quick diagram, arrows and all, then taps the corner. "I'll schedule maintenance to help you with that."

There's a rhythm to his words, a sound of control. Every suggestion is a command, every correction a small act of ownership.

I want to say it's overkill. I want to say it's unnecessary. "That saves what? A fraction of a nanosecond?" I shrink a little in my seat at my cavalier attitude. I don't want to seem ungrateful.

Kade levels a serious look at me. "That fraction could be the difference between life and death. *Your* life and death.

"The entry door is solid, which is good. But the peephole is misaligned. You can't see the landing. That's a vulnerability." He scribbles again. "I'll get that fixed, too."

He stands, smooth and unhurried, and takes a slow lap around again. He notices everything: the chipped mug on the counter, the orientation of the outlets, the proximity of the smoke detector to the range. He points out the spot where the carpet has peeled up.

"Potential trip hazard. In an emergency or struggle." He scribbles a note on his clipboard. "I'll have maintenance nail that down."

"I can have the landlord fix it." I figure that's the least I can do.

"No. It won't take but a minute while my guy is here for the other items. Any issues with the building?" He's facing me now. "Noise, plumbing, suspicious activity?"

"Nothing so far. Unless you count the neighbor's cat."

He almost smiles, then places the clipboard on the table. He rubs his thumb along the paper's edge as if weighing the next words.

"I know this is difficult," he says softly. "Starting over isn't easy. But you're doing well. Your work at the café, your integration with the community — it's all exemplary."

He looks at me, and for the first time, I see something vulnerable flicker behind the mask. His eyes are almost apologetic. "If you ever need anything, anything at all, use the phone. Don't hesitate."

Kade steps to the door, then pauses, with his hand on the knob. "I'll be in touch. Until then, remember to randomize your routes."

Standing in the center of my tiny kingdom, I let the new rules settle into the bones of the room. I check the time: 8:49 a.m. He was gone in twenty minutes, as promised. But it's the changes he left behind that will keep me awake tonight.

Evening pours through the window, slow and syrupy, turning the walls of my apartment the color of an old bruise. I sit on the sofa, legs curled, waiting. Kade said he'd return this evening to complete the audit, which probably means he's somewhere outside now, measuring the dusk in footfalls. I hear the thud of his shoes on the stairwell, the familiar pattern: two quick, one slow. I open the door before he knocks.

He steps in, with less business in his posture this time, but just as much intent. He stands by the window and looks out.

"Weather's turning."

I nod, unsure if he means the rain, the air, or the circumstances.

"I've got everything I need."

"What did you need this evening that you didn't get this morning?"

"Night survey. Needed to get a view from the outside, to see if there are any vulnerabilities."

"And?"

"The windows have sufficient coverage, as long as you keep the blinds closed at night."

I nod.

"One more thing. Limit your contact with Miss Mitchell. She's friendly, but talks too much. If she asks about your past, change the subject."

It lands like a slap. I start to object, but reconsider. "Kass?"

"Correct. Is that a problem?"

I shake my head while he starts a slow lap of the room, not touching anything this time. He stops, then turns to face me, a silhouette against the lamp in the corner. "May I ask you something, Tara?" His voice is gentle, but the question is a hook.

"Of course."

He steps closer, but not so close as to be improper—just enough that I can see the way his jaw tenses.

"Do you trust me?" The words freeze the air.

"I trust the program."

He watches me, waiting for more.

"And you?" I add, softer. "I trust that you want me safe."

He nods, as if this is both the best and worst answer I could give.

He stands in silence for a breath, then lowers his voice. "Trust is essential, Tara. In our arrangement. If I ever ask you to do something, no matter how strange or urgent, you need to do it. Without delay, without question. That's how people survive."

His hand lifts, slow and deliberately, and he places it on my shoulder. His grip is light.

"Can you do that for me?"

I nod, but my muscles beg me to flinch away.

He holds the contact for a moment, then lets his hand drop to his side. "Good."

I stand there, my pulse quickening in the hush. He closes the door behind him, soft and final. Outside, the last light of day dies. Inside, the blue phone is charging on the nightstand, a bright dot in a room of gathering dark. I watch it and wonder which of us will blink first.

CHAPTER 17

KADE

A week slides by in administrative increments: days measured out in recertification webinars and risk assessments, nights in the same chair, scotch levels dropping with the mercury. By Friday, the security contractor finishes upgrading Tara's flat: new locks installed, a second lock to reinforce the window, and an electronic peephole with a 180-degree view mounted on the front door.

The sliding glass doors of the grocery store hiss when Tara enters the grocery store. She doesn't notice me, though it is my job not to be noticed. I count the seconds it takes for her gaze to hit the convex security mirror above the entrance: three. She looks for shapes that shouldn't be there. She's gotten better at this. Last month, she drifted through stores in a numb daze. Now she plays rabbit, flicking glances to the endcaps and the perimeter.

Tara grabs a basket, not a cart, expecting a short stay. I keep my distance. There is an art to following without being seen. You become an artifact of the store. Nobody sees you until you make yourself known. I wonder if Tara knows I'm watching. I wonder whether she cares.

She lingers too long in the produce section, pretending to debate apples, scanning the colors, shapes, and shoppers, looking for anomalies. Her hand hovers over a green apple but retracts when a tall man in a blue work vest moves too close. The fruit goes unselected, and she drifts on. Every move catalogued, every hesitation noted.

At the self-checkout, she moves fast, scanning with more force than needed. I count four glances over her left shoulder, three to her right, and a final one to the convex mirror overhead. I let her finish bagging, step forward, and intercept her at the automatic doors.

"Hi, Tara," I say, voice set to soft authority. "Allow me."

She startles, reflexively clutching her bag to her chest like a child refusing candy from a stranger. Her mask cracks for half a breath when she recognizes me. Not necessarily my face, but my role—the one who holds her leash.

"I've got it," she says, voice flat. "Really."

She tries to sidestep, but the vestibule is narrow, and I block it with a single, easy step. She hates me for this, and I understand. She looks down. The washed and gray light outside leeches color from everything; it is that kind of day.

"You could just let me walk home."

"I could."

She pushes past me, breaking the standoff, and I let her go. I made my presence known, and that's enough. There's no point in making a scene, not in a town like this where everybody knows what everybody had for breakfast. I watch her stride across the parking lot, steps quick and uneven, until she disappears into the haze.

I wait a count of twenty before moving to my car. There's no hurry. The game is slow, and I have all the time in the world. Besides, I already know her next move. I've read her case files more times than I can count. Every time I do, I find something new. I write a note on the pad balanced on my thigh:

Subject increasing self-protective behaviors with handler. Signs of hypervigilance.

There are days when I think about telling her the truth—we aren't just watching for Bennett, we're logging her moves, her communications parsed for lapses—but it would only make her more paranoid.

I key the ignition and pull away from the curb. I drive slowly, tracing the road to the consulate, the sky the color of old bone. The real danger is always the one you don't see coming. I file the thought away for later, with all the others. I sip cold coffee from a travel mug, staring at the rain beading on the windshield.

My office is more like a tomb. The building is too quiet. I log in and go straight to the Wildfire file. My fingers move out of muscle memory—passwords, two-factor authentication, the little blue circle spinning, always hungry.

Finally, the file loads. I scroll through the summary again, my lips pursed. The summary page is different. Tara's address—the new one. Her street number is wrong by a single digit. I know I entered it as 401 Victoria Terrace. It now reads 410. This is the kind of typo you don't notice unless you've memorized every detail of the case. I check the edit history. Even the automated change log has been sanitized. Every edit, every file accessed, is logged with a timestamp and badge ID. The feed I'm looking at is choked with dummy entries—hundreds of system status pings that drown out any real activity. Classic obfuscation.

I scroll to a document titled "THREAT ASSESSMENT/BENNETT, T." There's a psych report here—the one I asked for—but when I try to open it, I get an error: "File not found. See system admin." My jaw clenches until I feel it in my temples. I dig deeper. The dummy entries started this morning, at precisely the time I watched Tara at the grocery store.

My fingers find the bridge of my nose and pinch. I sit with my eyes closed, thinking through the implications. I reach for the notepad I've dedicated to Tara's case. I turn to a new page and write, each word a nail in the coffin of plausible deniability: "Observed unauthorized edit to subject's file. See attached log. Retain for audit." I print the page, fold it in half, and staple it to the page.

I lean back, eyes closed, counting the seconds between the flickers of the light overhead. I breathe in, out—slow and measured. I feel the weight of the air, suspicion settling in. I remember Afghanistan, where the file said one thing, the orders another, and the truth was always a moving target. There is always someone else holding the leash, someone you can't see.

I know Maddie is coming before she knocks. Her footsteps are distinct. She enters, carrying a stack of case files—the kind of paperwork that used to fill boxes before we digitized our secrets. Today, they're props. A comfort to people who distrust screens. She's dressed in her usual bright colors—a floral blouse, yellow skirt, plastic badge lanyard covered in pins and puns. Her pasted-on smile. Her eyes scan my desk, my hands, the layout of the room. Maddie never stops gathering intel.

"Afternoon, sir," she sings, her tone just this side of mocking. "Got your assignments from the High Command." She drops the files on the desk. The top folder is thick, creased where someone gripped it too tight.

"Ryland keeping you busy?" I say, not bothering to look up.

She shrugs. "You know how it is. End of the quarter, everyone's a little testy. He says you're to review these old cases. Something about learning Werneth. I don't know. Seems to me that every case is different."

I flip the cover open. It's the kind of camouflage you use when you want to divert attention.

Maddie doesn't move. Instead, she leans on the edge of my desk, studying the iceberg picture on the wall as if seeing it for the first time. Maddie arrived here before me, so she's had plenty of time to see it.

"Thanks." I keep it neutral with her. "You can leave them."

She hesitates, and in that pause, I see the real Maddie—the one who scored highest in her class, who tracks every case like a bloodhound, who's desperate to rise above her current pay grade. She straightens up, and the smile flickers, then returns.

"Is there a problem, Maddie?"

"No. Not at all."

"Quick question. Did you change Tara's address in the system?"

"No." She sounds honest. The good liars always do.

"Who has access to the Wildfire files?"

She hesitates. "You. Me. Ryland, I think. Why?"

"No reason. Just making sure my ducks are in a row."

She releases a nervous laugh. "Just . . . don't work too late, okay?" Her hand hovers over the files, as if wanting to touch them, then she pulls back. "I heard the security system's acting up again. Power spikes."

It's not an empty warning. There were two blackouts on the security footage last week.

"Duly noted. Anything else?"

She shakes her head, hair bouncing slightly on her shoulders. "Nope. Just being thorough. You know me."

Maddie leaves, her footsteps vanishing down the hall. She's a counterpuncher, not a brawler. She's not going to make a move without someone telling her to, which means if I'm right to be suspicious of Maddie, she is a pawn.

CHAPTER 18

TARA

My eyes snap open to the glaring sun, pulse pounding, body braced for the coming workday. What the hell happened to my alarm? I remember halfway through my third shallow breath that it's my day off. The relief is so sharp it hurts.

Sunlight fingers the empty wineglass on my nightstand. For a minute, I let myself believe in a version of reality where nothing has changed—no intrusive consular officers, no government law enforcement officers haunting Werneth's streets, no secrets boiling just beneath my skin. I stretch my arms overhead and listen to the building settling around me.

I plan to walk to the bookstore, but the thought of stepping outside and bumping into Kade makes my chest cinch. It feels like he's everywhere. I don't want to risk another encounter.

I drag myself to the kitchen. Coffee beans in the grinder, filter fitted—the ritual soothing. I go through the motions and try not to dwell on how hollow the apartment feels since Kade did his inspection. He didn't change much, but somehow it feels sanitized.

I try to read yesterday's paper, but the words swim and vanish on the page. By my third cup, my nerves are shot. I pace the kitchen, wiping down the counters for the second time. I dig my phone from the pocket of my sweatpants and stare at it so long the screen dims and goes black. Then, before I can talk myself out of it, I pull up Nathan Ryland's number.

He answers after two rings, sounding exactly as I expect: brisk, military, not quite awake.

"Ryland."

"It's Tara," I say, then quickly add, "Wildfire." I cringe at how much I sound like I'm in a spy movie. If I am, send James Bond. Immediately.

Ryland is silent for a half-beat. "Is everything all right?"

I open my mouth, but no words come. "Yes. No. I just—" My throat closes. "Do you have a minute?"

He sighs. "Is this an emergency, or may I call you back in thirty minutes?"

"It's not urgent. I just have a question." I sink into a kitchen chair, dragging my legs up to my chest.

"Go ahead," he says, tone soft around the edges. "I'll make time."

I clear my throat. "Kade walked me home from the café. He said it was protocol. But—" I hesitate, listening to Ryland's breath on the line.

"But you found it excessive, overbearing?"

"More like unsettling," I say, voice barely above a whisper. "He also followed me to the grocery store. He's different from you. He's so—"

"Intense?"

"Yes." My head drops into my hand. "He never takes his eyes off me. Like he's memorizing everything I do."

Ryland laughs, a dry rustle of sound. "That's his job. Kade is very thorough. But I understand. He can come on strong."

I close my eyes. "Is he always like this?"

"Depends on the assignment. He's highly decorated. Led a dozen witness extraction ops in Eastern Europe, five in Southeast Asia. He's not the type to half-ass anything."

I can practically see Ryland squinting at a dossier through the phone.

"What day did he walk you home?"

"Two days ago."

"Hold a moment." There's shuffling, the clack of keys. Silence, except for the faint background noise of a news channel. I picture Ryland in a government office, blinds drawn, tie loosened but never removed.

After what feels like a century, he comes back. "I'm reading his case notes now. He logged an in-person sweep at fifteen-thirty. Standard for a protection detail during a heightened threat phase. Nothing unusual. Did he say or do anything that made you feel uncomfortable?"

I think of Kade's smile, precise as a scalpel. The way his gaze lingered on my hands, the arch of my neck. He hadn't done anything overt. Nothing obvious. It's all subtext. But Ryland isn't wired for subtext.

"No. I guess not."

Ryland seems to relax. "Kade is a pro. If there's anyone you'd want on your side in a crisis, it's him. Consider yourself lucky."

I roll my eyes at the ceiling. "Why would someone with his record want to be stationed in Werneth? No offense, but it's not exactly a hotbed."

Ryland's laugh is genuine, if brief. "None taken. I asked him the same thing. He said he wanted a change of pace. That after thirty years in the field, a few months in New Zealand sounded like a working vacation." Ryland pauses, voice softening. "We all run out of adrenaline sooner or later."

I pick at a loose thread on my sleeve. "So, there's no reason to worry?"

"Absolutely not. If anything, you should feel safer."

"I'll try."

"Good."

"Thank you."

He hangs up first, as always. I stare at the screen until the glow dissolves to black, and my reflection stares back. I feel a flicker of shame. Maybe the loneliness is getting to me. It doesn't matter. Ryland's words do what they're supposed to do.

I spend the day lazing on the sofa, binge-watching an Australian series. Their accents are so thick I have to turn on captions to follow along. I'm pouring water over tea leaves when my phone rings. The name on the screen is enough to make me smile: Kass, followed by a rainbow emoji and a smiley face.

I hesitate, remembering what Kade said. I answer anyway.

"Hiya," I say, trying for cheerful and landing somewhere in the vicinity of deranged.

"You busy?" Kass shoots back, her voice a burst of static and sunshine. "I had to kick a table of school moms out at closing. Needed to hear a sane voice before my brain unspools."

I glance at the clock. "It's not even three."

"Great! I'd love to meet you for happy hour when I get off. I'll buy the first round."

"That wasn't an invitation." I laugh. The memory of Kade's flat, unyielding voice pinches my mind. He'd been very clear that I should limit my contact with Kass. He'd called her Miss Mitchell, like she was an official hazard. I'd dismissed it at the time, but now the warning sticks.

"Can't," I say too fast. "I'm . . . uh, exhausted. Stayed up too late last night with a bottle of wine. Raincheck?"

Kass huffs. "You've gone old lady. I love it."

She doesn't push. She never does. We talk for another minute or two, trading gossip. When we hang up, the apartment is silent. I heat a bowl of soup and eat it in front of the TV. The glow bathes the room in cartoon blue. I try to care about the cooking competition on screen, but the only suspense I feel is a dull, persistent ache behind my eyes. By midnight, I'm sprawled on the sofa, blanket cocooned, every light in the flat on. I don't remember falling asleep.

The next morning, I wake with the hangover of too much nothing—a faint headache, a mouth dry as paper. By 6:05 a.m., I'm dressed and off to work, propelled by a hunger for normalcy. I let the salty air clear my head as I walk through town and join the slow trickle of pedestrians.

Kass is already at the café when I walk in. "Get your beauty sleep?"

I honestly don't know how she stays so perky all the time.

"Yeah, but I need coffee," I say with a big yawn.

The tables soon fill with regulars, and I have a break at the register. Two old men play chess by the window, the board wedged between their mugs. Near the back, two girls are hunched over a MacBook. A councilman I half-recognize from the newspaper is holding court with what I think is his staff. The group around him is dressed in sharp suits and crisp blouses. They nod and scribble notes, their eyes glued to him. When their meeting ends, they rise in unison, following him out the door in a neat procession.

By mid-morning, I've successfully eavesdropped on the entire café. The town gossips have moved on to a city council scandal. I wonder if that's what brought the councilman and his staff in. Ms. Whitfield is deep in conversation with a young mother, schooling her on how to teach proper manners. I think the mother is being polite because the child is a baby, maybe six months old.

The bell on the door jingles, and I glance up to see a man walk in. His dark hair is tousled from the wind outside. He's handsome but doesn't carry himself like he knows it.

"What can I get for you?" I ask with my widest smile.

"Uh . . ." He stares at the chalkboard behind me, his mouth gaping open as he decides. "So many choices. I don't know." His English accent makes me weak in the knees.

"What do you like?"

"It's not for me. It's for my sister. She's in the hospital and sent me. This is her favorite place."

"Who's your sister? If she's a regular, I probably know her order."

His eyes drift down to the counter. "Leesa Parker. Do you know her?"

"Yes, of course. She always orders a latte with an extra shot of espresso. What's it to be for you?"

"Long black, please. And I'll take a few of these pastries to go. Surprise me. What Leesa doesn't eat, I can give to the nurses caring for her."

There's tenderness in the way he speaks that pulls at my heart. "I'll get that started. Is Leesa alright? She hasn't been here in a few weeks."

He shakes his head. Sadness fills his face, and I instantly regret asking.

"She's, uh, got cancer."

My hand flies to my mouth; my eyes go wide. Leesa usually comes in after cycling—the poster child for fitness. She's told me about the triathlons she's been in all over the world. I'm shocked. I thought Leesa was healthy, strong. I know she's not much older than me.

"It's okay," he says to soothe me as he removes a card from his wallet.

I should be soothing him. Instead, I shake my head. "It's on the house. Tell Leesa her café gang is rooting for her. Can I get a name for the order?"

"Edmund." He smiles, his blue eyes crinkling at the corners.

I get his order together quickly, carefully selecting the best pastries in the case. I feel a familiar flutter in my stomach, but I work to suppress it. I place the box on the counter and close the lid. When I look up, he's staring at me. I feel the heat rush to my cheeks. I watch him leave. When he reaches the door, he spins around then smiles, nods Our eyes meet. I quickly look away, embarrassed.

I'm in the back, untying my apron, when Miss Sue's voice rings out. "We're closed."

Intrigued, I grab my purse and head out front. There's Edmund, standing tall and casual, and Miss Sue gives me a knowing, motherly nod. I can't help but grin as I make my way over to him.

"What brings you here?" I feel a flutter in my chest.

"I was in the neighborhood and thought I'd swing by to walk you home. Could do with a bit of fresh air."

Feeling a bit shy, I tuck a stray lock of hair behind my ear. Edmund extends his arm, and I loop mine through.

"I was gonna stop by the bookstore on my way home."

"Perfect." He smiles. "Maybe I can find something to help pass the time at the hospital."

The bookstore charmingly labels a cozy corner with checkered tiles nestled in the back as the "Coffee Nook." The espresso machine is a modest, compact model, dwarfed by the one we have at the café, but I find comfort in letting someone else take over the brewing. We settle into the plush armchairs, surrounded by towering bookshelves, and spend the next two hours in easy conversation. Our topics range from the mundane to the philosophical musings of our favorite authors.

We get up to leave, and I am genuinely sad. I could sit here all night and talk to Edmund, but I know he needs to get back to the hospital. On our way out, he asks if I think Leesa will like the book he picks up from a round display table. I scan the back cover and tell him it sounds suspenseful, if that's her type of reading. He nods and heads to the cash register while I look at the other books on display.

We step out onto the street. Edmund glances down at his watch, the leather band snug around his wrist.

"I can walk you home."

I shake my head gently. "It's okay, I don't live that far. Please, give my best to Leesa."

"I've been sitting around the hospital for almost a week now," Edmund says, leaning in slightly. "There's a place on the harbor I've been wanting to try. Perhaps you might join me there Friday night?"

My heartbeat quickens. I take in his hopeful expression, the way he fidgets with the cuff of his wool coat. He exudes a genuine warmth. I blink in surprise, my mind racing. A thousand reasons to say no flick through my head, but my mouth blurts out, "Sure."

"Great. I'll just jot my number down, and you can text me to work out the details."

Edmund fishes a pen out of his pocket and jots his number on the back of the receipt. After he finishes, I tuck it into my coat pocket.

He nods, with a small smile on his lips. "If you'll send me your address, I can pick you up. I'm thinking around five, so we can relax with a glass of wine before dinner. Is that okay?"

"Sounds nice. I'll see you Friday."

Edmund leans in and presses a soft kiss to my cheek. I walk home with the optimism of someone who, despite experience, hasn't learned that the most dangerous monsters often wear gentle masks. It's only later, in the quiet of the evening, that I realize I've let my guard down. And that's always how bad things start.

CHAPTER 19

KADE

Winter clings to Werneth like an infection. The fog settles over the harbor every morning, never quite letting go. I feel it in my teeth and under my fingernails—persistent and raw. The locals say it's a good sign, means the tourist buses will stay away, but even they hunch deeper in their coats, bracing against the sea's bite.

After Ryland's call, I need to recalibrate. He said my approach was too rigid, that a velvet glove was sometimes more effective than a closed fist. At first, I assumed he meant to undermine me, test my pride, but I see the truth in his words. I've given Tara space, pulling back and observing from a distance.

It's my job to help her find a balance between vigilance and paranoia. Both are essential, but when I first met her, it was obvious paranoia ruled the day. The way she flinched if anyone got too close. The look she gave everyone as if they were a threat, the blue phone always nearby. I've seen that brand of fear before, and I know how quickly it can mutate. Trying to stay sharp, but living at that pitch too long—something's bound to snap.

This morning, she is different. She lets her hair hang loose, her hands smoothing her apron with a distracted elegance. She smiles more, seems to interact with others more naturally. The possible contributing factor: Edmund Harrison Bramston III.

He is what the program calls a "peripheral variable," which means he's not a threat, not an asset, but something that requires monitoring. When I ran his name through the system, there was nothing—no criminal, financial, or professional red flags. The passport was legit; the medical visa is authentic. He's here to care for his terminally ill sister. The diagnosis is tragic and verifiable. I trailed him to the hospital one afternoon and watched as he sat at her bedside for three hours without checking his phone once. Still, every fiber in me searches for an angle, an opening, a sign that this man is anything other than what he appears.

The clock tower on the church chimes, and I cross the street. My boots leave wet ghosts on the tiles as I enter the café. The inside is a prism of condensation, the kind that amplifies the scent of burnt espresso and failed pastries.

Tara stands behind the register, finishing up with a customer. She looks up when the bell announces my arrival. I'm not the only one who notices the change in her: the regulars, the wanderers, the odd backpacker who drifts through all seem to treat her now with something like deference, as if she's become more firmly stitched into the fabric of Werneth. She offers a smile. It is small, precise, but genuine. I remind myself not to overinterpret.

"The usual, Wes?" she says so casually that I am having difficulty getting used to this greeting.

I nod. "And a table, if you've got it. I'm meeting someone for lunch."

She scans the seating area. "Take the window. Less draft from the door."

I settle in, facing the street. It gives me a full range of sight lines—the front entrance, kitchen door, and side alley. Tara brings my coffee herself, setting it down with the cautious grace of a server who's seen too many scalded hands. She leans in a little closer than normal.

"I made it extra strong for you."

"Thanks." I genuinely mean it.

"When's the mystery guest supposed to arrive?"

"In fifteen or twenty minutes, but who's counting?"

"You're early?" She cracks a smile at her attempt to make a joke.

"If you're not fifteen minutes early, you're late." I do my best deadpan look and suppress laughter when her smile quickly fades.

"Military, right? My dad used to say that. Drove Mom up the wall."

I feel the smile freeze on my face. "Something like that."

Her lips twitch, but she lets the silence stand. She is learning, too, about the power of restraint. She slides a laminated menu toward me.

She moves off, but not far. She glances at my reflection in the espresso machine, as if double-checking my reality. I taste the coffee—bitter, earthy, a roast that pretends to be more sophisticated than it is. I drain half the cup in two swallows. My body requires fueling, not coddling.

Tara flits between tables with a steadiness I would have doubted weeks ago. She lingers longest at the old couple's table, laughing at a joke I can't hear. I try to imagine her before the program, before the reams of incident reports and the parade of faces like mine.

The wind outside sharpens, rattling the window frames. I lean back and check the time. Six minutes until noon. A new presence interrupts the café's low hum: tall, heavy, parka zipped to the chin. Police Chief Dave Dobson. The radio dispatcher called him "the mayor in blue," though he prefers to be addressed by rank. He's younger than most chiefs I've dealt with, but his hair has already surrendered to the cause.

He stops at each table, dispensing greetings, news, a shoulder to squeeze, or a hand to shake. When he finally reaches me, he gives a nod that's both professional and personal.

"Kade. Hope you're settling in."

"Trying to, Chief. Coffee's decent."

"Tara, love, flat white, please?" He addresses her with the familiarity of someone who's mapped out every inhabitant of his town like pieces on a board.

She brings the coffee, eyes flicking from him to me and back. I watch the tension at the corner of her mouth, the way her hands flutter before settling at her sides. She doesn't linger.

Dobson leans in, voice pitched low. "We appreciate you being here, you know. Out-of-towners usually attract notice, but you've been discreet."

"Discreet is my job."

He sips his coffee, gaze steady over the rim. "That's not how the Yanks do it on TV."

I smile. "We leave the theatrics to your end of the world."

He laughs, a low, genuine sound. "You'll fit in. Just don't expect to find decent barbecue."

We talk around the point for a while after Tara serves our lunch. We cover the weather, rugby, and the upcoming festival at the harbor. He brings up the recent spate of burglaries along the waterfront, asks if I've seen anything suspicious. I tell him the only thing suspicious is the price of gasoline, and he grins again. The rapport is textbook, but I know there's an undercurrent—he is probing, and so am I.

He set his empty cup aside. "You here long, Mr. Kade?"

"Depends. My superiors are hoping for a quick acclimation. Less risk, less cost."

Dobson considers that. "Werneth's quiet, but people talk. If you need anything, you come directly to me, not the boys."

"That's understood."

He stands, adjusts the zipper on his parka, and gives a little salute to Tara before heading for the door. She watches him go, then shoots me a look that's equal parts amusement and suspicion.

Tara clears my table. "He's nice, the Chief. Not what I expected."

"He's the man you want in your corner." I drain the rest of my coffee.

The residue is thick at the bottom, as if something vital has settled there, out of sight.

She leans in close and lowers her voice. "It's not like my experience with the police in the States was all that stellar. They didn't exactly set the bar high."

I sense the meaning behind the words but let it pass. I've read her file. I know the police didn't help her even when she begged and pleaded. She had to hire her own private investigator to gather the evidence the police could no longer ignore.

The day is half gone, and I have reports to file, patterns to analyze, and budgets to prepare. Badging in through the rear entrance and heading straight to my office, I disable the screen lock, pull up the system dashboard, and open the Wildfire file. I enter an update, which I know Ryland checks.

SUBJECT: QUINN, TARA (FKA KATHRYN CARAWAY)

ASSESSMENT: Hypervigilance significantly reduced. Asset no longer requires enhanced monitoring, direct or indirect.

ADVISED: Continue standard protocol.

The lie fits as comfortably as my shoes. I'm about to log out when my desk phone rings, accompanied by a flashing red light, denoting it's a call on a secure line. I lift the receiver, enter my six-digit pin.

"Kade." I answer quickly.

"Secure call from Deputy Bill Cooper."

"Yes, put him through."

There's a three-second delay, then the click and squawk of an encrypted line. "Kade?"

I recognize Bill Cooper's voice immediately, the way all his vowels collapse inward, like a building scheduled for demolition.

"Cooper. How's everything in the Motherland?"

He grunts, which passes for humor. "Good enough. Look, I'm sending you that doc you were looking for. Just hit your inbox. Had to dig for this one. Wildfire psych eval was buried deep."

My pulse slows, the way it does when you're about to open a body bag. "That's interesting."

"But I got it. The bastard worked in IT at one of the local departments. His record reads like a whole pile of favors called in, if you ask me."

I hear the bitterness in his voice, the kind you only get from years of watching the system grind good people to pulp. I refresh my email. The file arrives, and I rescue it from quarantine by security protocols.

"Okay, I have it. Walk me through it."

Cooper's voice drops a register. "Narcissistic Personality Disorder. Delusional features, obsessional ideation. High-functioning, but with a streak of predatory fixation."

I scroll through the report. The phrases leap out, each one more damning than the last:

- Lacks empathy; compensates with performative charm.

- Fixates on objects of desire; seeks to possess, not relate.

- Reacts poorly to boundaries or rejection; escalates behaviors to restore perceived control.

"Classified as a predatory stalker," says Cooper. "Not the type that wants a relationship. Just wants power."

"Which means the asset is only safe as long as she stays invisible."

"Or submissive. But you and I both know that neither lasts."

I close the report. The screen reflects my face, harsh and colorless. "You said the evaluation was suppressed?"

"Yeah. The department probably figured it would make them look bad if it got out since the perp was one of their own."

"So you think the locals were holding out on handing this over to us?"

He grunts again. "Wouldn't be the first time locals snuffed feds."

"Thanks, Bill. I owe you."

"Keep your head on a swivel."

The line clicks dead, leaving a whiff of static and the lingering aftertaste of American politics.

I forward the file to Ryland, tagging it URGENT. Then I sit in silence for a moment. The program wants us to believe that changing the name and changing the country changes the outcome. But the old self always leaks through in habits. I stand and walk to the window, watching the flagpoles tremble, remembering the language of predators. It's the stillness before the strike you have to watch for. The silence means something is about to change.

Tomorrow, I will check in on Tara. I will say nothing about the report because the program is right about one thing: knowledge doesn't set you free. It makes the cage smaller.

I log off and lock the office. Outside, the world is the same. The wind is only wind, but I can't shake the feeling that something is hunting in it.

Chapter 20

Tara

Despite being July, it's winter here in the southern hemisphere, wrapping the town in drizzle and relentless winds. Directly south is Antarctica—the winds carrying up from the polar ice cap, whipping through the mountains, standing guard over Werneth. When the wind comes in from the north, there is nothing to break it from coming off Tasman Bay.

Damp stone and dead blossoms lend a certain gothic bleakness to the town, but no one else seems to mind. The children still chase each other outside, shrieking along the harbor's edge. The old men at the café still smoke under the awning, nursing their flat whites, wind be damned.

For reasons known only to the program minders, I am summoned to the Consulate Office. Kade's text arrives just before dawn:

KADE

Please come to the office 15:30

ME

K

Tugging my puffer jacket tighter around me, I nestle my hands deep in the pockets as I plod through the chilly air toward the café. Kass, as always, is already there working the dough when I arrive. We navigate the familiar routine and emotions of the day. Kass makes me laugh, customers test my patience, and the espresso machine vexes me. It's another typical day—until it isn't.

I arrive at the consulate to meet with Kade.

"Hi, Tara." Maddie waves enthusiastically.

"Is he here? I've been summoned."

"Conference room." She shoves a piece of candy in her mouth, wipes her hands on a napkin, and gestures for me to follow. "He said to bring you straight back."

By the laws of bureaucracy, this means it is absolutely bad news.

The conference room is at the end of a hall that smells of air freshener. Maddie knocks twice, then swings the door wide with a ceremonial flourish. Inside, Kade hunches over a folder, his black suit jacket thrown over the chair behind him.

"Tara, good, you made it." Kade's all business, but his mouth twitches as if he's suppressing something.

I remove my coat and stuff it in a chair, then sit in the one next to it.

"Apologies for the short notice. I have a brief, purely procedural matter to discuss, then you're free to enjoy the rest of your day."

Brief is not a hallmark of government workers. Procedural is.

Kade loosens his tie, a signal that I should relax, too. "We need to discuss your interactions with Edmund." He says the name as though they're friends.

"I'm having dinner with him tonight. He's only here temporarily. It's not like this will go anywhere. It's just dinner." Even as the words leave my mouth, I know it's not just dinner to him. It's a potential threat, a leak that might need plugging.

"Harbor View tonight?"

I'm surprised when he asks this; it takes a second to register. Then I remember the texts Edmund and I exchange are on the blue phone. I don't have a personal cell phone simply because I would look ridiculous carrying two phones around. I nod, biting back a sarcastic comment.

Kade opens the folder and shuffles some papers. "We just need to review your cover story for any holes, and then you're done. This is when most cases experience a breach. I'm just trying to be proactive."

I narrow my eyes. "Do you surveil him, too?"

His silence is answer enough.

I sit back in my chair and scoff. "Unreal," I whisper under my breath.

Kade drums his fingers on his mug. "If he asks questions about your past, what do you do?"

"The same thing as when anyone else asks. Deflect. Distract. Laugh it off."

He nods, satisfied. "It sounds like I don't need to remind you of the program rules. I think you'll handle yourself just fine."

The meeting lasts all of five minutes. Maybe it is procedural after all—a box for Kade to tick on a government form that boasts a string of numbers and letters in the bottom right corner. *Asset was reminded of her obligation to the program—check.*

I can't shake the feeling that something's shifted. He was relaxed in a way I haven't seen before. I shrug it off. Tonight, Edmund has reservations for us at the fanciest restaurant in town. In any other state in America, it would be called a diner dressed up with white tablecloths. In Werneth, this is their fanciest. I've bought a blood-red velvet dress to be warm yet sexy at the same time.

By the time I get home, my hair has frizzed into a wild crown from the mist. It won't hurt to get ready early. Edmund is driving Leesa's car, and I'm grateful I won't have to brave the icy elements to the restaurant. I start the shower, letting the water heat up. When I see steam billowing out of the bathroom, I know it's ready.

My hair is halfway between a wild animal and a warning sign. I wrangle it into submission with a curling iron, burning my knuckle only once. I dust color onto my cheekbones, then add a reddish-brown lipstick. When I inspect myself in the mirror, I realize the effect I've achieved is less "date night" and more "cruel Victorian governess." I don't hate it.

The dress comes next. I lay it across the bed, fingers smoothing the velvet. It's heavier than I expected, the lining thick and luxurious. There's a sharp sting of guilt as I snip off the price tag and slide the garment over my head, but it vanishes when I catch my reflection. The square neckline frames my collarbones. The sleeves hug my arms, but the skirt flares just enough to suggest movement, even when I'm standing perfectly still. I smile because I see someone I recognize in the mirror.

I'm still barefoot when Edmund knocks.

"Edmund?" I say through the door, knowing full well who it is. I have the super peephole Kade installed.

"Just me," his voice hums through the door.

I slip on my only decent pair of heels, feeling composed and ready, at least on the outside. He looks edible in a navy wool suit and a crisp shirt the color of storm clouds.

"You clean up well."

He smiles, eyes soft. "So do you. Wow."

The *wow* isn't performative. He stands there for a beat, just looking at me, and I flush under his gaze.

He lifts his hand, revealing a gift bag. "I, uh, got you something. It's not much."

I smile at his thoughtfulness and invite him in.

"You can open it now, if you want. We've got time before the reservation."

The tissue paper is matte black, with a silver ribbon perfectly tied into a bow. I want to hate him for being so perfect, but I feel this strange, fizzy delight.

Inside is a book. I run my thumb along the dust jacket, then look up at him. "How did you know I've been wanting to read this?"

He shrugs sheepishly. "Lucky guess."

I smile, all teeth. "Thank you. Do we have time for a glass of wine?"

He looks over my shoulder at the open bottle of wine and my half-empty glass on the counter.

"Allow me."

Edmund tops off my glass while I get one out of the cabinet for him. We settle onto the couch, the book in my lap.

"Go ahead. Let's read the first chapter together."

My voice is steadier than I expect. He listens, nodding. It's a thriller novel, and the hook comes quickly. As I read aloud, he becomes animated. His face and his hands mimic the passage, and I do my best to read through the smile on my face. Chapter one ends on a cliffhanger. Edmund checks his watch and says, "We don't have time for more." We leave for the restaurant.

The Harbor View is a glass box set on the pier, suspended over dark water with lights shimmering off its subtle current. Soft jazz plays in the background, just loud enough to create a cocoon of privacy around us. Our table has the perfect view, a tea light candle that hints at romance, and —what? What is that?

My heart clenches, and my body goes numb. Nestled in the center of the crisp white tablecloth—like a warning shot—is a single yellow rose. My eyes dart around the restaurant. None of the other tables has a rose. Only this one. Deliberate. Intentional.

No. It can't be.

A cold chill creeps through me. Todd's words slice through my head, an icy blade of memory. *"On the day I kill you, I will send you a dozen yellow roses to cover up the stench of your rotting corpse."*

The restaurant blurs, sound tunneling down to white noise. Edmund's face hovers, concern etching lines around his eyes. His lips move, but I can't make out the words.

I stare at the rose. It taunts me. He's found me. He's here.

My pulse hammers in my throat. I scan the room, searching for a familiar face in the dim light. Every shadow looks like him. Every clink of silverware sounds like a gun being cocked.

"Tara?" Edmund's voice finally breaks through, gentle but alarmed. "What's wrong?"

I can't speak. I shake my head, mute with terror.

Edmund leans forward, folding his arms on the table. The ring of his cell phone interrupts him. The ringtone makes me jump. Todd's had the same one. Edmund turns the phone off, sliding it back into his pocket.

"Sorry about that. I left the ringer on in case Leesa needs me, but it's just a mate back home."

Over his shoulder, I see Todd's face, and the illusion collapses around me. The clatter of silverware and plates, the murmur of conversation—every noise in the room stings like a slap. I blink. I look again. He's gone. Not gone. The table next to us, turning his head as though he's pretending not to watch.

I'm sure I'm imagining it until I see him again, slipping past us. I think it's Todd. I think it's him, but it's the server, with his mouth twisted in a half-smile. It's not really a smile at all. I can't breathe. My throat is dry and raw. My hands tremble in my lap.

The walls close in tighter, squeezing the air out, suffocating. I push my chair back, my movements jerky and wild. Panic seizes every muscle.

"Excuse me, I need . . . I need . . ." I don't know what I need.

"Tara—" Concern rises in Edmund's voice.

I'm hyperventilating, chest heaving. I watch as Edmund stands, bracing myself for him to walk away. My vision blurs and bends, his figure distorting like I'm underwater. He doesn't leave. He's right beside me, extending his hand. I take it. It's solid, firm. He leads me through the tangle of tables. The world slows down, catches up to me as we walk out into the night. Cold air cuts through the fog, and I'm not gasping anymore.

Edmund looks at me, not with judgment but with a painful kind of understanding. "What can I do? You're shaking."

"Take me home."

He wraps his arm around the small of my back and gently guides me to the car. Quick but not rushed. Careful. Making sure I'm right beside him. That's when I see it: a shadow shifting across the street, then gone. For a second, my heart seizes, convinced it's Todd. Or Kade. Or something worse. But the harder I look, the more it appears to be nothing at all.

My flat is dark and familiar. The panic doesn't vanish, but it fades.

I'm not sure whether I find it comforting or stifling.

Edmund stands by the door. "Do you want me to spend the night on the couch?" It's as though he already knows I'll say no when I really want to say yes. He reads my silence.

"You don't have to."

Edmund ignores my no and walks into my bedroom. I stand in the doorway and watch as he fluffs my pillow and pulls back the duvet. He lifts the spare pillow and takes it into the living room, dropping it on the sofa.

"I'll sleep here tonight." He makes it sound so casual. I hear the concern underneath.

He moves to the kitchen, flicks the kettle on, not even pausing.

"I'm sorry about dinner. It's not fair to you." I hear myself as though from miles away, exhausted and unsteady.

"Life isn't fair," he says. "That's how I know it's worth it."

I adore him for that. I walk away, into the bedroom, and close the door. I change into yoga pants and a T-shirt. I fetch a spare blanket and place it next to Edmund, not meeting his eyes.

"This is for you." I wonder how long this can last. I wonder what will happen when he realizes I can't give him what he needs, that I'm too broken to give him anything at all. I wonder if it matters to him. It should. But as he lies down on the couch, I know it doesn't.

CHAPTER 21

KADE

There is a ritual to pouring scotch. First, the ice: a single cube, a cold tooth in the glass. Then the scotch: viscous and angry, cut-glass, gold, poured to just below the rim. I have always admired the way scotch holds light. It doesn't shimmer or sparkle; it absorbs. I take a sip and stare at the wall while my mind plays the tape of the night, as I always do. Frame by frame, analyzing each moment.

The yellow rose was a test. I will admit this to no one. The program has rules, and the rules are to protect the asset. We do not introduce unknowns; we do not escalate trauma, and we never, never taunt the past with parlor tricks. But the rules are for people whom the Marshal Service can trust to follow them.

I am not one of those people.

The test was simple: introduce a variable, measure the reaction. We could have done it in a controlled environment, with paperwork and two-way mirrors and someone from Behavioral sitting three feet to my left, chewing a pen. But the field is the only place that counts. Out here, every data point is pure. It is unfiltered; it is violent; it is true.

When Tara noticed the rose on the table, her hands went rigid, fingers curled into claws. She did not breathe. Then she catalogued the room, logged every escape route, and checked every face for the one she never wants to see again.

Tara looked in my direction, but past me as Edmund ushered her to the car. I was background radiation—the world's oldest trick. She saw what I wanted her to see: a specter, a shape that belonged to every dark night she'd ever survived.

Could I have intervened? Could I have slid into her line of sight, let the illusion break, allowed her to take comfort in the artificial security I represent? Sure, but that would have been for me, not for her. It also would have violated the thing I respect: the purity of the test.

The test is not over.

I set the glass down and wipe condensation from my hand. I open my laptop, prop it on the coffee table, and log into the program portal. Assets are supposed to log every anomaly within twelve hours. Even if they don't, we can access the blue phones, the shadow archives that track every keystroke and spoken word. But I prefer the old-fashioned way: let the asset do the work.

The log is empty. No mention of the rose or the shadow at the restaurant. Not even the expected vent about "anxiety spike" or "potential trigger." She thinks she can handle it.

I drink to that, to her, and to the empty chair on the other side of the room that's not waiting for anyone. I refill the scotch, this time without ice. The room is cold, but not as cold as I am. The trick with drinking is to always fall asleep on the upswing. If you miss the window, you wake up with a brain full of spiders and a mouth full of ash.

In one swift motion, I tip the glass back and let the cool liquid slide down my throat before rinsing it under the tap. I head to the bathroom, brush my teeth, and go through my nightly routine. I pick up my phone, squinting at the screen. Tara should have reported in by now, but there's only silence. The clock reads just after midnight, 00:37. I'll give her until noon.

I close my eyes, waiting for sleep, or something close enough to it. I wake at 06:18, sober. I don't bother showering. There's a point at which the chemical residue on your skin becomes part of you, like a second, secret fingerprint. I wear it like a badge, or a warning. I make coffee. It's instant, cruel, and exactly what I deserve. Mug in hand, I settle behind my laptop. Remote logins used to be impossible. In the early days, you had to show up at the office, badge in, and sit under fluorescent lights. Now they expect you to do the job from wherever, whenever. The tech is better, but the work is the same: heavy, endless, and indifferent to the people who do it. I enter my credentials—the whole dog-and-pony. The Marshal Service tells you it's for security, but really, it's so you'll never forget who owns you.

Although I know every line of the psychological evaluation of Todd Bennett by heart now, I read it again. The brain is a leaky bucket, and repetition is the only way to fill it. This guy is a deranged monster. But that's not news to me. This chameleon knows how to vanish into the fabric of his surroundings. The burning question is: what sets him off? What provokes his inner chaos? What ignites his dark impulses?

I mine the document for clues, insights into Bennett's fractured psyche. Childhood trauma. Abandonment issues. A desperate need for control. It's all here—the blueprint of a broken man. Levers to pull. The report is clinical, sterile. But between the lines, a plan emerges. I lean back; the pieces fall into place. Hazy at first, then sharpening into focus. It's a risk, but one I calculate carefully.

Time moves at a snail's pace as I wait to see if Tara will report the incident. Pacing, I check my watch: 11:58. Two minutes, two eternities. Noon arrives—nothing. I give Tara more time. An hour. Then another. The third one arrives, and I have a new appreciation for her. Strong. Resilient.

I'm envious watching her navigate the complexities of a developing relationship. It's like watching a delicate dance. From afar, I observe the little moments—the way she smiles at Edmund, the way their laughter echoes. It's completely unexpected, if not inappropriate, that I delight in witnessing the unfolding of their bond. My own life, wrapped up in the clandestine world of federal law enforcement officers, hasn't allowed for such enduring connections. It's a demanding career; many of us struggle to maintain personal ties. Yet, seeing her succeed where I haven't, I feel a mix of envy and respect.

On the kitchen table, my briefcase sits, locked and latched. I open it and sort through the rubbish: pens, paper, receipts, a bag of almonds that expired in the previous fiscal quarter. Below this is the one thing that matters: the flip phone.

I pop the battery and slot in a new SIM. The screen lights up with a green, idiot glow, and I punch in the number. The line connects. I wait for the click, the one that means someone is there.

"Status update. No changes. But there have been some . . . complications." I shift my weight. My free hand drifts to the holster concealed beneath my jacket. "Nothing I can't handle."

A cough—not human, more like a digitized bark.

"Trust has to be earned in this business. And re-earned. I'll be back in touch."

The phone is slick with sweat when I thumb it shut. I remove the SIM, break it in half, and put it in the microwave. Thirty seconds. There is satisfaction in destroying things. It's the only real power left.

Outside, the wind rattles the window, angry and insistent. I watch the cloud bank roll over Werneth, smothering the town in its gray gut. Soon, the rain will come. I stand by the window and wait for it. We are what we pretend to be. I'm just better at it.

CHAPTER 22

TARA

Kass is already behind the counter when I arrive for my shift. She's wearing a bandana patterned with yellow sunflowers, which makes her hair look like a brush fire. She gives me a look. "You made the muffins already?"

"They're in the oven." I keep my voice low, hoping she'll take the cue and leave me alone.

No such luck.

"So." Kass leans on the counter, elbows splayed. "When are you going to let me live vicariously through you?"

"What do you mean?" I feign ignorance. I put the pastries out, stacking scones like building blocks, dusting the display case with sugar.

She barks a laugh. "Don't play dumb. Details. I want details about your date. Harbor View. That's like . . . the prom for people in this town who aren't twelve. How was it?" She cocks an eyebrow.

I try to keep my face neutral. "It was fine."

"Fine?" She stretches the vowel. "Why are you just holding out on me? I wouldn't. I would tell you *everything*."

No one fools Kass. She hops onto the counter, feet dangling, arms crossed like a stage director waiting for the cast to screw up. "You didn't answer your phone. So, obviously, something happened."

"I'm not holding out."

I want to forget about the yellow rose. The way my heart stopped cold in my chest, the way the world shuddered into darkness for a few minutes. I want to tell her I spent my days off making sure I locked my front door and latched all the windows.

Instead, I say, "It was fine. Really."

Kass slides off the counter and edges closer, the café suddenly too small. "Did he say something to upset you?"

"No. Maybe I just don't want to talk about it."

Kass watches me for a long beat, and I feel the weight of her gaze landing everywhere I don't want it. She softens a little. "Okay, okay. But I can tell when you're lying. Your voice gets all flat, like a robot."

The oven timer dings. I wipe my hands on my apron, extract the muffin tray, and ignore her. Not that it helps. I can feel her staring.

The morning builds. People file in; the day carries on, oblivious to the chaos inside me. I keep to my station behind the counter, relishing the anonymity that comes from being invisible in plain sight. That's why I didn't see him come in. Edmund appears at the end of the counter, hands in his pockets, leaning forward like he's got all the time in the world. His hair is damp, slicked back as if he walked here through a storm, which is possible, given the sky is already threatening a tantrum outside.

He waits for me to notice. When I finally do, I freeze mid-motion, a milk pitcher in one hand, the other gripping the edge of the counter. He holds my gaze for a second, then smiles. It is a real one, not the kind people use to hide things.

"Hey," he says, voice soft.

"What'll you have?" I try to sound casual.

"Flat white. Please."

I start the order, forcing myself into the muscle memory of coffee-making. I tamp, steam, and pour, feeling his eyes on me the whole time.

He studies me. "Look, if you're avoiding me because the other night—"

I fumble the cup. It hits the counter hard enough for the coffee to slosh over the edge.

"Sorry," he says. "I didn't mean—"

"It's fine." I wipe the cup clean, then push it across the counter to him. Our hands nearly touch, but not quite.

He doesn't pick up the coffee right away. "I'm not good at this, but I think I owe you—"

"It's not your fault." My voice is low, tight.

He nods. "My mom had panic attacks. Growing up, I thought everyone's mom hid in closets when the mail came or hyperventilated at the grocery store. When I got older, I learned how to help her through them. I understand."

I stare at him, unsure whether to feel gratitude or shame.

He gives a small smile. "It's okay. Really." He sips his coffee, grimaces, and then laughs. "Scalding. See, I'm not even good at drinking coffee."

The tension breaks, just a little.

I force myself to laugh. "You should have ordered the tea."

He sets the cup down, then leans in. "Are you free tonight?"

"Why?" I think of the book he bought me, still untouched from where we left off that night.

"Because I still owe you a dinner. We don't have to go anywhere. I'm an excellent cook. Leesa's still in the hospital, and her kitchen is sitting unused, unappreciated."

The quiet confidence, the not-pushing in his voice, makes me nod before I realize I'm already agreeing.

He grins, boyish and surprised.

"I'll bring wine," I say, because that's what people do.

"Deal." He drains the cup in one go, wincing as it burns. "See you tonight at seven?"

I nod again, then busy myself with the pastry case, pretending to rearrange the croissants as he leaves. I watch his shape recede, then vanish into the mist outside, already unsure whether I said yes because I want to, or because I'm incapable of saying no.

Maybe it doesn't matter.

Maybe it's the same thing.

Kass glides in, grinning like she's won something.

"Sooo . . . another date?"

"Yes," I mutter, my hands busy with nothing.

Kass lets out a squeal.

The taxi driver doesn't bother with small talk; he lets the heater hum and the radio mutter static as we wind up Mt. Atawhai. I hold the bottle of wine like it might run away. The book from Edmund sits in my lap. Below, the harbor and the town shrink to a string of fairy lights.

At the top, the taxi swings into a narrow driveway and stops in front of a house carved directly into the mountain. The windows glow yellow against the dark sky. The house is concrete, not the warm kind with wood trim and flower boxes, but bunker-gray with sharp angles and glass, perched like an animal crouched against the elements. I didn't take Leesa to favor such a modern style. Not that I know her well. She comes in after cycling and talks about the triathlon she's training for. Or, at least she did before her cancer diagnosis.

I fumble with my purse, pay the driver, and let the wind slap my face awake as I get out. My hair whips across my eyes, blinding me. The taxi peels away, leaving exhaust in its wake. I stare at the silhouette of the house, the glowing rectangles of windows, and feel like I'm at the edge of a cliff. I steady myself and head up the stone steps.

Edmund opens the door before I knock, as if he's been waiting the whole time. "Hey. Come in. It's freezing."

Inside, it's a different world. Concrete walls, yes, but softened by rugs and Leesa's medals hung on bright ribbons. Light pours from standing lamps, and a pellet stove cranks away in the corner, scattering a burning scent into the air.

Edmund helps me off with my coat, then takes the wine with a half-smile. "This was a good year for the Marlborough region. I can't wait to try it."

He leads me through the living room, past a bookshelf packed with everything from travel guides to tattered mysteries. There's a blanket tossed on the sofa and a mug on the coffee table.

The kitchen is barely bigger than a closet, but food claims every surface. Bowls of chopped vegetables, a pan of something simmering, bread warming in a towel. The stove is working hard, rattling the lids of the pots.

"Make yourself at home."

Smiling, I'm not sure how to do that, as I hover at the doorway and shove my hands in the pockets of my jeans. "It smells amazing."

Edmund grins, a little sheepish. "Thanks. I learned from my grandmother."

He pours me a glass of wine, sets it on the counter, and hands me a cutting board. "Can you slice these?"

He gives me parsley, a knife, and a bowl. I gratefully accept the task, glad for the distraction. The first few minutes are silent except for the crackle of the stove. Edmund checks the pot on the stove, stirs, and then lowers the heat.

"You're good with a knife," he says.

"Occupational hazard."

He glances over, and his look is soft, as if he doesn't want to scare me off. "You okay?"

I nod, focused on the parsley. "Just tired."

"Long day?"

"Long week." I keep my head down.

We work side by side, and the kitchen shrinks around us. He passes me bowls and spoons, talks me through each step as if we're on a cooking show. After a while, the silence stops being heavy and feels companionable.

He asks about work, and I tell him about the café. He asks about Kass, and I say she's basically my parole officer. I ask about Leesa, and he tells me she's doing better, but the treatments knock her flat for days at a time. He says it's easier being here than back in England. The two of them are all that's left—their parents died several years apart.

I ask about his job, and he shrugs. "Project manager, nothing interesting. I like fixing things, but people are harder than buildings."

I smile, surprised at myself. "I'll drink to that."

He uncorks the wine, pours us each a glass, and holds his up. "To fixing things that don't want to be fixed."

I tap my glass to his, feeling ridiculous, but the wine is smooth, and it heats my stomach.

Edmund plates the food with care. Chicken with herbs and lemon, roasted vegetables, and garlic bread. He sets the table, lights a stubby candle, and stands back to admire his work. For a moment, the room looks like it belongs in a magazine, not in a mountain bunker overlooking the world's edge.

The food is good, better than I expected. It tastes like effort and intention, not just calories. Then he looks at me, his eyes soft and open. "What was life like before you moved here?"

I almost choke on my wine. The answer unspools in my head: desperate, hunted, small. "Not much different." I realize it's not a lie.

"Did you like living in the States?"

I think about the house I left behind. The nail holes on the walls where memories once hung. My shoe collection. Oh, how I miss my shoes.

"Not really. Werneth is quieter. It suits me."

"Why'd you leave?"

I want to say I was running. Instead, I say, "Needed a change."

He lets the lie settle, then nods. "Fair enough."

I am so used to interrogation, I almost miss the kindness in his questions. He's not prying. He's just trying to get to know me.

Edmund tells me a story about Leesa from childhood. I keep eating even though I'm completely full. Finally, he places his knife and fork at six o'clock on the plate. I do the same and declare it the best meal I've had all day. He gets the joke.

He glances at the book I brought. "You want to read now?"

"Sure, let's read." I'm relieved he hasn't asked about my panic attack. I'd prepared a story about being a divorcee and not having been on a date in years. I'm glad I didn't need it.

Edmund retrieves the book, and we settle onto the sofa, shoulder to shoulder. He opens the book and hands it to me. My hands are steady for once. Chapter two, exactly where we left off. He listens. I stumble over the words at first, hyperaware of his knee pressed against mine, his arm draped casually over the back of the sofa. As I read, his body softens, his breathing slows, and I feel the warmth of him seep into my skin.

The words fill the room like light. At some point, I look up. Rain snakes down the window, blurring the world outside. I feel warm. Safe. Almost happy. Which means, I suppose, that the other shoe is about to drop.

He's looking at me as if he wants to say something. Instead, he reaches out and tucks a strand of hair behind my ear, then lets his hand linger there. The silence between us is warm and heavy, a blanket I don't mind wrapping around myself.

He moves closer. I let him.

He kisses me. Gentle at first, then with more intent. His hand caresses the side of my face, thumb tracing my jaw. I let all the fear, hunger, and loneliness pour out. Nothing matters—not the wine, the food, or the storm outside. Just his mouth on mine, the taste of rosemary and salt, the sound of rain beating on the windows.

When we break apart, I'm breathless.

He rests his forehead against mine. "You're full of surprises."

"You have no idea."

We sit there, silent except for the storm, which is louder now. Maybe the wind has picked up, or maybe the world wants to remind me that nothing good lasts.

I look past him, out the window. The darkness is almost complete, but for a split second, I see movement. A shape, a shadow—something that flits past the glass and disappears.

My heart stops. I bolt upright. My gaze locks on the window.

Edmund follows my eyes. "What is it?"

"Nothing." The word comes out raw, unconvincing.

He squeezes my hand. "You sure?"

"Just thought I saw something."

He stands, moves to the window, and peers out into the night. "Nothing there. Just the wind."

But I saw it. I know I did.

He sits back down, puts his arm around me, and we lean into each other, watching the candle burn lower and the wine run out.

It should feel safe. It almost does.

I can't help looking at the window, waiting for the next shadow to flicker by. This moment, this warmth, this almost-happiness is only borrowed, and the world is waiting to take it back.

CHAPTER 23

KADE

The house is silent except for the steady rhythm of my breathing and the high-pitched whine of the air vent. Weekends stretch on endlessly, with Sundays being the hardest. As a kid, Sundays meant dressing up for church in our best clothes and gathering for a big family dinner around the long oak table, with laughter and chatter filling the air. Now, Sundays stand as a stark reminder of my solitude in this vast world. Accomplished, but alone.

After a five-mile run, I head to my makeshift gym in the bedroom to lift weights. That kills an hour. I take a shower and hear the sharp chirp of my phone. I quickly rinse, turn off the water, and wrap a towel around my waist. The screen glares at me: INCIDENT REPORT—PRIORITY 3

It's from Tara, time-stamped 13:10. My pulse quickens, and without bothering to dry off or dress, I bolt straight to my computer, adrenaline surging.

Logging in takes longer than I want, but I finally get in. I pull up the Wildfire case and double-click the new activity. The asset claims a "shadow" followed her from the supermarket to the harbor footpath. She lost visual. The rest is detail—steps, street names, times, a grainy photo of the empty street. There is no physical evidence; there is barely emotional evidence, except in the run-on sentences that leak her stress.

I let my mind idle before I dial her number. She answers so quickly; I think maybe she's testing the system.

"Kade?" Her voice is unsteady.

"I'm here. I show that you are at home. Are you safe?"

"I think so. I've checked all the doors and windows."

"Okay. I can come over and take a look around if you want."

"No . . . no, it's fine."

"I read the report, but can you tell me what happened?"

There's a pause, a hitch of breath. She begins, slow at first, then with increasing urgency. The supermarket, the footsteps, the figure that followed her. I make affirmative noises, letting her unspool the story at her own pace.

"Can you describe the person?"

"Well . . . I never . . . no, I didn't actually *see* anyone following me. It was just a feeling. I'm sorry to have alarmed you, but you told me to trust my gut and report anything."

"You did the right thing, Tara. I'll retrace your steps and stop by to check on you."

"You don't have to do that, Kade. It's Sunday, after all. I'm sure you have better things to do."

I glance around my empty place. In my head, I think, *Not really*, but out loud, I say, "It's fine. This is my job. I'll head over in a few minutes. If you need anything before I get there, call me."

My steps to the bedroom are urgent, purposeful. I quickly dress. Before I leave, I return to my laptop. I previously assigned Maddie the task of monitoring Edmund's social media presence. Unlike me, she grew up immersed in social media, and she's quite skilled at it. In fact, she seems to be skilled in all things technical. She's probably spent countless hours tracking Edmund's online activity.

I open the update and scan the content. Edmund's feed has been quiet over the past few days. No new posts, no interactions. But Maddie has flagged something potentially concerning. At first glance, it appears routine —a few posts about Edmund's latest adventures, some likes and comments from his friends. But then a detail catches my eye. It's in the background of a photo—grainy and barely visible. I drop a box around it and send Maddie a message to have the photo enhanced.

The relationship I've cultivated with Chief Dobson has paid off. I open a browser and log in to the Werneth Police Department portal. I pull up the street surveillance system. Not because I expect to see anything, but because the act of watching feels like penance. I queue up the street cameras closest to Tara's flat; scroll through archived video between 12:45 and 13:45. There's a silhouette behind Tara. I see Tara, hunched and urgent, moving quicker than normal. I can tell from her movements that she believes she is in danger. I zoom in. A hat blocks the man's face. A brief flare of a cigarette, then a turn at the mouth of an alley.

The air outside has a crisp bite of winter as I climb into my sedan. I take a circuitous route, scanning for anything out of place. The streets are mostly empty, with a few scattered pedestrians—nothing out of the ordinary. I park a block away from Tara's and approach on foot, senses heightened. I walk around the stairwell, checking underneath it. I move to the back. No obvious signs of tampering. I take the stairs two at a time and rap my knuckles against the door—three sharp taps.

Tara opens the door and immediately wraps her arms around my neck. "Kade."

This moment is genuine for her; it's not just a test to check the system. The tightness of her hug tells me she's truly relieved to see me. This is a good sign I'm earning her trust. I quickly glance around her apartment.

"The apartment is secure."

She's already prepared a mug of tea, so I sit with her at the kitchen table while she sips.

"Thanks, Kade. I feel silly for making a fuss."

"It's all good. How was your date with Edmund on Friday night?"

Her expression tells me it didn't go well. She looks down at her mug.

"Fine," she nods. "Great."

I know otherwise because I was there. She still doesn't fully trust me, or maybe it's the program she's unsure about. I've seen this before. Most assets cycle through the same arc: paranoia, threat, false alarm, regression, then slow stabilization. The first is always the hardest to endure, for both sides. The difference is that I know it's an arc. I know the next stage before it comes.

I stand up, and the chair scrapes loudly against the floor. "If you need anything, just call me."

"Thanks for coming over, Kade. I really appreciate it."

When I get back home, I slow the playback of the street cameras. I take it frame by frame. I see a shadow behind her, always a half-step out of frame. The camera grain is too thick for certainty. I log this, too, but under my notes, not the official record. The shadow is probably nothing.

Later that evening, my phone vibrates at 20:30. This time, it's a calendar reminder: 08:30, the consular briefing. I need to log an acknowledgment in the system or risk a scolding from Ryland.

INCIDENT TYPE: SURVEILLANCE/PSYCHOSIS

NOTES: Asset reports suspected pursuit. No independent verification. No witnesses.

ADVISE: Monitoring.

Monitoring, but no escalation. I save it, then run a finger along the scar at my wrist. It's a straight line of hardened skin, a byproduct of a different sort of vigilance, from a life where risks came with shrapnel, not tedious notes. Sometimes I press my thumb into the ridged tissue to remind myself that things hurt for a reason. I should feel sorry for her, but what I really feel is a kind of kinship: the mutual certainty that nothing good lasts, that every moment of peace is a trick of the light.

The overhead lights switch to motion-sensitive as I walk down the hall. There's no sound but the slap of my shoes against cheap carpet. Maddie isn't due in the office for another hour.

I settle in behind my desk, log in to the system, and open the Wildfire case on my screen. I pull up Todd Bennett's details and reach for the phone. The line rings five times before a man answers, his voice thick.

"Customs, Jenkins."

"This is Kade, U.S. Embassy. Need a quick check on a travel restriction." I rattle off Todd Bennett's details.

Jenkins sighs. I can picture him squinting at the screen. "One moment."

While he clatters at the keyboard, I stare at the burn mark on the desk, a perfect black oval where some other functionary must have left a cigarette to rot. The furniture never forgets.

"Got it," Jenkins says. "Flag is active. No activity, no border crossings logged."

"Thanks. Log any notifications to my direct line."

Jenkins grunts, and I hang up. Another box to tick.

There's a silence after the call, heavier than before. The silence you get the minute before a firefight, when the world seems so impossibly still that you doubt if anything will ever move again. In the old days, this was where you checked your ammo, counted the seconds, and prayed.

At 08:25, I log onto the videoconference, which stutters once before opening the window. Ryland's stern face appears. The backdrop is his office, littered with printouts and a single dying potted plant.

"Kade," he says, like it's a question.

"Morning, sir."

He reads from his second monitor, not bothering with the preamble. "Your asset filed an incident. You believe it's credible?"

"I believe she believes it. But there's no corroboration. No witness, no physical trace. Closest thing is a street cam with a possible tail, but the footage is inconclusive."

Ryland grunts. "They always are. I don't need this to escalate."

"It won't. There's no sign of operational breach."

He narrows his eyes. "How are things?"

I let the silence work. "She needs a reason to trust someone. You know that."

He shifts and sips from his "#1 DAD" coffee mug. "Tell me about the boyfriend."

"Edmund Harrison Bramston III. British national. Here on a medical visa to care for his terminally ill sister. Clean record, minimal Internet presence, no flagged associates. Maddie is monitoring him. Bramston's not the risk. The risk is the psychological stressor."

Ryland's mouth twists. "Of course. Every asset is a time bomb, but the clock starts ticking faster when you introduce variables. Intimacy is the classic trigger."

"I advised against it." That's only half-true. "She's built for conflict. If she doesn't have an enemy, her mind invents one."

Ryland laughs. It's a dry, sharp sound. "You think she's inventing the incident?"

I shake my head. "No. I think she's rehearsing for the moment he does show up. She wants to prove to herself that she can survive it again."

Ryland leans back, folding his hands. The light on his side flickers, shadowing his jaw. "What's your next move?"

Swallowing, I glance down at the neat line of pens in front of my keyboard. "I confirmed the flag on Bennett's passport with Customs. No activity. My plan is to monitor, de-escalate, and document. If there's an actual breach, I'll know it before she does."

He stares at me for a long moment. "You sure about that?"

It's a test, but it's also a warning. I play my part. "No doubt."

He nods, as if that's the right answer. "Keep her compliant. Don't let her spiral. If you need resources, you have them."

"Yes, sir."

He ends the call, leaving me with the afterimage of his face. I lean back and run a finger down the side of my tie until the knot relaxes enough to let me breathe. A delivery truck somewhere outside reverses, its beep a steady pulse. I think about Tara counting shadows as if it's the last one she'll see. I wonder what it's like to live with that level of uncertainty.

Maybe I already know.

I slide my hand into my pocket and pull out the gold coin I carry with me. It is five Afghanis rupees, a relic from my time in Afghanistan. I run my thumb over the battered ridges until the nerves in my hand go numb. I remember a night in Helmand Province when the dogs wouldn't stop barking, and my entire squad sat in the dark waiting for the breach that never came. The not-knowing was worse than the violence that followed.

CHAPTER 24

TARA

I t's Monday, my day off, which means the world expects me to do nothing, but the world has never quite understood what I do. The apartment is a mausoleum. I wander its tight orbit from kitchen to couch, all movement silent, like I am the ghost, not the haunted. The only living thing is me, and even that is debatable after the last twenty-four hours.

I haven't set foot outside since the incident yesterday. There was nothing out of the ordinary except that, halfway home, I got that tingling sensation that someone was watching me. Following me. Step for step.

When I told Kade, I half-expected him to respond the way the police did in the States. There's no evidence that someone was following. Even if there were, I was on a public street. Everyone has the right to walk down the street. Instead, Kade lowered his voice as if the air could transmit our conversation as a warning to whoever was out there.

Now it's noon, and the shadow has curled itself up in the bottom of my lungs, making every breath a little tighter. I haven't eaten. I haven't showered. The news flickers in the background, a perpetual loop of tragedy and weather updates. It's like a screensaver for civilization's slow decline.

I've vacuumed the entire apartment, reorganized the medicine cabinet, and refolded every shirt I own. The noises from the street like the muffled shouts, a dog barking, the distant chime of a tram all seem orchestrated to maximize my unease.

I push myself into the shower. The spray needles my shoulders, numbing the itch of memory. Afterward, I stand in front of the mirror, trying to see myself as someone else might— a girl in a strange city, lines under her eyes, hair pulled back too tight. No distinguishing features, nothing to mark me as worth following. I practice smiling, just to see if I still can. The reflection does not cooperate.

Back in the living room, I make a lunch I do not want. I eat in small, robotic bites, savoring the melted processed cheese. My blue phone dings to signal an incoming text message.

> **KADE**
> Checking in

> **ME**
> All quiet.

> **KADE**
> Let me know if anything changes

He never uses a period. It makes me trust him more. I sense something beneath his words—not concern, exactly, but a sort of engineered empathy. Like a doctor who's memorized the script for delivering bad news. I imagine him in an office somewhere, feet up on a desk, scanning a wall of monitors. Or maybe he's driving through the neighborhood in an unmarked sedan, mapping escape routes.

Knowing he is checking in makes me feel lighter, like my body won't rot in the apartment for days before anyone comes looking for me. I clean the kitchen and reorganize the fridge by food group, then alphabetically. I check every lock and window.

The silence grows claws. By mid-afternoon, I've started reading the labels on cleaning supplies, comparing the warnings and the empty threats about eye contact and skin irritation. I wonder how long it would really take for someone to break in. Not long, probably. The glass in this rental unit is thin enough to punch through with a closed fist.

I think about yesterday's shadow. Maybe he was just lost. Maybe he didn't see me at all. Or maybe he was waiting, learning my patterns, cataloging the minute inefficiencies of my security.

I check the door three more times. Still locked. The afternoon collapses into itself. Outside, the sky is the color of wet cement. The town below my window is silent, the usual clamor of people muffled by clouds. Even the gulls have gone somewhere better.

The urge to call Kass is overwhelming. She's the only one I know who can crack a joke so brittle and sharp it leaves me in a fit of laughter. I open the contact screen, thumb hovering over her name.

Don't.

Kade's warning is a specter in my head. "Keep your distance."

The logic is unassailable. Kass talks to everyone, tells everyone everything, and it wouldn't take much for a clever listener to become a leak. Still, the need for comfort is a physical ache.

I close my eyes and picture her instead: standing behind the counter, curls forced under a paisley bandana, face lighting up when she spots a familiar customer. The way she would lean in and whisper whatever local gossip she'd harvested that morning. I wonder what she's telling people now. Probably nothing, I decide.

My thoughts drift to Edmund, and I can't help but smile. I shoot him a quick text to let him know I'm thinking of him. He responds almost instantly and asks if I want to meet at the park overlooking Phoenix Bay for an impromptu picnic.

I arrive early with a quilt, our book, and a chilled bottle of Pinot Grigio. I spot him under a tree, barely holding its last yellow leaves, with an ancient tartan blanket stretched over the lumpy ground. There is a charcuterie board, complete with a wedge of cheese the size of my heart, and a row of precisely halved figs. The champagne is on ice, and a large bottle of water beads with condensation. Edmund sits cross-legged, back straight, arms folded. He looks like someone who's spent his whole life being told he's not enough and trying to prove otherwise by always being exactly what the moment requires.

Edmund notices me at the exact moment the wind snaps the hem of my dress like a flag in retreat.

He smiles.

I melt.

"Hey. You made it."

"Wouldn't miss it. You brought enough food for a rugby team."

He shrugs sheepishly. "I didn't want you to go hungry." He glances at the Pinot Grigio. "And I see you've come prepared."

"It's my only party trick," I say. "Show up with alcohol, leave before anyone asks me to dance."

"Not today." Edmund motions for me to sit.

I hesitate, scanning the periphery. There's an old woman feeding ducks with a bag of stale bread. A man sprawled under a newspaper, shoes off, sun on his neck. No one even looks at us. I settle onto the blanket, crossing my legs at the ankle in a way that feels polite.

Edmund starts pouring. I take a sip, letting the cold wine seep into my chest. He serves me slivers of cheese, wedges of pear, and crackers arranged with geometric precision. We don't talk about anything substantial at first. Just the texture of the cheese, the weirdly sweet wine, and the blanket that bunches up every time we move. The air is thick with birdsong—it sounds like someone winding up a clock and letting it run down. The wind keeps coming, sometimes warm and sometimes sharp, flipping the pages of my book.

After a while, Edmund leans back on his elbows. "Read to me?"

I scoot forward and lean my head into the cozy space between his hip bone and his ribs. I pick up the book and turn to where we left off. The words flow from my mouth as he strokes my hair. The plot thickens, and three suspects emerge. I reach the end of another chapter, my mouth dry.

"So, who do ya think done it?" I ask teasingly. Edmund has already refilled my wineglass, but I sit up and reach for a bottle of water instead.

"I think it was the neighbor, Collette."

I throw my head back and laugh. "Not possible. She's a red herring just to throw you off. Don't fall into the author's trap."

Edmund laughs, then lets the silence have its way with us. He doesn't speak, but I feel him watching me. Not the way men like Todd did, but with a patience I find foreign.

"Where are you from, really?"

I turn the plastic fork in my fingers, pressing the tines into my thumb until it hurts. "Born in Mississippi. Then lived in Georgia. Now here."

"That's a long way to run."

"You think I'm running?"

He considers. "I think maybe you're tired of being chased."

The fork snaps in my hand, and a glob of cheese lands on my dress. I wipe it off with a paper napkin, then make a show of checking my phone for the time.

It's only half-past six. I want to go home, but the idea of my little flat is intolerable. I realize that I'd rather be here, next to a man who asks questions and then doesn't punish me for the answers.

"What about you? What's your story?"

"Born, raised, and still living in Northampton. It's about an hour outside of London. My dad passed from cancer, probably because he built houses and was around a lot of asbestos before they knew it was dangerous. Mum passed eight years later, out of loneliness, I think. So, it's just me and Leesa now."

Edmund's face goes sullen. I don't mean to, but I reach over and touch his wrist. It's just a gesture, not an invitation, but he covers my hand with his. His skin is cold, but the pressure is warm.

"There's a girl at the consulate, Maddie. She's got this way of talking that makes you think she's harmless, but really, she's cataloguing everything. Like she's already figured out how you're going to die."

"That's grim," Edmund says, but his tone is careful.

I try to laugh, but it comes out as a cough. "Sorry. I'm bad at small talk."

I think of dusk back home, how the shadows stretched to the Gulf, the air so thick with humidity you could choke on it. Here, the dusk is sharper, and the cold seeps into my skin.

"I should get you back," he says, rising. "Or you could come to Leesa's with me."

"Fine," I say like it's an imposition. "But if I disappear, you'll be the first suspect."

He grins. "Deal."

We pack up the remnants of our picnic and head to Leesa's car. He offers me his arm. I know this drill: the ritual of the walk, the opening of car doors, the performance of decency. Still, I let him escort me, if only to remember what it's like to be protected by someone who doesn't expect to be paid back in flesh.

He unlocks the front door and leads me down a narrow staircase to a basement lined with wine bottles and dried garlic braids. There's a fireplace — wood, not gas. Edmund lights it, and the air fills with the scent of sap and ash. We sit on a battered loveseat, and he pours two glasses of something red that tastes expensive.

"Did you know the town was once destroyed by a fire?" I tuck my hair behind my ear.

"Werneth?"

"Yeah. The whole town was on fire . . ." I tell him about the bucket brigade.

"Oh, that's why it's called Phoenix Bay. The town rose from the ashes like a phoenix. I get it."

The silence afterward is not awkward. It's heavy but not suffocating. I shiver, even though the fire is roaring. Edmund gets up and finds a blanket in the cabinet. He drapes it around my shoulders, then sits back down, closer this time.

"Do you ever think about starting over? Just burning down the old life and seeing what grows from the ashes?"

He nods. "Everyone deserves a second chance."

That's the phrase that does it. The old church language, so out of place on this side of the world. I don't kiss him. He doesn't kiss me. It's more like the space between us collapses, the blanket bridging the gap, our bodies tipping toward each other as if magnetized.

Our lips meet, tentative and dry—the way two people kiss when neither wants to be first. I pull back almost immediately, my heart in my throat. He waits. His hands are in his lap. His breathing is measured, patient.

I look at him, scanning his face for the telltale signs of danger. I see none. I lean in again, and this time he meets me halfway. The kiss is longer, less afraid. My hand rests on his thigh, the fabric of his jeans rough against my palm. He puts his arm around me, but it's not possessive. Just a weight, a presence.

I let him hold me. I let myself be held.

The wine, the fire, the blanket—all make me slow, languorous. I settle into his side and feel the tension in my spine unravel.

"I don't want to be alone tonight," I say, my voice almost too soft to hear.

"You don't have to be."

I wonder if the old me—the one who kept an incident log and checked the locks twice every hour—would recognize this version. The one who lets a man fall asleep beside her and believes that, maybe, second chances are real.

CHAPTER 25

KADE

The digital ghosts are hungry today. So am I, as I comb through the audit log on the Wildfire case. There's an entry that catches my eye. No memo, no context, just a sterile line item: "Incident Wildfire: Handler Override."

Handler Override. That means it was Ryland. Why would Ryland run an override on my case?

I click deeper, fingers drumming a military cadence. The log is clean, but not too clean. It's like someone wanted it to look aboveboard but missed a fingerprint. I recognize the pattern. Ryland always erases twice, never three times. He says it saves time, that no one ever checks that deep. I do.

The log entry leads to a dead-link file with a name. Lawrence Hyde. I stare at the blank screen, watching my reflection there. The office shrinks into itself, narrowing my vision to the only evidence a human being occupies this space: a framed photo. Courtesy of Ryland, a gift when I first arrived in New Zealand. Meritorious Service Medal ceremony. I'm in full dress, jaw locked, eyes bruised by the flash. Next to me, Ryland—taller, thinner then, his smile a gash cut into marble. I can't remember the moment I received the medal, only that when it was over, he squeezed my hand until I felt the bones grinding.

"You earned this in Afghanistan," he'd whispered.

I'd earned far more than a medal in Afghanistan—a lifetime of regret. Ryland knew that better than anyone. His words echo in my mind, a haunting refrain from our conversation about this case when I transferred to New Zealand.

"Wildfire. Delicate case. It's not personal, so don't make it personal," he'd said, his voice smooth as polished granite. But with Ryland, it's always personal. Every move calculated, every piece positioned just so on the chessboard of his ambition.

I'd accepted, of course. Ryland, whose requests are always orders thinly veiled as choice, could sign an execution order and then go home to prune his rosebushes. His hands always perfectly clean.

I know this because he was my lieutenant over in Afghanistan. I'd just made sergeant before the deployment. A private in my squad was always finding ways to irritate everyone with his antics. We called him "Private Pain in the Ass," and he wore it like a badge of honor. He strutted around the barracks with a cocky grin, as if the nickname were a medal pinned to his chest. He never missed an opportunity to live up to it.

Ryland assigned us a mission. Two teams, two targets. Just as we were gearing up, he abruptly changed the plan, redirecting the parameters and leaving my squad to handle the aftermath. We went in, and it was chaos. Five wounded, one dead.

My finger traces the rim of the cup. My eyes lock onto a spot on the wall, but all I see is Private Thurmond's face staring back at me. I remember his hearty laughter echoing in the mess hall. The sharp crack of the gunshot rings in my ears, the moment he crumpled to the ground replaying in my mind every time I close my eyes. I see it on a loop when I try to sleep. The scotch helps.

It was friendly fire that killed Thurmond. A bullet from one of our own. Ryland wasted no time slipping into damage-control mode.

"It's straightforward. Follow the chain of command," he said, his voice cold and unwavering. "You sign off as his sergeant, and I'll do the same as your lieutenant. He'll take the fall. He's been a thorn in our side anyway, so no one's going to question it."

"I can't do that." My conscience was screaming.

"It's an order. It's necessary, Sergeant Kade. I'm not going down for this," he insisted, his eyes hard and unyielding.

I signed, but only because Private Pain in the Ass agreed to take the fall for Ryland. I was awarded the medal, while Private Pain in the Ass was dishonorably discharged. Ryland's record is spotless, while the truth lies buried with Private Thurmond.

Like I said, Ryland's hands are always perfectly clean.

I shake the thought. The past is a dead planet. Nothing grows there. I need to have a call with Ryland, but it requires careful preparation. If I come at him head-on, he'll restrict my access by noon. I should play it soft —probe, not attack. Let him believe he's still holding the leash.

The internal messaging system shows that Ryland is online. I type him a quick message that I need five minutes. He immediately sends me a link to a video call. I'm surprised, but not really. The video call will show his superiors that he's in a meeting.

My hands are steady, but my chest is electric. The screen flickers, then Ryland's face appears.

"Good morning, sir," I say, my voice as flat as a printout.

He smiles back, all teeth. "Kade."

"About the override—" I keep my tone casual, like I'm mentioning the weather.

"Yes?"

"I noticed the log. I didn't realize you were running parallel observation."

A pause. He measures the silence with a scale. "It was a situational necessity."

"Care to elaborate?"

He doesn't flinch. "No, I don't. Suffice it to say, the incident was handled."

I let the words hang. "You think she's stable?"

"She's functional. That's enough."

I drum my fingers, making sure he hears it. "If you're worried about my methods—"

"I'm not. If I were, you'd already know. Your asset's safety is paramount, but so is the integrity of the program."

I nod, then change course. "You remember that night in Taji? When the comms went down and you rigged that antenna out of scavenged wire?"

He blinks, thrown off by the pivot. "We had to, or the whole city would have gone dark."

"You always did what had to be done. Even if it meant breaking the toys."

"What made you bring that up?" He leans in, the webcam warping his face. "For reasons you know, I don't like talking about Afghanistan."

"If you ever need to talk about that night, you know I'll listen."

Ryland goes silent for a second, then snips it. "Anything else on the Wildfire situation?"

"Yes. Minor concern regarding external contamination." I keep it vague, but not too vague.

Ryland's silent. "You think we have a leak?"

"I think," I say, carefully, "that someone has been moving files on the network."

He breathes once, heavily. "You checked the logs?"

"Twice. Mind if I have Maddie run an analysis?" I let the implication hang. Maddie is his person, not mine.

"Yeah." I hear the edge in his voice. "She's thorough."

"She's excellent." I lay the flattery on thin and obvious. "You always pick the right people."

"I'll authorize Maddie to investigate. Quietly. If there's anything anomalous, it comes directly to me. No intermediaries. Understood?"

I grit my teeth. "Understood."

He disconnects without another word.

For a second, I listen to Ryland's voice looping in my head.

He's onto me. Or maybe he wants me to think he's onto me. It's going to be a long week. But at least I know who's playing on my field.

The only way forward is caffeine. The hallway is empty. At the end of the corridor, the kitchen light glows jaundice-yellow. I pause at the threshold. Voices carry in these old buildings, but I know the sound of Maddie's. She's in there, low and urgent, talking to someone. Maybe the coffee machine. Maybe a ghost. Maybe someone on the other end of a phone.

I step to the side, flattening against the wall. The conversation is a river with boulders—broken, choppy, and hard to follow.

". . . can't delay, it's already in the log . . ." Maddie's voice, sharper than usual, is stripped of its normal treacle.

A low answer, inaudible. The reply is a hiss, indistinct, something like ". . . you handle it . . ."

I hear the clink of ceramic on Formica, then a deep sigh. "No, I don't think he suspects me, but hold on . . ."

The phone is muffled. Steps. A drawer slams. Maddie resumes, softer, but I'm good at reading tone when the words fail. She's worried. Maybe scared. Maybe for herself. Maybe for someone else.

The clatter of the coffee machine drowns the rest.

I step back, move to the fire door, and push through with a bang. Maddie's at the sink, rinsing her mug.

She turns, and her mask is perfect. "Hey, Kade. I'm making a fresh batch. Want one?"

"Definitely."

She wipes her hands on a paper towel. "Got some weird request from Ryland. Know anything about it?"

"Yeah, we can talk about it later, though. It's not urgent."

Maddie pours two mugs and hands one to me. She doesn't fidget, doesn't crack under the weight of my stare. If she's nervous, it's under the skin. She leaves, not looking back. I stand there, listening to the echo of her footsteps.

The cup is heavy in my hand. I stay in the kitchen re-running the fragments of Maddie's call through my mind. Nothing adds up. Nothing ever does. But the numbers are getting close. Tomorrow, I'll check the audit logs again. For now, patience is the only weapon left.

I can't stay at the office. I'll obsessively check the logs. I pull out my phone and Google the hospital.

"Werneth District Medical Annex. How may I direct your call?"

"Yes, I'd like to send flowers to a friend of mine in the hospital. Can you tell me what room Leesa Parker is in?"

The operator pauses. I quickly rattle off her date of birth to confirm I'm not some random stranger. I'd prepared for this and looked her up in the system. It works.

"She's in room 312."

"Great. Thank you."

When I arrive at the hospital, I duck into the floral shop on the first floor. I pay cash for a nice arrangement and instruct the worker to just sign the card "From your friends at The Cottage Café," and ask they deliver them to Leesa's room tomorrow.

At the Werneth District Medical Annex, the third floor is a labyrinth of glass, polished tile, and strategically placed wall art. I stroll past Leesa's room, the door slightly ajar. I see Edmund sitting in a chair next to her bed, talking to her. She's asleep. I keep walking. Twenty paces to the left is a small area with vending machines and chairs. I take a magazine from the table and grab a seat, pretending I'm reading. When it comes to surveillance, I am a very patient man.

My patience is rewarded when Edmund emerges from Leesa's room. He stands in front of the elevator. I wait until the doors almost close and jump in.

He turns, startled, then smiles politely. "What floor?"

I look at the panel. He's already pressed the basement. "Basement, thanks."

"I'm headed there, too."

"Yeah?"

"Coffee out of the vending machine is terrible. They have a cappuccino machine in the cafeteria."

I smile and nod politely. "Cafeteria. That's where I'm headed. Thanks for the tip on the coffee."

"No worries, mate."

"Are you Australian? English?"

Edmund laughs. "English. Let me guess . . . you're American?"

"How'd you know?"

We both laugh this time. The doors slide open, and the smell of floor wax and disinfectant overwhelms me. We're about to go our separate ways when I make my move.

"You know Tara, right? The barista at The Cottage Café?"

He colors, the faint flush of someone who's on the precipice of love. I've seen this look before. Before he can respond, I speak. "She's a friend of mine. The Americans tend to congregate abroad, you know?"

I say this specifically because Edmund attended a social for British expats in New Zealand. Leesa's a member of the group. I imagine he was going on her behalf to apprise them of her condition.

Edmund nods, studying my face.

I look down and shake my head. "She's had it rough."

"I figured as much, but I don't pry."

"That's good. She's not fond of attention." I glance around the room, lean in just a little. "Between you and me, she's been hurt more than she lets on."

"We probably shouldn't be discussing this."

"You're right. Just friendly advice. You seem like a good guy, but you're leaving soon, right?"

A wince, brief but honest. "I . . . probably. I'll need to get back once my sister—"

"I'm sorry. Look at me being the one to pry." I hold his gaze, as soft as I can manage. "It's just . . . just that she's not in a state for heartbreak. Not again."

He sits with that. The overhead lights flicker, or maybe it's just the blood in my temples.

"Did she ask you to talk to me?" His voice drops to a whisper.

"No," I answer, and it's true. "I just look out for her. Used to know her back in the States. There was an incident. She doesn't talk about it. She probably won't." I let the words hang there for a beat. "She deserves peace."

He nods, slow and heavy. "I never meant . . . we're just friends."

"Maybe keep it that way. Sorry if that was awkward. Probably best not to mention this to her, eh?"

He tries to smile, but it's forced.

"I'll keep your sister in my prayers." I give him a light pat on the back and walk across the cafeteria to the coffee machine. I don't want coffee, but I've got to play the part. I do not look back. My hands are steady, breath even.

Mission accomplished.

CHAPTER 26

TARA

I pretend I'm not waiting for his text. I ignore the phone on the kitchen table while I dress for work, as I lace up my boots, as I tie my hair in a ponytail, and as I eat the same breakfast as yesterday, and the day before: toast, marmalade, coffee. I count out the seconds before my resolve cracks, and I tap the phone awake. The screen is a desert. I toss it onto the couch and leave it facedown. If he wants to reach me, he knows how.

Outside, the wind has a needle's edge as if someone honed it on the ocean and sent it across the sea to find me. The walk to the café is longer than it should be, each step set to the slow rhythm of failure. I force my mind to catalog the colors of dawn, to imagine what Edmund would say if he saw the mist burn off the harbor, the flocks of oystercatchers sweeping low over the breakwater. He'd say something clever, something sly, and then look at me like I'm the most beautiful disaster he's ever seen.

The Cottage Café is already alive with the scent of espresso and the high, chemical shriek of the steam wand. Kass is behind the counter, head down, wrestling the grinder.

"Morning, Tara," she chirps, then coughs as a powdery cloud puffs up into her face.

"Morning."

"You hear from your Brit?" Kass's hands work the portafilter, tamping with ruthless precision.

I shrug, which is easier than explaining the hollow in my chest. "Hospital, remember? He said his sister's not doing well." I want to believe this is all it is.

"Right." Kass's eyes go wide, tragic. "You want me to make you a flat white before we open?"

"Thanks." I glance at the phone again. Still nothing.

By half-past six, the morning regulars drip in. By eleven, they're all here. Peggy Whitfield, two retired fishermen, and a pair of exhausted moms with strollers. I pour myself into the rhythm: order, serve, clear, repeat. But every lull in the noise makes me think of him, and every clatter in the alley makes me flinch.

By two, the shift drags. I check my phone—again, again, again—like a lab rat pushing a lever that never dispenses a pellet. No calls. No messages. I scroll through our last conversation, searching for a clue, some hint I missed.

ME

How's Leesa? Dinner this evening?

EDMUND

Stable. I'll be at the hospital all week.
Raincheck.

ME

Of course. Let me know if you need anything.

That was five days ago.

Kass leans on the counter, watching me. "Want me to text him? Maybe the guilt trip works better from a stranger."

"He's not the type to ghost." It comes out of my mouth sounding almost defensive. The conviction feels thin.

Kass shrugs. "Maybe he's busy. Hospitals are shit, right?"

"Right." The word tastes bitter.

I nearly say, "I'm scared." Not of Edmund, but of the hole his absence has left, and of what else might fill it.

Instead, I say, "I'm just tired. Sorry I'm being a downer."

"His silence says a lot more about him than it does about you," Kass says, her voice gentler than I've ever heard.

Kass nods thoughtfully. "Pinball at Harry's? It always works for me."

I almost laugh, but the sound sticks in my throat. I shake my head and meander home with the steps of a woman who will die alone. I sit by the window, staring at the street. A woman walks a dog. I remember when I used to walk my dog—before all of this, before the old life was taken away. I'd scan the shadows, and keep my keys tucked between my fingers like brass knuckles. After Todd, I told myself I'd never let another man make me feel like that again.

I watch an old flick, the volume low. It takes too much energy to fix dinner, so I don't bother. I wake up on the couch at three o'clock in the morning, the TV screen humming. I look at the phone screen, expecting nothing.

A text. I have to read it twice to be sure it's real.

Edmund

Thanks for the flowers. Leesa loved them. Been busy at the hospital.

A small, bright rush of relief. Then confusion: I didn't send any flowers.

I stare at the message and move from the sofa to the bed. I continue staring until the screen darkens and sleep claims me. I wake with my phone still in hand, cradled to my chest. I check the message again.

Edmund

Thanks for the flowers. Leesa loved them. Been busy at the hospital.

This is a classic Miss Sue move. It's my day off, so I quickly dress and check the time. It's nearly eleven, so the morning rush will be over, and the lunch rush will not have hit yet. I pull my hair back and secure it with a tie, then head to the café under the guise of coffee.

Kass is singing a cheery tune under her breath.

"Kass," I say, and the word comes out too loud.

She jumps. "Jesus, Tara. You okay?"

"Did anyone—" I pause, steadying my voice. "Did you send any flowers to the hospital? To Leesa?"

She wipes her hands, brow furrowing. "No. You want me to?"

I shake my head. "No. It's just . . . he texted. Said thanks for the flowers. I never sent any."

"If anyone did, it was probably Miss Sue. She loves that stuff." Kass nods her head toward the kitchen. "She's in her office if you want to ask."

I wait for my flat white in a go-cup before crossing through the kitchen into Miss Sue's office. It's tiny, like it was built to be a storage closet. There's no desk. Her laptop sits on a piece of plywood held up by sturdy, solid boards affixed to the wall.

"Well, look at that." Miss Sue pulls down her reading glasses. "What brings you in?"

"Coffee. Mine doesn't taste the same at home. I prefer our coffee here."

Her shoulders shake with a genuine laugh. I can't help but smile. "Sounds like you're just as dedicated a customer as you are an employee."

I take a sip from my cup. It's hotter than I like, burns going down, but I manage a smile, anyway. I can't help it. Miss Sue is infectious.

"Oh! I almost forgot . . . Edmund asked me to say thanks for the flowers."

"What flowers?"

"I don't know. I thought maybe you sent flowers to the hospital for Leesa."

Miss Sue looks genuinely confused, then her cheeks flush. "I probably shoulda done."

"Somebody did, and Edmund's thanking *me* for it."

"Maybe the cards got mixed up, or maybe Edmund misinterpreted who they're from."

Kass slides up beside me as I'm leaving. "Want a shot of something in your coffee?"

"I'm fine. It's just—" I lower my voice. "It's weird. That's all."

Kass puts a hand on my arm, quick and firm. "If you need anything, you say so."

"Thanks." I wave her off, saying I'll be fine. The lie is almost warm on my tongue.

The rest of the day is a blur. I compulsively check my phone—no new messages, no missed calls, no evidence that anyone has remembered me, except the lingering message. I reread it, searching for a hidden meaning or a code only I would understand.

I take a screenshot. It's muscle memory from when I had to document every offbeat thing Todd did. Back when nobody believed he was stalking me. The screenshots were evidence then. Now, it's comfort.

The sun is tracing its arc through the sky. The wind tunnels off the water. I walk fast; my keys laced through my fingers. Another comfort from my old life. Every sound is a potential footstep. Every parked car is a watcher. I round the corner onto Victoria Terrace and see the familiar sign for Werneth Fine Frames. The "r" still looks weary to me.

Mr. Holloway steps out, turning the key in his stubborn lock. He glances up at me, his hands never pausing. "Afternoon, Tara."

"Closing early for a snoozer?"

He snorts, metal clicking under his hand. "Something like that. Business is slow."

Mr. Holloway wears his loneliness with the same off-the-rack dignity as his brown cardigan. Even when he's needling me, it's with an undercurrent of hope that I might bite back. Sometimes, I do.

He gives the door a final shake, satisfied. "You're home early yourself."

"Trying to make good choices," I say, though it's a lie. I only ever make the same mistakes, repackaged.

Mr. Holloway ticks over my shoulder, the way people do when they're preparing you for a big reveal. "The other day, a man stopped in. Not local. American accent. Didn't want to buy a frame, didn't even look at the displays. Kept his hands in his pockets—"

My breath hitches in my throat. "What did he want?"

"Asked about who lives upstairs. Said he was interested in moving in, but he never asked about the rent." Mr. Holloway shakes his head. "Just wanted to know if you were quiet. If you kept to yourself."

Something inside me flips—quick and cold. "Did he give a name?"

"Told me his name was Lawrence Hyde. You know him?"

When I hear the name "Hyde," I immediately think of Todd. I often described his behavior as "Jekyll and Hyde" because he would quickly switch from Southern charm to volatile. I quickly dismiss the thought. It's paranoia talking.

I shake my head. "No. But if he comes back, maybe offer him the premium matting package. Drives away all sorts of undesirables."

He chuckles, relief flowing in. "Will do. You take care."

The stairs up to my flat creak with the weight of ancient wood and newer anxiety. I drop my bag, toe off my boots, and pause to listen. The apartment is silent except for the hum of the old fridge and the faint murmur of traffic outside. I scan for any signs of intrusion. None. Not that I really expected one. Sometimes, paranoia is just another name for practice.

I reach for my phone and dial Kade's number. It rings twice.

"Kade."

"Got a minute?"

"Sure, go ahead."

"I ran into Mr. Holloway, the frame shop owner. He says a guy was asking about me. Someone named Lawrence Hyde."

I hear Kade inhale sharply, then exhale, as if calibrating the weight of the conversation. "What kind of questions?"

"Am I quiet? Do I keep to myself? That sort of thing. Claimed he wanted to move in upstairs but didn't ask about the rent."

"That's odd. Did he describe him?"

"No, but he said the guy had an American accent."

"Describe Holloway's demeanor. Did he seem rattled? Or like he was fishing for gossip?"

"Honestly, it was hard to tell. He's the type who treats everything as a prelude to a true-crime podcast. But yeah, he seemed off. Not scared, just . . . off."

"Okay." The silence is different this time, not waiting to be filled. I hear him breathing, slow and even. I hear a pen click in the background. "You feel safe?"

"Define safe."

He ignores the joke. "I'm happy to come over if you need me to."

"No, I'm fine." I twirl a lock of hair around my finger.

"Since we talked, you don't have to log it through the app. I'll triage it from here."

"Kade?"

"Yeah?"

"One more thing. Edmund thanked me for flowers that I didn't send."

"Oh." His voice drops, almost a sigh.

There's another pause. I let it sit.

"It's probably a mix-up by the florist. I don't think it's anything to be concerned about."

I hang up first. The call leaves an aftertaste. Something is changing in the air. I can taste it on the back of my tongue: metal and old smoke. For a long time, I lie on my bed and stare at the ceiling, waiting for my mind to stop spinning. It's not Lawrence Hyde; it's Kade's reaction that keeps me awake.

CHAPTER 27

KADE

The office is dead quiet. I like it this way. I close the door, slip back behind my desk, and roll the name "Lawrence Hyde" around in my mouth. It tastes fake, like chewing on a plastic coin.

I try to pull up the dead-link file that first coughed up that name. The system blinks—error—then defaults to the dashboard. I try a second time, using the cached directory, and it's as if the file never existed. That's not normal. Even a sanitized file leaves a shadow, some digital bruise. But here: nothing.

Every instinct tells me not to run the name through the system, don't enter it anywhere it can be traced. Painfully, I've learned what happens when I chase shadows too directly. Instead, I open the Werneth PD access portal and run a side-channel to the town's camera system. I find the one at the intersection of Victoria Street and Victoria Terrace. The main drag curves uphill toward the frame shop. I set the feed to four-day history, double speed. The software runs a summary: "No unusual events." Which means nothing.

I take it back to 1.5x and scrub the video with my eyes fixed on the feed.

There's nothing out of the ordinary. A white delivery van, a postman, Mr. Holloway taking out a stack of cardboard. Then, at 13:21, two days prior, a figure steps into the frame. He's wearing a black overcoat, and what looks to be gray slacks and brown leather shoes. Not a tourist, not a local. The coat fits too well, and the gait is balanced, purposeful. I pause and drag the cursor back.

He stands outside the frame shop for fifteen seconds, watching the window, then steps inside. Six minutes later, he leaves, hands in the coat pockets, head tilted down. Whoever it is knows there is a camera. He never —not once—looks in the direction of the lens.

I run it again, slower. After he leaves the shop, he walks between two buildings. Out of sight. The man's posture is clean, military. No hesitation at the curb, just a single pivot. The coat, though. It's too tailored. It reminds me of what Ryland always says: "Dress to blend but always dress for respect."

The third time I watch, my scalp prickles. The walk is measured, deliberate, not hurried. If this is Ryland, he's not doing a good job of trying to hide. If it's not Ryland, someone wants me to think it is. I rewind the footage. The man's build is almost right. Ryland was always a half-head taller than me, more ex-rugby than ex-military, but the camera angle makes everyone seem shorter.

I loop it again. No one else enters or leaves the shop all day. That part is normal. I run a cursory check on the neighboring businesses. No one lingers, no one follows the man. There is, however, a light-colored sedan that circles the block twice: once at 12:03 and again at 13:14. The same sedan? Maybe. The plate number is a grainy blur. Could be a rental, could be a decoy, could be nothing. In this business, every nothing adds up.

I minimize the feed, lean back in my chair, and close my eyes. I roll the name again, softer.

"Lawrence Hyde." It sticks in my throat. I think about the dead-link file. About the sanitized log. Whatever's going on, I'm not supposed to see it. But I do. The man on the camera almost looks like Ryland. Almost.

I pull out the flip phone from the bottom drawer. I pop the back, slide in the SIM card, snap it shut. The phone boots with a mindless jingle. I dial the number by memory.

It rings forever. On the eighth cycle, a click.

I wait for a voice. Instead, a dry cough.

"Go."

I keep my voice level. "Query on Wildfire. Are you familiar with the name Lawrence Hyde?"

I nod my head as I listen to the response.

"No, I haven't run the name through the system. Logs appear to be scrubbed on my end. Anomalies, maybe. But too many to be system lapses."

A silence. I hear paper shuffling before he speaks again and I listen carefully.

"Negative." I run a hand across my chin. "I don't want anything logged in the system until I can figure out what's going on with the logs. Asset is secure. Unnerved, but secure."

He hangs up without saying goodbye. It's a small favor. I remove the SIM card, take out the clippers, and destroy it. It feels good—decisive—a show of control over at least one variable. I shove the remnants in my pocket for the microwave later, when I get home.

Who is Lawrence Hyde? It's the not knowing that rots my stomach.

I walk down the hall. Maddie is at the front desk, waiting for visitors who never come. I'm not sure I even know what she does half the time. My steps are light down the hallway until I see the back of her head come into focus. She's on her personal phone, texting. Probably her mother or a friend.

"Maddie?"

She whirls her chair around with a sudden, forceful motion. The phone flies from her grip, landing on the desk with a thud that echoes through the lobby. Her eyes widen in shock, her face a canvas of startled guilt.

Maddie gasps, a hand pressed to her chest. "Kade, you scared me!"

I assess the situation. Her cheeks flushed crimson. Maddie blinks rapidly, no direct eye contact. She glances at the phone on the desk like it's a loaded gun. She's hiding something, but I don't have time to dig into it now.

"I'm so sorry, I didn't hear you coming."

There's an edge to her voice. It could be because I startled her, or it could be that I caught her doing something she shouldn't be. I dismiss her apology with a flick of my wrist, my face giving nothing away. "Never mind that. What did you find in the logs?"

"Just routine maintenance. The system was reorganizing files for optimal performance—I confirmed with Tech in D.C. Nothing suspicious."

I cross the lobby and lower myself into a visitor's chair, the cheap upholstery creaking beneath me. "Standard procedure, is that right?"

"Exactly. You happened to access it during the reorganization cycle. That's why you hit those dead links."

I hold her gaze without speaking. The silence stretches between us like taffy. She fidgets, then breaks.

"I've been chatting with Ryland since my transfer from Auckland. I'm looking to advance beyond analytics into something with more teeth." She leans forward. "Do you think I have what it takes to be field-certified?"

The question almost seems like a joke. She's dressed in a leopard print blouse, a black pencil skirt, and a bright red belt that matches her shoes and lipstick. Blending in has never been her style. Plus, the fact that you can hear her before you see her spells disaster for an agent. "Why would you want to work in the field? With your technical expertise and sharp mind, you're most valuable as an analyst. The field is risky."

Maddie's mouth drops open in disbelief. "Risky? I know the protocols inside and out. I'm ready for more responsibility. I want to make a real difference, not just stare at screens all day."

I see her determined expression. I can't deny her aptitude with analytics, but field work requires a whole different skillset. "Look, I appreciate your ambition. But field certification isn't something the service hands out lightly. There's a reason most agents spend years working their way up."

Her brow furrows, defiance flashing in her eyes. I stand from the chair, the cheap upholstery giving a groan. It's a power move, of course.

"Here's a test run for you. When Tara finishes her shift tomorrow, walk her home. Pay attention to everything—her behavior, the environment, potential threats. Take mental notes. Then report back to me. Consider it your first unofficial field assessment."

Her bright eyes are wide, and her lips are parted in a silent scream. "Alright. I can do that. Easy."

"Remember, this isn't a game or a drill. Take it seriously. Lives could depend on your observations in the field."

"I understand. I'll treat it like a real mission."

"Good. Because it is a real mission." I turn to leave, then pause. "And Maddie? Be discreet. The last thing we need is Tara getting suspicious or asking questions."

"Of course. I know how to be subtle." She flashes a confident smile.

I glance at her desk—the scattered pens and sticky notes. I return to my office, thoughts churning. I need to talk to Ryland about Maddie. Something doesn't sit right. The phone rings while I drum my fingers on the desk. He picks up on the third ring.

"Ryland."

"It's Kade. We need to talk about Maddie."

A pause. "What about her?" His tone is guarded, defensive.

"Is she fully vetted?"

"What makes you ask?"

"I just caught her on her personal phone, looking guilty as hell when I walked in."

Ryland sighs. "Kade, she's a young woman. They're always on their phones these days. It's probably nothing."

I lean back in my chair, unconvinced. "Maybe. But lower-level employees like her are susceptible to breaches. If the right person comes along waving enough cash . . ."

I let the implication hang.

"You think Maddie would commit treason?" Ryland's voice rises in disbelief. "That's absurd. She worked directly under me here in Auckland. Her loyalty is unquestionable."

"I'm not accusing her of anything," I clarify, trying to diffuse the tension. "But we have to consider all possibilities. Even the uncomfortable ones."

Ryland sighs heavily. "Look, Kade, your concern is noted. But I'm telling you it's the product of your imagination. You want this case to be something it's not. This case is a walk in the park for you."

"Yes, sir." The words taste bitter as they leave my mouth. "She tells me you two have discussed field certification."

A dry laugh crackles through the phone. "Ambitious girl. But between us, she belongs behind a desk."

"My thoughts exactly. Still, I've assigned her to escort our asset home tomorrow—gives her that field experience she's craving."

"Wait—you just implied she might be compromised, and now you're putting her near the asset? Make up your mind, Kade."

I pinch the bridge of my nose, frustration simmering in my gut. Ryland isn't seeing the bigger picture here. "It's not about making up my mind. It's about evaluating risks and gathering intel. If there's even a chance she's compromised, we need to know."

"And you think having her walk the asset home will reveal that?"

"It's a controlled test. I'll be monitoring the whole thing."

Ryland's sigh crackles through the line. "Fine. But I'm telling you, you're barking up the wrong tree with Maddie. She's one of our most promising young analysts."

"Noted. Hey, let me ask—"

"Go."

"You didn't come to Werneth and not have dinner with me, did you?"

Ryland laughs. But I know him. It isn't a real laugh. "Not a chance, buddy."

The line goes dead. I set the phone down. It's what he didn't ask that irks me.

Maddie. Her loyalty is "unquestionable," according to Ryland. Maybe he's talking about her loyalty to him. She is hiding something, and I intend to find out what it is. I pull up her personnel file on my computer, scanning the details. Stellar performance reviews, glowing recommendations from superiors, including Ryland. On paper, she's the perfect employee. In my gut, she's a liability.

CHAPTER 28

TARA

The shift is over. My hands reek of espresso and dishwater. My mind hums with the static left by a creepy phone call. I'm halfway out the door, keys in my fist like a set of claws, when I see Maddie waiting on the sidewalk. She's bundled up in a lilac parka, her hair a glossy brown helmet, and for a second, I don't recognize her. Her smile jumps ahead of her, too eager, as if she's been waiting a long time and has rehearsed how this will go.

"Tara!" She says my name like a bright bead popping on a string.

I blink at her. "Hey. You lost?"

She laughs, a small, mechanical sound, and tugs the hem of her coat. "No, I'm just early. Kade sent me to walk you home."

I do know Kade. I know him better than I want to. This isn't his style. He doesn't coddle. He especially doesn't send staff out in a down jacket as an escort unless something's up. The thought curdles in my gut, but I nod.

"You hungry?" Maddie asks quickly, like maybe she'll get to say her lines and scurry back inside. "The office will pay for it."

"I just spent eight hours surrounded by food. But thanks." I start walking, and she falls in at my side, her boots keeping pace with mine. There's a nervous energy in the air, the sense that the town itself is waiting to see which of us will speak.

We make it a block in silence before she tries again. "How's work going?"

I glance at her. Her cheeks are raw from the cold, but her eyes are clear, sharp as salt. "It's not that bad."

"That's not what I hear. Word is, you're the only one who can handle the morning crowd without throwing a cup at someone."

I snort. "They haven't seen me on a bad day."

The wind whips around the corner, and I tuck my chin into my coat. She mirrors the move. Her hands disappear into the sleeves, fingers curled tight.

We pass the florist's shop, where condensation smears the windows and stems and petals press against the glass in a funhouse display. I don't look too closely. I don't want to see if yellow roses are there. I keep my eyes on the sidewalk, on the half-frozen gum and the beer bottle caps lodged in the curb. The sun is already draining out of the sky, leaving a gray, metallic shimmer on the street.

Maddie breaks the silence again, softer this time. "How are you really doing, Tara?"

The question lands like a stone in my stomach. I'm not sure if she means the job, the program, or the way I spent last night counting the minutes between each creak in my apartment. Maybe she means all of it. I give her the answer she expects. "I'm fine. Better than before."

She nods. "Good. That's good."

We walk in step. Our shadows braid together on the sidewalk. I watch the way she glances at every parked car, down every alley. She's not subtle about it. She's not trained like Kade, but there's a discipline to it.

After a block, I test the waters. "Is Kade really that worried about the incidents I've been logging, or did he just want an excuse to get you out of the office?"

She grins, but it's a reflex. I can't tell if I caught her off guard. Maybe she doesn't know about the incidents. I don't know how much a receptionist at the consulate is privy to.

"He worries about all his cases."

I let the silence stretch to see what she'll do. She fills it, eventually.

"He said it's been rough. Panic attack, or something?"

I exhale, watching the mist of my breath tumble ahead. "Which one?"

"You want to talk about it?"

I shake my head. "No offense."

She shrugs, accepting it. "I get it."

We reach the crosswalk. The wind off the harbor picks up, cutting through my layers and threading a chill into my bones. I steal a look at Maddie. Her face is tight, eyes scanning the intersection, lips pressed into a thin, colorless line.

It's her turn to probe. "I'm not seeing anyone following. These incidents, has there been someone following you?"

The question is too direct. Now I'm the one caught off guard. "What do you mean?"

She shrugs, but her shoulders hitch a little higher than normal. "I just . . . Kade's whole job is to keep you safe, but you know, it helps if you let us know."

"Us." She says it as if there's a whole committee on the project, and maybe there is. Maybe I'm the only one naïve enough to think otherwise.

I keep my voice flat. "No one's following."

She nods, but the muscles in her jaw work overtime, chewing at the inside of her mouth.

A pack of teens cut across our path, shrieking over a bag of chips. The noise jars me, but Maddie barely flinches. She's locked in now, running a script.

I try a different angle. "Has anyone heard from Todd?"

The name hangs in the air, electric and toxic.

Maddie's eyes flick up, then away. There's a tiny quiver at the corner of her mouth, a micro-smile that dies on arrival. "No. The embassy would know if he left the country."

I nod, letting the answer wash over me. She's not lying, but she's not telling the whole truth either. I know the drill. I've played this game before.

We walk in silence until I see the frame shop; the windows are dark. Maddie slows, letting me take the lead up the stairs to my flat. I unlock the door and hold it open for her, but she hesitates on the threshold.

"Do you want to come in?" I ask politely. *Please say no. Please say no.*

She hesitates. I give her an out. "I'll be fine. Thanks for the walk."

She smiles too quickly. "You sure?"

I nod. "Yeah. I'll lock up behind me."

"Alright. I'll see you later, Tara." Maddie says it as if we'll be meeting for happy hour after work.

I watch her turn and start back down the stairs, hands jammed in her coat pockets, head down against the wind. If it were Kade, he'd stay on the landing until he heard the click of the deadbolt lock.

I cross to the window and look down. Maddie's still in sight, her lilac coat a bright smudge against the charcoal street. She walks with a purpose, but not a destination. After a minute, she stops, pulls out her phone, and makes a call. I can't see her face, but I imagine the way she'll recount the walk, the way she'll frame our conversation to Kade.

I watch until she disappears around the corner. I run my thumb along the edge of the windowpane, cold biting into the flesh. For a moment, I wonder what it would be like to be on the other side of the glass, to be the watcher instead of the watched. Then I remember that it doesn't matter. On either side, you're still alone.

Sunday is my day of rest when the world recedes to a low hum. No work, no Kass, no Kade. Just a space where, for a handful of hours, I can pretend I am no longer the product of someone else's nightmare. I make breakfast slowly, savoring the violence of the knife through toast, the hiss of coffee hitting the mug. My hands move with method, not grace. Standing by the window, I eat a piece of toast, the plate propped on the palm of my hand, and watch as the street below stirs from its coma. No sign of anything except gulls picking at a pizza box by the bus stop.

At eleven, I force myself out the door. The bookstore smells like dust and lemon cleaner. There's a man in a flat cap in an armchair by the window, reading a French cookbook and eating potato chips from the bag. He licks his fingers after every page, then makes a face, as if he's just remembered he hates himself. I know the feeling.

I'm early, of course. When I said I'd meet Edmund at noon, I meant sharp, but I couldn't stand the silence of my flat and the steady tick of time in my head, so I came almost an hour ahead and wandered the aisles, picking up books I have no intention of buying. I'm in the thriller section, spine-out, when I hear his voice.

"Hi," he says, voice hoarse.

I close the book about a woman who poisons her husband for the life insurance, then feels bad about it. I think about buying it, just to see if she gets away with it in the end.

"Hi." I try to smile, but it doesn't stick.

He looks awful. Deep circles are under his eyes, and stubble climbs up his cheeks like moss on a headstone. His hair is disheveled. He smells like the inside of a cab.

He rocks on his heels, then shoves his hands in his pockets. "Sorry for not calling," he says.

I shake my head, dismissing it. "It's fine. I figured you were busy with Leesa."

A single nod. "Yeah." Then, after a breath, "She's worse."

I look for something to say that isn't a cliché, but my mind serves up the classics anyway. "I'm sorry."

He shrugs. "She's sleeping most of the time. The doctors say it won't be long now."

His eyes go glassy for a second. I wonder if he'll cry. I'll have to hug him if he does. I cross my arms, hugging the book to my chest.

"I can leave you alone. If you need to be with her."

He shakes his head again, slower this time. "I wanted to see you."

I nod, but I don't know what he wants from me. Distraction? A polite way to end things without either of us having to say it?

He glances at the book. "Is it good?"

I look at the cover. "It's about a woman who kills her husband."

He snorts, a pale ghost of a laugh. "Foreshadowing."

We stand there in the aisle, like strangers waiting for the other to speak first. Outside, the sky is a colorless smear, threatening rain. Inside, the world shrinks to the space between us and the overhead lights buzzing.

He clears his throat. "I'm leaving soon."

I feel it then. The click of inevitability. "Back to London?"

He nods. "After the funeral, I guess."

I look down at my boots. I was a placeholder. A plot device in the narrative of his grief. I want to hug him. Instead, I set the poisoner's book back on the shelf and walk down the aisle, hoping he'll follow. He does.

"I liked the other night," he says, voice soft.

I remember the picnic, the reading on the couch, the taste of his kiss, and the way his hands felt.

We reach the children's section, where the shelves are lower and the chairs are plastic. There's a mural on the wall of cartoon giraffes and penguins in scarves. I sit, knees folded under me like a child in time-out. He sits across from me, somehow folding his entire six-foot frame into a space designed for a toddler.

He looks at his hands. "Leesa's not doing well and . . . well, I just . . ."

My heart drops. I know what he's going to say. I spare him. "You need to be with Leesa right now. It's okay. I understand."

"You deserve better than some guy who's going to leave in a few weeks."

"We had a great time together, Edmund. I'm happy we did. I hope we can keep in touch, in case I make it over to London one day."

He smiles. "You always sound so tough."

"I'm not." That's the truest thing I've said in weeks.

He leans forward, elbows on his knees. "I'll miss you."

I take his hand and hold it for a moment, the way one holds a bird that's crashed into a window. Gentle, but with the knowledge that it's already half-dead. "I hope Leesa doesn't suffer."

He squeezes my hand. "Me, too."

We sit there until the man with the flat cap gets up, leaving the bookstore silent but for the hum of the lights. He doesn't even buy the cookbook whose pages he turned with licked fingers.

When I finally let go, Edmund stands, sways, then steadies himself.

"Goodbye, Tara."

"Goodbye, Edmund."

I watch him leave, his shoulders hunched against the wind. Then I turn and wander the aisles one last time, breathing in the paper and dust—the scent of endings and beginnings.

I'm not ready to date. I'm not ready for much of anything, except this: the knowledge that letting go doesn't have to hurt as much as holding on.

I can't bring myself to go back to my empty, barren flat. I make a slow shuffle, tracing the spines with my finger. I am halfway to the new releases, and I freeze.

There's a man.

He stands at a window, next to the door. The street's bright, cold lights him up, backlighting his frame.

He's built like a battering ram. Broad shoulders. Thick neck. Big hands.

He takes off his sunglasses. Tucks them into his collar.

His hair is short. Iron-gray fuzz.

Every cell in my body goes electric. It's not Todd. It can't be. Todd is on the other side of the world. The probability he's in Werneth is zero. But my brain does not care about probability. It cares about the posture, the way he tips his head, the slow roll of his shoulders as he reads. My mouth goes dry. The blood drains from my face so fast I grip the edge of the display table to keep upright.

I want to get a look at his face. I try to look, but he's angled away—a profile at most. He picks a book off the shelf, thumbs the pages, and puts it back. I tell myself to breathe.

I can feel my pulse in my teeth. I'm already backing away, eyes darting for the exits. I knock a stack of paperbacks to the floor. The noise is nothing—a whisper—but it feels like an explosion. I have to get away. Away from the bookstore. Away from the man who can't be Todd. Away from the sickening sense that my past has finally caught up to me.

CHAPTER 29

KADE

A sharp knock at my office door sends a jolt through me like an electric shock. Maddie's personnel profile is splayed across my screen. She slips in without waiting for an invitation or even an acknowledgement, eyes wide with concern. Thankfully, it's strategically turned away from the door precisely to guard against moments like these. I lock my computer anyway. The way Maddie did when she realized I was standing behind her.

"Tara's here. She's really upset. No appointment. What should I tell her?"

"Put her in the conference room."

I yank at my tie, loosening it with a deliberate, exaggerated motion, though it's all for show. I'm processing the details from Maddie's personnel file. Her hometown is uncomfortably close to Bennett's, which leads me to question who she was messaging.

I stride into the conference room, feeling the tension crackle in the air. Tara is pacing like a caged lion by the windows, her black denim and boots adding to her fierce demeanor. Her hair is twisted up, secured with a pencil. She doesn't even glance my way.

"Tara." My tone is warm yet probing. "What's going on?"

She whirls around to face me, eyes wild. "I saw him. At the bookstore. He was right there, in front of me." The words tumble out, fast and jagged.

I run through a quick assessment. She's sweating under her collar, fingers tapping a rhythm on her forearm, eyes glassy. Every sign is familiar: the tight jaw, the way she squares her shoulders as if she's about to take a punch. This is what real fear looks like. I close the door.

"Slow down. Who did you see?"

"Todd." She spits the name like venom. "Same build, same walk."

I keep my face neutral, but my mind is racing ahead. This is a new level of panic for her. I jot down a note, keeping my eyes on the paper.

"Okay. Tell me exactly what happened, from the beginning. Start with the name of the bookstore."

Tara looks directly at me. She doesn't see me. There's a difference. One you internalize in my line of work, and the one where you end up retired early, badge in a shadowbox, teeth in a glass. It's the difference between being trusted and, in Tara's case, not being trusted.

The story spills out of her, all sharp edges and missing pieces. I listen, nodding at the right moments, letting her purge. When she's done, she collapses into the chair, spent.

"Alright. You're safe here."

I take the seat opposite. I want her on my side of the table, but her demeanor suggests the separation is necessary. I'll work to change that.

I cap my pen, considering. "Did he see you?"

She shakes her head. "Of course, he saw me."

"I understand how frightening this must have been. But Tara, the likelihood that Todd Bennett made it into the country undetected is extremely low. We have a flag on his passport. If he enters the country, we'll know about it."

I let the silence balloon between us.

"Sit tight. Let me go to my office, make a call. I will help you figure this out."

Tara nods.

When I open the door, I nearly run into Maddie holding a coffee mug with bubble gum pink lipstick smudged on the rim. She staggers back, sloshing coffee onto her hand. She hisses in pain but manages to keep her grip on the mug.

I don't have time to decipher her expression or the way she cradles that mug like it's a grenade with the pin pulled.

"Excuse me," I mutter, shouldering past. "Stay in the room with Tara."

I need to get to my office, need to start pulling threads before this unravels completely.

I go straight for the phone. My fingers punch in the analyst's extension. The twitch in my jaw the only tell that my composure is slipping.

"Embassy ops, Gower."

"Need a sweep on flight manifests for the last seven days. All U.S. inbound, full passenger lists. I'm sending you the details of who I'm looking for." My fingers are racing feverishly over the keyboard as I send Todd Bennett's details.

Gower makes a noise that might be a laugh. "You expecting trouble?"

"That's why you're on payroll, Gower."

"I need a case number."

"It's in the details I just sent. Customs has his passport flagged, but he may be entering on a shell ID."

He clicks keys for a moment. "How soon you want it?"

"Priority."

He sighs, but the respect is there. "Give me the day."

Before the phone settles onto the receiver, I'm out of my office and heading back to the conference room. I stand in the doorway.

"Thanks, Maddie. I'll take it from here."

She pats Tara on the shoulder and walks out of the room without making eye contact with me. I shut the door behind her.

Tara's eyes glisten, wide and shimmering under the fluorescent lights, as she tilts her head slightly toward me. Her eyebrows furrow, and her lips part slightly, as if she's about to speak but holds back, silently imploring me for help.

I take my seat opposite her. "Did you see a face?"

She hesitates then shakes her head. "No."

I nod, make a show of caring. "Anything else?"

She shakes her head again.

"Okay. I have an analyst in Auckland reviewing flight manifests. We're on an island. If Todd got in, somehow bypassing the flag we have on his passport, I'll know."

I match her silence for a minute. "Look, I was never good at discussing feelings."

She laughs, a knife-edged sound. "That's a surprise."

I smile at the dig. I know I deserve it. "The service . . . they make us see someone. After. But all the shrink wants is to check off a box."

"After what?"

I take a coin from my pocket, run my thumb along its grooves. I hesitate just long enough to get her attention.

"We were on a mission overseas when all hell broke loose. Gunfire. Deafening. Relentless. Troops scattered in every direction, desperately seeking any shred of cover they could find."

She throws a glance at me, sharp and quick as lightning. I stand rigid, turn to the window, my back to her. One hand burrows into my pocket, while the other flips the coin with a nervous energy. I hold the memory at arm's length, viewing it with the cold detachment of a coroner examining a corpse.

"You know, there's always that one guy who thinks he's invincible, like rules don't apply to him. He was a thorn in my side, a constant challenge, so I kept him close. Needed to keep a leash on him. I grabbed onto his vest and pulled him with me. There was a blast that produced a cloud of tiny sand particles that pricked your eyes. You could barely see through it."

I turn and look. Tara's eyes are fixed on me, hanging on every syllable I utter. She's like a fish on a hook, swimming toward the boat.

"We took cover in a building. It was nothing but rubble. It had been bombed out, but not recently. I crouched low, navigating through the debris, slipping out to the side to loop back to the street and retaliate against whoever ambushed us. My lieutenant was in front of me. Private Pain in the Ass was glued to my six."

I pace around the conference table with deliberate slowness, building tension with each step. I pull the chair next to her and drop into it. I'm close enough to feel the air shift between us, but not close enough to crowd her. My elbow is braced on the table, a single finger pressed to my temple, as if holding my skull together.

"I thought I was invincible. I had a rack full of ribbons and reached sergeant before we deployed. This was my first command." I place the coin onto the table with a metallic clang. My finger traps it with a slight tremor. "But I was terrified. Comms were in chaos. Voices clashing and yelling. Through the haze, I caught movement. Heard a gunshot. A body erupted. He was one of ours. Thurmond."

I pause, let the image fester between us.

"A grenade went off somewhere close. Everything around us was on fire, including Thurmond. Or what was left of him. I couldn't leave Thurmond behind. The fire was intense."

I unfasten the cuff of my sleeve. I roll it up. I show her the burn scars on my arm. I do a quick assessment of her in my head. Her posture is soft. Her eyes track my scars. Her hard shell has melted away into something pliable. Something I can work with.

I speak slowly, deliberately. "Every single time I close my eyes, I see Thurmond burst into pieces. Over and over."

"That's awful. How do you deal with something like that?"

I hear something new in her voice: a reluctant need to know. A desperate, almost tortured curiosity.

"I had nightmares about it for a year. Still do."

She speaks without looking at me. "What did the therapist say?"

"That I should focus on moving forward."

"Did it work?"

I smile. "No."

For a long time, the only sound is the hum of the fluorescent lights.

Finally, she says, "Why are you telling me this?"

"Because I know what it's like to think you're already dead."

I see her soften as she considers this. I take the coin, press it into her palm. She tries to resist, but I close her fingers around it.

"You think this is going to fix me?"

I shake my head. "No. But it might remind you that you're not alone."

She holds the coin tight. Stares out over the table. "What happened to the rest of your squad?"

"Some made it out. Some didn't." I watch the reflection of the sky in the window. "You lose people in this line of work. You lose parts of yourself, too. But I will not lose you."

She draws a deep breath, chest rising like she's about to scream. Instead, she exhales and throws her arms around me in an embrace.

"Thank you," she softly whispers into my chest.

Mission accomplished: I have her trust.

CHAPTER 30

TARA

There's a hush in the conference room that makes every sound magnified. Each tick of the government-issued clock sounds like a countdown. I am left in a room too large for waiting and too bright for comfort, while Kade works his brand of calm, clinical damage control behind closed doors.

The latch clicks, and I tense. Maddie enters, humming tunelessly. She carries two takeout menus like victory pennants, and her smile is an offensive display of unbroken teeth and optimism. "You've got to eat," she sings out.

"I'm fine." I blurt it out reflexively, like telling the nurse I don't need help out of the wheelchair—even though I do.

"Nonsense." Maddie places the menus in front of me, flipping one open. "We're ordering in, and Kade says it's on the office. Office budget, not his personal, but still. I think we should make it count, don't you?"

She's dressed in a bright red sheath dress with a novelty necklace shaped like little sushi rolls. Maddie radiates a kind of caffeinated energy that makes my molars ache.

I let the silence grow, half hoping she'll shrivel up in it. But Maddie is the kind of woman who draws power from emptiness. She sits on the table in front of me, leaning in like we're co-conspirators instead of government employee and liability.

"I narrowed it down to Thai or Indian, but then I remembered the last time I had the Thai I paid for it. In the bathroom, if you know what I mean." She shoves the Indian menu closer. "You ever try masala dosa?"

"No."

"It's life-changing. You should." She's already scanning the pages, highlighter at the ready. She highlights her own choices as she goes, marking up the page like she's correcting a child's math homework.

"The pay here is practically non-existent. I'm basically living on ramen and frozen yogurt. But the benefits are pretty good, and Ryland says you have to look at the whole package, not just the salary." She giggles, then looks up at me like we're sharing an inside joke. "So, when the food is on Uncle Sam, I'm going to make the most of it. Want the chicken entrée to take home for later?"

I shake my head, not even knowing what "later" is going to be like. I guess it depends on the call Kade is waiting for in his office.

"We're also ordering dessert. It's a moral imperative."

My eyes drift to the window. I half expect to see Todd's face, or maybe just his shadow, slip across. The hum of the fluorescent lights drills down into my spine. Maddie notices, of course. She notices everything, even if she plays dumb about it.

"You know," she says, her voice softer, "you're lucky to have Kade. Most of the handlers just want to push you through the process. Paperwork, signatures, on to the next case. But he really cares. You can tell."

I don't respond. The only thing I can tell is that everyone in this office has perfected the art of sounding sincere without ever meaning a single word.

Maddie twirls a pen between her fingers. "I'm putting you down for the saag paneer and a side of garlic naan. That's, like, everyone's favorite, but if you're not feeling it, I'll just take it home." She grins. "Honestly, I always order double because by the time the food gets here, I've changed my mind at least twice. You have to hedge your bets, right?"

I want to ask what she actually does here. Every time I've seen her, she's at the reception desk. She said she's a program analyst, but I've seen the way her hands shake when she types in the password to her own computer. If she's an analyst, I'm the Queen of England.

She gathers the menus I haven't even touched from the table. "You just relax, okay? I'll be right back."

As she stands, she leans close enough for me to smell her peppermint gum and the cheap rose-scented lotion she uses by the gallon. "If you ever want to talk about . . . anything, I'm not as young as I look. I know what it's like." Her voice falters, just for a second, and I catch a flicker of something—sympathy, maybe, or something sharper and more personal— but it vanishes before I can grab onto it.

"Thanks," I say, and it comes out flat.

"Back in a jiff." With a little salute, she vanishes down the hall.

Silence returns to the room. I count the seconds it takes for her footsteps to fade, and then I'm left with only the clock and my own restless heart pounding out a warning in a strange Morse code I can't quite decipher.

I can't focus, can't even remember what a normal day is supposed to feel like. All I want is for Kade to give me the debrief, tell me the plan—or at least pretend to. Instead, the minute hand crawls, the door stays shut, and all I have is the aftertaste of fear in my mouth and the endless echo of that man at the bookstore.

When the door swings open, I want it to be Kade's imposing silhouette. Instead, it's Maddie, clutching her phone. She sidles up next to me and sits—not at the far end of the table, not in one of the other eight chairs, but in the one right beside me. I can feel the warmth of her knee and see the dent her weight makes in the cushion.

"You okay?" Her voice is syrupy with concern. "You looked kind of white when you came in before. Not to be weird, but I know panic when I see it." She flashes a sympathetic grin. "I get it. When I started here, every time Ryland yelled for me from his office, I'd sweat through my whole outfit."

I want to snap at her that nobody in this building actually cares about what happens to me as long as the paperwork is tidy and the scandal is contained. But I just nod, let her project her own history onto me, let her think we're two of a kind.

"Did you have a favorite place to get coffee back home? You know, before. My roommate and I, we used to rate every café near campus for their oat milk lattes and their Spotify playlists. I mean, there were three, so it was a short competition. But still." She laughs and lets the silence open for me to fill.

"I didn't really have a favorite," I say. "Mostly just whatever was close."

Maddie leans in a fraction more, as if proximity can draw out the truth. "My theory is, it's not about the coffee. It's about the atmosphere. Like, you get used to people knowing your name, asking you if you want your regular. It's comforting, even if the place is trash." She kicks off her heels and wiggles her perfectly painted toes. "I think that's what I miss most. Just being known. You know?"

I look at her and wonder if she rehearsed this conversation in the bathroom mirror. If someone told her to play the empathetic big sister and report back on my mental state. I can almost hear Kade's instructions, even the way he'd phrase it: "Don't push but see if she'll talk. See if she's about to break."

I turn away. "How long have you worked here?"

"Not long. But I've been with the agency for two years. I was supposed to go to DC, but Ryland offered me a fast track if I came to New Zealand first. I worked for him in Auckland before he sent me to Werneth to gain field experience. Which is a joke, because nothing happens here. Until now, obviously. I'm basically the youngest person working under Ryland, so I get all the weird jobs. Inventory audits, website updates, sitting with people who are having a tough day."

She looks at me sideways, eyes full of regret. "Sorry. I know you probably don't want to talk about any of it. I just . . . sometimes it helps to have someone who isn't, like, paid to analyze your every word. Like a friend, not a therapist."

I want to say, "You're not my friend. You have no idea what I've been through," but the words stick in my throat—too sharp to risk in the open air.

"I'm fine," I say again, quieter this time.

She doesn't look up as she says, "I heard about the guy at the bookstore. Freaky, right? I wouldn't be surprised if it was him." She flips her phone over and over in her hand. "We had a training about stalkers in grad school. They're always more persistent than anyone expects. You think you've seen the last of them, and then—bam! There they are, right where you thought you were safe."

I feel the hairs on my arm rise. "You think it's him?" My voice was barely audible.

Maddie shrugs, an artful performance of innocence. "I dunno. I'd be freaked, too."

Her words drop into the space between us, like an ice cube down the spine. I want to ask what she knows, if she's just guessing, or if Kade has told her more than he's told me. But her face remains bland, unbothered, as if she's talking about weather patterns or reality TV.

"If it is him, Kade will take care of it. He's kind of a legend, you know. Even Ryland respects him, and Ryland doesn't respect anybody."

There's an intercom on the wall. It buzzes, loud and tinny, like an electric shock. Maddie jumps up, relief flooding her face. "That'll be lunch.

I'll go grab it." She turns, already halfway to the door, then pivots back. "Don't go anywhere. I mean, you can, but . . ." She trails off, then winks. "Back in a sec."

The door swings shut behind her, leaving me in a vacuum, ears ringing. I realize I'm gripping the chair so hard my nails have left little half-moons in the vinyl arm. I press my palms together and try to steady my breathing, but every time I close my eyes, all I see is the ghost of Todd's face.

Maddie reappears with a brown paper bag the size of a toddler. She cradles it in her arms, setting it gently on the table as if it's a gift and not just an overpriced takeout order. She produces a stack of compostable utensils and little plastic tubs of chutney, mint, and some radioactive red stuff.

"Feast time!" she chirps. "Hope you're hungry, because I went a little nuts." She unpacks the containers, each labeled in black marker: lamb vindaloo, saag paneer, chicken tikka, chana masala, a parade of naan, samosas, and rice pilafs. I count seven different curries, all supposedly for two people.

"Pick whatever you want," Maddie says. "It's all my favorite. Seriously, you can't go wrong."

I stare at the medley of food. "How many favorites can one person have?" I mutter.

Maddie laughs. "Oh, like, a million. I change my mind hourly." She scoops a mountain of basmati rice onto her plate and douses it in two different sauces. She eats with abandon, chasing every bite with garlic naan, the bread torn and slathered with bright green chutney. For all her petite energy, she consumes food like a marathoner, not even pausing to wipe the speck of curry that lands on her chin.

"Is Kade coming?" I ask.

Maddie shakes her head. "He's eating at his desk. He likes to work while he eats. Two birds, one stone thingy. He's all about efficiency. Don't worry, as soon as he knows anything, he'll come out. Until then, it's just us girls." She rolls her eyes, a parody of solidarity. "Which, honestly, is probably for the best. Kade's nice, but he's kind of intense, don't you think?"

"I guess."

I try a forkful of the lamb, for lack of anything else to do with my hands. I chew slowly, not tasting anything. The food sticks to my teeth. My stomach's a knot, but I keep going, if only to keep Maddie from asking why I'm not eating. She keeps up a monologue about the time Ryland tripped on a wet floor sign and tried to blame Maddie until the camera footage proved otherwise. She eats, talks, and gestures with her fork.

"I heard you like to cycle. Do you miss it?" She's fishing for something, maybe rapport, maybe just proof that I'm not a lost cause.

"I haven't ridden a bike in a long time. Not since the move."

"That sucks. I always think, if I had something like that, I'd just force myself to do it. But I guess it's different when you're, you know. In the program."

I set my fork down, suddenly exhausted from the small talk. "What is that supposed to mean?"

For once, Maddie doesn't smile. She wipes her hands on a napkin, slow and deliberate, then folds it into a perfect square. "I'm just trying to make things less terrible, even if it means being annoying."

I feel the food congeal in my stomach. We sit in uneasy silence for a minute. I pick at the naan, peeling it into strips, stacking them into a little cairn on my plate. Then Maddie licks her spoon clean, and sighs.

"Honestly, you don't have to like me. You don't even have to trust me. But if there's something you need, just say it. Even if it's just to get out of this room for a few minutes."

I look at her. She's too bright, too young, but underneath, I can't help but wonder: is she friend or foe?

She collects the containers and begins stacking them back into the bag.

"If you want, I can ask Kade to speed things up. Or, you know, delay. Whatever you need."

"No," I say, too quickly. "I just want an update."

She smiles. "Me too, Tara." She stands and takes the bag, leaving the room a little quieter, a little less claustrophobic.

I sit alone again, the sharp tang of mint and masala clinging to my tongue. I ponder the insidious nature of losing friends. Not with the violent finality of a bullet or a knife, but with a relentless barrage of a hundred tiny doubts that gnaw at your core until they taste like fiction.

I wonder if, when the time comes, I'll know which of these strangers to trust.

CHAPTER 31

KADE

The office is never truly quiet. Even with the double-paned windows and the off-brand white noise, there is always a whine at the edge. It's an artifact of fluorescent lights, of electrons bleeding through walls. I never touch the lunch Maddie brings me. I let it linger on the corner of my desk, sweating saffron and tomato. It forms a wet, sticky halo underneath.

Ryland answers on the first ring.

"Ryland." His voice carries the same bite it did when we shared a safe house waiting for the rain of bullets that never came.

"Kade." I match his tempo. "Brief update on Wildfire."

A beat, maybe the scratch of a pen, maybe the sound of another call waiting on his end.

"Proceed."

"She's convinced herself that Bennett's here." I hear my voice flatten out. Every syllable drilled into compliance. "Three incidents now. Last one, she claims direct visual. Gower's checking flight manifests, but so far nothing."

"Why Gower? You've got Maddie. She's an analyst."

"I've got her in the room with the asset right now."

Ryland inhales slowly and nasally. I imagine the air must filter through a mile of skepticism before reaching his lungs.

"I can't afford for another resource to be used."

"Gower's already on it."

There's a long silence that makes me feel uneasy.

"If Gower finds a credible threat, you are to initiate safe house protocol. Understood?"

"Understood. At present, I have her contained."

"Contact the safe house. Guy's name is Stony. Make sure he is prepared for a possible guest. Keep me apprised once you have Gower's report. And, Kade—"

"Yes, sir."

"Learn to trust your staff."

The line dies. Not even the decency of a goodbye.

Ryland's last statement is exactly what I am afraid of. Trust Maddie. As if it were that simple.

Through the wall, Maddie's laugh spikes, then cuts off. I hear her shoes click toward my door. I don't bother to hide the food. She opens the door a crack, peeking in with those chipmunk eyes.

"Tara asked for an update."

"Tell her to sit tight. I'm working the phones. Checking all incoming flight manifests. I'll be in to talk to her when I can."

"Who's check—"

"Don't. Ever. Leave her unattended." I don't raise my voice. I don't have to.

"If she makes a run for it, that's your career, not mine."

Maddie nods, retreats, and closes the door with exaggerated care. I trust Gower. I trust Cooper, but Maddie is a wildcard—a variable I can't solve for. She's too eager, too bright-eyed, and too much Ryland's creature to be trusted with anything that matters.

My office is twelve degrees colder than the rest of the building. I keep it that way. When you live your entire career in the slipstream of other people's disasters, you learn to crave the clarity of cold. I dial the secure line, muting the speaker and flipping the switch that patches me through the consulate's security grid. It takes a code, which is supposed to make me feel like it's secure. The line clicks, then hisses, then opens.

"Cooper."

"It's Kade. We've got a problem."

He's half a world away, but I need his help. I glance at the clock—it's ten in the evening for Cooper.

"What's going on?"

"We've had a possible sighting of the Wildfire case's primary."

"How credible?"

"Enough that she is spooked. Right build, right voice, same tailing pattern. Can you get the locals to do a welfare check to make sure he is there? I want eyes on him until further notice."

"You want me to check on him personally?"

I consider the question, but only for show.

"Between you and me, brother, something's not right. Every time I access the database, I find more holes than data. Files get moved. The local authorities have been told to keep it off the books. Ryland wants a storybook ending for this one."

Cooper is silent. I watch a gull spiral down to the parking lot, land beside a strip of broken plastic, and pick at the edges with precise, mechanical jabs.

"Give me a coupla hours," he says.

I kill the call and toss the receiver onto the base. It's just past sixteen hundred, and the world is waiting for my next move. I let it wait.

My phone rings, a pulsing light. I check the tiny screen on the outdated phone procured from another lifetime. Gower, finally.

"Checked the aviation manifests," he says, not bothering with hello. "Last three months, all points of entry. No Bennett. No known aliases." His voice sounds like he was phoning from the bottom of a well.

A sense of release—not quite relief—spreads through my chest. I loosen my tie, which was already two buttons slack, and let my head tip forward until my forehead nearly touches the desk.

"Good work, Gower. Push on vessels next. Ferries, cruise ships, anything that floats. He might have come in under a blind spot."

"Unlikely." I can almost hear his eyes roll.

"Do it anyway. Thorough is thorough."

A pause.

"Copy. Anything else?"

I think of Tara, her face etched with the jittery certainty of someone who'd seen a ghost.

"Keep an eye on local networks. If there's chatter, I want to know before Ryland does."

"I'll set up an alert."

The line clicks, and the call ends. I sit for a minute, alone in the afterglow of procedure. The office is still, but the hum in my skull keeps time. I think about the safe house and protocols and how, despite all the precautions, there is no shelter from what Tara carries in her head.

I give myself a full minute to smooth out my expression, to put every muscle back into its appointed place. Then I leave the office, the clack of my shoes against the industrial carpet loud enough to make the corridor flinch.

The conference room reeks of curry. Maddie's attention flickers upward the second I enter. She tries to fold her features into a neutral mask, but doesn't quite make it—empathy leaks at the corners.

Tara sits next to her. Hands folded, eyes fixed on a spot just left of center. She looks even smaller than before, like someone who has shrunk to fit inside her set boundaries. Every joint is drawn in tight, a study in containment.

I hold the door, nod once to Maddie. She takes the cue, rises with the speed of someone fleeing a crime scene, and slips out. Her scent lingers, artificial rose.

I close the door with the slow care of a funeral director and cross to the chair Maddie vacated. For a moment, neither of us speaks.

I fold my hands on the table.

"Tara."

She doesn't look up.

"Did you find him?"

I shake my head. "He isn't in New Zealand. Not in the past three months, at minimum. My analyst cross-checked every flight manifest, every possible alias. There's nothing."

She lets out a sound. Relief, maybe. Disappointment, probably. Her fingers splay on the tabletop, the nail beds a raw red. She looks up at me, and her gaze hits me like a thrown rock.

"You don't know him like I do."

"Maybe not. But I know patterns. I know how these things escalate. Right now, there's no evidence he's here. If anything changes, we'll be the first to know. But you're safe to go home."

I wait for the words to sink in, then I press on. "Keep your phone on you. If you see anything, call me directly. Day or night."

"And if he's already here?"

"We have a protocol. I won't hesitate to get you to safety if there is a credible threat."

We sit in the stale quiet, neither blinking. I can see the war play out behind her eyes: a part of her wants to believe, and a bigger part refuses to.

"Go home. Get some rest."

She stands, but there is a moment when she hesitates, as if she might collapse back into the chair. On her way out, she pauses at the door.

"He always said he could get past anything. That he knows people. Do you think that's true?"

"I think that was true in the town you lived in. He worked for the police department. But you're in New Zealand now. Safe."

Tara grabs her purse and her coat, then looks at me.

"This book. I was looking at it when I saw him. I ran out without paying for it."

I observe her looking down at the floor. There is shame there. She clutches the book to her chest like it's a lifeline, saving her from drowning in her guilt. I take my phone out of my pocket and gesture toward the book. She lays it down on the table, and I take a picture of it.

"I'll go by the store and pay for it myself."

She nods. As she walks past me, I see that her hands have finally stopped shaking.

I leave the conference room just in time to see Tara turn out of the hallway into the lobby. I trace her route, stopping just shy of where the carpet meets tile. From here, I see Maddie in her native habitat. She looks less like an analyst and more like a student cramming for a pop quiz she's forgotten. She pecks at the keyboard with a velocity that suggests muscle memory, not thought.

I pause. Maddie is messaging someone. Internal. I steady my breathing to lean in and identify the system's in-house chat avatar in the corner of her screen. I hate the avatar the system assigned me. I recognize the one on her screen because I chat with him often. Ryland. From this distance, I can't make out the words. Squinting won't help.

I step forward and clear my throat. Maddie flinches, not dramatically, but enough to confirm her guilt in some tiny, administrative way.

"Oh! Hi there, Kade."

"Let me know when you have a moment. In my office." My voice is purposefully gentle at first, but pitched to override any polite refusal.

She nods, and in the span of a single breath, locks her computer and smooths the hair that never quite stays in place. I turn and walk away, with an extra slow cadence to give her time to catch up.

She hovers in the doorway of my office, knuckles white on the frame, exactly one minute and twelve seconds later.

"Come in." I don't look up from the page I was pretending to read.

She slides into the visitor's chair, crossing and uncrossing her legs. This tells me she is uncomfortable, trying to make herself comfortable. I keep pretending to read.

When she settles into the chair, I set the paper aside.

"Big day at the office today, huh?"

"I'll say. Unusual activity for this office. For sure."

I fold my hands on the desk.

"How's Tara?"

Maddie gives a little half-shrug, aiming her eyes at a spot over my left shoulder.

"She's shaken, but I think she'll be okay. I talked her down."

"How so?"

She blinks. "Just . . . girl stuff . . ." She lets the sentence dangle, as if the next word was too big for the room.

"That's interesting. Did you observe anything or come to any conclusions?"

She hesitates. Just a beat, but in my line of work, you can measure lifetimes in the spaces between answers.

"She's tough."

I let her bask in the silence to see if she will fill it with more while I decide if I want to press her.

I give her the bureaucratic smile and pivot. "Since I arrived at this duty station, we've never really talked." I push my chair back from the desk and throw a leg over my knee. "Tell me about your family. Are they in the States?"

Maddie reacts as expected. Her face lights up. She tells me about her mom in Alabama, her sister who just passed the bar exam, and cousins I don't care to know anything about.

"I saw a UGA coaster on your desk. Did you go there?"

Of course, I know she did. I've read her file. But I also know this is the college Todd Bennett attended. Decades apart, of course.

"Guilty." Maddie lets out a small laugh that was supposed to be casual, but it rattled around the room like a coin in a tin cup. Her throat bobs, and she drops her gaze to the edge of my desk.

I drum my fingers once, slowly.

"Are you in touch with anyone from the States? Friends, perhaps?"

"I don't know what you want me to say."

That got her. The pink rises to her cheeks. She fidgets, then quickly stops herself when she realizes she's doing it.

If this were any other person I was interrogating, this is when I would turn up the pressure, but it's Maddie, and I consider that she's in communication with Ryland.

"I didn't mean to pry. I just thought you did such a good job keeping Tara calm that I'd get to know you a little better. I really appreciate your help today."

Part of me means it, and the other part of me—well, the words taste like vinegar on my tongue. She's up to something.

Maddie looks directly at me, eyes wide.

"Thank you so much. That means a lot to me, Kade."

I let her sit with that, let the shame do its work.

Somewhere, someone is watching, waiting for me to make a mistake.

I intend to disappoint them.

CHAPTER 32

TARA

The stairwell smells like a feral cat has died. I drag myself up the flight of stairs, half expecting to find its corpse on my doorstep. My flat is unchanged. It's still a rectangle carved from plaster, with cost-cut corners that show. The radiator spits heat like a nervous tic, and my bedroom window looks out over an alley.

I close the door and thumb the deadbolt twice—once isn't enough. I press my forehead to the door. Nothing stirs outside, but I listen until I can map the outside sounds. I drop my purse by the door, then glance at the balcony. The bar on the sliding glass door that Kade installed is still in place. Everything inside is exactly as I left it. It always is. I dutifully text Kade, as promised.

ME

Home

KADE

Everything good?

ME

Yep

KADE

Call if you need anything

My muscles are still wired, tendons humming beneath the skin. I replay the conversation with Kade in my head. His smile, all orthodontic perfection and synthetic calm. "You're safe to go home." He had said it like he was tossing a dog a treat.

The word "safe" means nothing when it comes from law enforcement. Kade is no exception. I've heard it before, in rooms colder than the consulate conference room, sitting across from police who ran fingers over my incident logs and called them all "coincidences."

The deputy's face flashes through my mind, with his mustache trimmed within regulation. His eyes glazed as they flicked through my log, the screenshots I'd collected, the times and dates, each one logged with the neat obsession of someone who knows she'll have to prove her own sanity.

"He's never physically harmed you," the cop had said, voice bored as a weather forecast. "You can't charge a guy for being in the same public places as you. There's no evidence to suggest he was in your backyard."

"But he was," I told him.

"Okay, but can you provide evidence of this?"

"No. But I know it's him. It's always him."

He smiled like a man who had already solved the puzzle. The answer is "nothing happened." He called it a "domestic matter." Said I should "get a restraining order, if it would make me feel better."

I move to the window and watch the street outside, counting cars. Every time a headlight sweeps the wall, my body tenses. I replay the man at the bookstore, second by second, until I can taste the bile in the back of my throat. It was Todd. I'm sure of it. I don't care what Kade said. He *is* in New Zealand, and I saw him. I don't feel fear. I feel hatred.

Pure, white-hot hatred. He's not a man anymore but a force of destruction, a black hole in a too-small universe. I imagine him at my door, pale and smug, waiting for me to open up and let him in.

I imagine killing him—that split second when I take back control, when I become someone he can't predict or contain. I can see it so clearly, it's almost real. I want to smash something. To scream until the walls come down. I consider arming myself, but the kitchen knives are so blunt they couldn't puncture a tomato, let alone a man's skin. I snatch one from the drawer anyway. The weight of it feels surprisingly empowering in my hand. I storm across the apartment, into the bedroom, and rip a pillow from the bed. I drive the knife deep into the fabric, the blade slicing through. I practice the sound I'll make when I lunge, the words I'll say when I watch life drain from his body. My heart pounds with relentless fury. My breaths are ragged. I drop to my knees, my back against the bed, and cradle my head.

I want to march down to Kade's office and force him to admit that he can't protect me, that he won't even try, that all his hollow assurances are just another way to shackle me to my own terror. But I know what happens to women who raise their voices. They get written off as unstable, hysterical, and a risk to themselves and others. The best I can hope for is a thicker file. The worst is a padded room, a diagnosis, another fucking prescription. I think of the stories I've read—women who disappear in broad daylight, women who file reports and are never seen again. I think of the statistics, the odds, the way the world is tilted so far against us that even breathing feels like an act of resistance.

I'm done hiding, done waiting for someone else to save me. If Todd wants a confrontation, he'll get it. I hope he comes tonight. I hope he tries.

I was never safe. But I was never helpless, either.

If he comes, I'll kill him.

I wake to the beat of the alarm at 5:30 a.m. My neck is cramped, my mouth dry. My jaw is locked from grinding. Another day, another performance at the café.

I check my phone. No calls, no texts. I unlock it and scan through my messages, then the spam folder—just to be sure. Nothing from Kade. Nothing from anyone. Except a coupon for pizza.

I dress in the same uniform as always: khaki pants, a white button-down shirt, and a threadbare cardigan. Twisting my hair into a knot, I secure it with two bobby pins.

The normal routine would be to walk. Even in the rain. Three blocks, ten minutes if I take the direct route. Instead, I open my phone and pull up the taxi app. Routine is the enemy.

I wait at my window; arms crossed over my chest. I wonder if Mr. Holloway, the frame shop owner, would know if I vanished, if I were murdered overnight in my apartment. I shouldn't be thinking this way.

When the cab pulls up, I take the stairs two at a time, keeping my head down. The driver leans across the seat, popping the lock with a cheerful click.

"Morning!" he says, accent flat and local—maybe second-generation Kiwi.

I nod and mumble my destination, "The Cottage Café," even though he already knows. The app always knows.

Inside, the cab is over-warm and smells of air freshener—that sickly pine they use to mask old tobacco and spilled coffee. I wedge myself into the backseat on the passenger side. His name tag reads "Samir." The driver is maybe in his forties, hair thinning at the crown, cheeks bristling with yesterday's shadow. A gold chain peeks from under his collar.

The speedometer flickers to eighteen, then twenty, then back again. He taps the wheel in time with the blinker.

We hit the first light. A man in a lime-green safety vest pushes a trolley stacked with plastic bags. For a split second, I think it's Todd. Same slope of the shoulders, same way of looking past people rather than at them. My throat closes, and my hand goes rigid on the seatbelt. The man turns his head; it isn't him, not even close. The panic drains out, leaving my muscles leaden.

"Rough night?" the driver asks, like he's seen it before.

I give a non-committal noise, focusing on the world outside. At the next corner, a woman with a stroller waits at the crosswalk. She glances at the cab, at me, then back at her phone. Nothing dangerous, nothing memorable. Still, I clock her shoes, the color of her scarf, the size of the child's hand wrapped around the stroller's bar. I catalog every detail in case I need to recall it later.

Every parked car becomes a threat, potentially there to surveil me. I realize how ridiculous these thoughts are in my head. I am losing my grip. The line between reality and paranoia blurs again, like it did in the States. I try to contain it, but I am stunted by the inertia of fear.

"I used to work mornings," he says, voice thick with nostalgia. "Paper route, back in Sri Lanka. Never could sleep in after that. Mornings get in your bones, you know?" He laughs, expecting a reply.

I nod, forcing a smile. I memorize every detail. People reveal themselves in their smallest stories.

"Ever see the dolphins, out by the wharf? They come in close this time of year. Sometimes right up to the seawall. I take my daughter down when I can." He glances at me, trying to read if I'm the kind of person who likes dolphins.

"I've seen them," I say, though I haven't.

The roads are empty as we reach Victoria Street. Samir slows to a crawl, squinting.

"Here we are," he says, easing to the curb.

I pay with my phone, hoping it will erase me from his memory.

The lamplight outside throws gold lines on the front glass of The Cottage Café at 6:18 a.m. Inside, the air is so still you can hear the flour settling, the snap of eggshell, the faint bubble of yeast in the sourdough starter.

It's my favorite time, before the world arrives to ruin the peace. Kass is off today, so it's just me and Miss Sue for opening. I slip into the back room, drop my things, and pull on the apron. Miss Sue is at the prep table, sleeves rolled to the elbow, hands deep in a bowl of dough the color of wet sand.

She doesn't look up when I enter. She never does. She just says, "You're in early, love," in the same tone she'd use to point out that the milk's about to sour.

"Took a cab." I wash my hands and grab a knife. Carefully, I line up the tomatoes and draw the blade through the first one. I try to focus, but watching the blade tear through the tomato brings me a sense of pleasure. Peace. If Todd shows his face, this is the knife I will use.

She glances over her shoulder, eyes narrowing. "You look tired."

"Didn't sleep." That's true enough.

She slides a tray into the oven and wipes her hands on a towel, turning to face me fully for the first time. "That boy keeping you up again?"

For a half-second, I think she means Todd, and my throat closes. But of course, she's talking about Edmund.

"No." I return to my slicing. "I'm not seeing him."

"My, you don't mess around. Dropped 'em like a hot potato, eh?" She says it with a hint of challenge, as if testing for a deeper reason.

I shrug.

"I'm sure your tall drink of water is out there." She moves past me to the espresso machine, gesturing for me to sit. "Go on. I'll pour."

I obey. The chair is cold, but the promise of coffee warms my hands in anticipation. Miss Sue works the machine with precision. She brings two mugs to the table and sets one in front of me.

"Drink," she says, and I do. It's strong, bitter, and perfect.

She sips her own, cradling the cup between both hands. "Want to talk about it?"

"There's really not much to say."

She's quiet for a moment, letting the silence breathe. "My sister used to say that, too. After her divorce. But then she got a dog. It was a mean little thing. Hated everyone but her. She let it sleep in her bed, fed it from the table."

I can't picture Miss Sue with a sister. I can barely imagine her as anything but elemental, conjured into existence in this kitchen.

"Is that what you're recommending? Pet therapy?"

She grins. "It's worked for stranger cases."

I finish the coffee in three long pulls and stare into the dregs. "I keep thinking about the women who end up on those podcasts. You know, the true crime ones. The last thing anyone remembers is 'She was always so quiet. She never caused trouble.'"

Miss Sue's eyebrow shoots up.

"Are you worried that'll be you? Reduced to a footnote?"

"I think I already am."

This is one of those moments the program warns you about. The moment when someone is kind, caring, and seemingly harmless. You let your guard down, your worries spill out, and suddenly there is a risk. I shift uncomfortably in my seat. I shouldn't have said anything. I regret it.

She reaches across the table, her hand resting briefly on mine. Her palm is warm, the skin paper-thin and strong as parchment. "If you want my advice, don't give them the satisfaction. Cause trouble. Scream when you need to."

My small talk is stitched together from scraps, held together by caffeine and the need to keep moving. I rinse pitchers, refill sugar, clear plates. My body knows the drill better than my mind. But my mind is a traitor, always darting ahead.

Miss Sue eyes me with that piercing gaze. "You're jumpy as a cat on tin, Tara. Don't tell me it's the weather."

"Sorry, I'm just distracted."

She shakes her head. "If someone's bothering you, you tell me. I know people. I can handle it."

"Thanks, Miss Sue. If it comes to that, you'll be my first call."

A timer beeps in the kitchen, shrill and insistent. I'm relieved. Miss Sue stands, smooths her skirt, and checks the oven. The smell of baking scones floods the room, sweet and yeasty. The sky outside softens from black to blue. The world stirs, slowly. We work in quiet harmony until opening.

The quiet is dangerous. That's when my thoughts spiral. I picture Todd, pacing like a wolf, smiling, making plans. I tell myself he can't reach me here, but the logic never sticks. Fear has its own gravity. So does rage.

CHAPTER 33

KADE

There's nothing more unsettling than fluorescent light at three in the morning. It glows cold and pitiless, leaching the color from everything it touches: the battered desk, the government-issue wall clock, the file folders stamped Confidential in the same faded font. My office smells like burnt coffee and disinfectant.

Cooper hasn't called back. That means Bennett's trail in the States is cold. The bastard can't be that slippery. Gower's scrutiny of the flight manifests isn't foolproof. Bennett might slip in under an alias. A fake passport is risky—border security should catch it unless he's got inside help. Unlikely, but not impossible. The tension in my chest tightens like a vice.

I wake up the computer and turn my attention to the digital trail I've been tracking. The log file fills half the screen. It should be a static document, unbreachable, a perfect record of every digital footstep in the system. But the lines don't add up. Last night's batch job, the one that should have swept new records into the central archive, is missing twenty-three entries. Gone, not even a fingerprint left behind. That's impossible. Unless someone with root access wanted them gone.

I lean forward. My chair protests with a weak hydraulic hiss.

Most people don't notice computer logs. They're just timestamps, trailing slugs of data— never meant for civilian eyes. But I've spent my life reading between the lines. The silent gaps, the misaligned hashes, the emptiness that should be an entry. I scan through the active user logins. It's a short list. Only Ryland, Maddie, Bill Cooper, and I have access. I discount Bill Cooper immediately. Those credentials haven't been used since Tara got here.

Maddie's user ID appears twice. The first is a clean login. The second is buried in a block of admin commands, well after midnight, running a diagnostic tool. She's good. Too good. If she wanted to cover her tracks, she'd do more than just delete a file. She'd seed the logs with dummy entries, create a pattern, maybe even pin it on someone else. She's got that in her— all wide-eyed innocence and nervous giggles.

But this work is crude. The kind of sloppy a rookie would make. Or someone who believes they are above reprimand. That points me to Ryland. He's a decade my senior, and every year of that gap is fossilized in his bones. He knows just enough to get himself in trouble. He's a by-the-book man, but he cuts corners when nobody's auditing his moves. Or he thinks nobody is.

I check the timestamps. The tampering happened at 02:17. I close the log and open a shell window. I type in the root command, watch the prompt flicker, then run a forensic script. It pings through the system in under a minute, leaving a digital report card on my desktop. I cross-reference every file touched in Wildfire over the past forty-eight hours. Four anomalies: a cluster of system binaries recompiled from source, a deleted shadow file with the name Lawrence Hyde, and two files that weren't there before.

Lawrence Hyde.

Maddie's account had access to all of them. She's a common denominator I can't ignore. But this doesn't feel like her doing. I know her digital signature is self-destructing macros. I know the way she names her temp files after Greek gods. These are bland, utilitarian—no, this is Ryland's speed, his flavor. If he did this, he's better than I thought, or someone's teaching him. I wouldn't put it past Maddie. She's so eager to curry favor with Ryland.

I jot everything down in my field notebook. Paper and ink, always. Old habits from my first career. I flip back a few pages, to the case that started all this: the Caraway situation, the stalker, the endless cycle of court orders and broken boundaries. Todd Bennett. His name is circled three times. Underlined twice.

I remember the last meeting with Ryland. He was fidgety, the way men get when they've made a deal with the devil, and the ink is still wet.

"We need to keep it tight," he told me. "No leaks."

"Why *this* case? We shouldn't be anywhere near Bennett."

He smiled, a thin, papercut smile. "Keep your friends close and your enemies closer, right?"

I hit print on the log file and stand. My legs ache from sitting too long. The printer in the hall rattles to life, stuttering through the early morning. I walk out to collect the papers. I flip through the sheets, double-check the data. Twenty-three entries, gone like they never existed.

I return to my office and shut the door. I thumb through my notebook, searching for a pattern, a crack I can wedge a crowbar into. Maddie's too clean. Ryland's too obvious. But someone did this. Nothing stays erased. Not really.

History always repeats, just never in the way you expect. The hum of the electronics pushes me into the past. There's always a moment just before dawn when the body forgets where it is, and the mind slides sideways.

I think about the last time I erased something. Afghanistan. Sand in my mouth. Heat so thick it could peel the skin from your bones. The stink of sweat, gun oil, and fear. I was a twenty-six-year-old sergeant and still believed in the rules. Ryland outranked me. He was my lieutenant—square-jawed and upright, all West Point bluster under the grime. Todd Bennett was a private, older than the rest, but always with something to prove. A real pain in the ass.

That fateful day started the same as all the others. Patrol, report, and wait for the clock to run out. Except this time, the road was quiet. Too quiet. We knew the script, but still, we walked right into it. Mortars hit us from the ridge, small arms fire from the old schoolhouse. We dove for cover, but there was nothing except a bombed-out courtyard and an overturned truck. Ryland called for air support, but got nothing but static. Comms were down. I heard Bennett's breathing— ragged, like he was running up a mountain.

We huddled behind the truck. Ryland was bleeding from his arm, but he wouldn't admit it. I patched him up, hands shaking. Bennett stared, lips moving in silent calculation.

"We push through," Ryland said, already on his feet. "We flank and move fast."

Bennett hesitated. "We don't even know how many there are."

Ryland gave him a look that could freeze a river.

"That's why you're a private and I'm a lieutenant."

Classic Ryland move to pull rank. I almost laughed. Almost.

We ran, keeping low. The air was needles and sand and sound. Bullets chewed up the dirt, sparked off twisted rebar. We made it to the far wall, blasting through a doorway, barely hanging on. Ryland led, I covered, Bennett followed. We cleared each room, the floor crunching under boots.

That's when it happened.

A figure in the smoke. Ryland's gun was up. A shot. Then another. The echo was endless.

When the haze cleared, I saw the body. Not a fighter, not an insurgent. One of ours. Maybe twenty, maybe younger.

Ryland froze. Bennett looked. I checked the wounds. There was nothing I could do to save him.

Thurmond.

"We have to report it," I said.

Ryland shook his head. "No comms. We finish the sweep, then go back. Get our story straight."

Bennett was shaking, staring at the dead kid.

Ryland kneeled, checking for signs of life. He put the radio in the kid's hand, and pressed his thumb against the transmit button.

"He was relaying enemy positions," Ryland said. "That's what we say."

I wanted to vomit. I was caught in that liminal space between obeying an order and doing something I knew was wrong.

We pulled the body out, and left it near the entrance. Ryland's hands were steady, deliberate. Todd's were not. When we get back to the FOB, Ryland pulled me aside.

"Look, it was an accident. I can't go down for this. Bennett's going to say it was friendly fire. You're his sergeant. Sign off on it. I'll do the same."

Ryland could be very persuasive. I followed the order. Nobody noticed, because nobody wanted to.

The next day, CID interviewed us. Bennett's story didn't match ours. He hesitated, stuttered, changed details. Ryland never faltered. I parroted what I was told.

A week later, Bennett was dishonorably discharged. Misconduct. He sent letters, emails, increasingly desperate, then angry, then nothing at all. Ryland got promoted. I got a commendation. The incident became a footnote, lost in the dust of a hundred others.

But I dream about it. Thurmond's empty eyes, the way Ryland closed the report with a perfect signature and never looked back.

In the distance is the sound of a garbage truck reversing. In my office, knees locked, sweat prickling under my collar. For a moment, the overhead light flickers, and I expect Ryland to be standing there, telling me to get it together.

But it's just me. And the knowledge that Todd Bennett has every reason to hate us.

"This is why I need you on this, Kade," Ryland had said when he called about transferring me to this post in New Zealand. "You know Bennett. You can anticipate him."

I shake the memory loose. I need a plan. I close my notebook, stand, and stretch the ache in my back. I run a finger along the seam of the desk, feeling for hidden tape, a mic, anything out of place. Paranoia is a survival skill.

I hear a noise. I can tell it's Maddie. Her walk is brisk, head down, clutching a folder so tight the paper crumples at the corners.

She doesn't see me. I watch her from the shadow of my open office door. She enters the server room, swipes her badge, hesitates, then steps inside. I wait. Thirty seconds. One minute.

Then I follow.

The air in the server room is frigid, racks humming with a pulse that matches my own. I keep to the far wall, listening.

Maddie is hunched over the terminal, typing fast, eyes flickering from screen to screen. She pulls a USB stick from her pocket, slides it into the port. The screen fills with a wall of code, then blinks black.

She's copying something. Or planting it.

I step closer. "Couldn't sleep?"

She jumps, then turns, the mask already in place. "Just trying to get a head start on the day. You know how it is."

I nod. "Want some help?"

She pauses, then shakes her head. "I got it, thanks."

I pretend to leave, but linger outside, listening to the click of her keys. When she finally exits, I duck inside and check the terminal. The logs are wiped. The USB is gone.

The key to a proper trap is to make it look like nothing's changed. I set up a new subdirectory, bury it three folders deep, and name it in the agency's default lingo: Archive_2Q. The directory is empty except for a single text file—another canary. The filename is long and technical, including a string only I would notice: opFor_3rdSquad_LOG.txt.

Inside the file, I see the kind of information no one would care about unless they were looking for it. A list of names, all scrambled; dates that don't match any other documentation; a test message in a language I barely remember. It's bait, but also a warning. Anyone who touches it leaves a fingerprint. If they're clever, they'll try to wipe the access logs. But I've got a shadow process running, writing everything to an off-site backup through a channel nobody else knows about.

It feels like overkill. Then again, so did armored doors. That's why I'm still alive.

I'm deep into an unrelated budget review when a reminder dings. I have a briefing with Ryland.

"Morning," he says. He's shaved, eyes red-rimmed but alert.

"Morning."

"Anything on Wildfire?"

I shake my head. "Just the usual."

He pauses too long, as if expecting me to volunteer something. He runs a hand over his tie, straightens it even though it's already perfect. Finally, he says, "Keep me posted. There's a lot riding on this."

He means his job. Maybe more. I send Maddie a quick message.

Me

Need you to run a diagnostic on the intake server, ASAP.

Maddie

On it! Will loop back after.

Always the overachiever.

Outside, the streetlights flicker off as the world is waking up. Something moves in the shadows, or maybe it's just my imagination.

CHAPTER 34

TARA

The silence never holds. The bell above makes a sound like a shot glass striking marble— sharp and immediate. Kass throws herself through the door, the entire bell mechanism dislodged.

"Shit, I am so sorry, Tara—shit, shit, I know, I know, you're going to kill me!" She's still talking as she barrels across the tile, arms up in mock surrender, hair spitting out of her headband in wild, springing coils.

My stomach churns with a surge of primitive electricity, the instinct to flee fighting the instinct to collapse. I ground myself behind the counter.

"I slept through three alarms. Actually, four. The phone was dead and my aunt borrowed my charger. She's in Christchurch for the—whatever, but I don't have a charger, and so—" She cuts herself off, breathless, and peers at me like she's expecting a citation.

I manage a thin smile. "You're here. That's what matters."

Kass blinks, lips pursed. "Okay but what about Miss Sue? Is she here? Tell me she's not here."

"She's here," I say, low and flat. "Muffins are already done."

"Of course they are," Kass groans. She spins a dishtowel into a noose and mock-strangles herself, which, I guess, is her way of making light. "I'm going to be dead. She's going to skin me. The Phoenix Festival is today. Like, today-today. Parade's running right past our door. You're going to want to brace. Crowds'll be worse than the Queen's Birthday, and twice as needy."

Kass nods, muttering to herself as she goes to the back and yanks an apron from the peg. She slaps it on, double knots it, and then pivots in the direction of the kitchen. She's a perpetual machine of motion, running on something close to mania.

Six-thirty comes, as it always does: slow, then all at once. At first, it's just the regular caffeine-deprived customers. Miss Sue emerges from the back, hair pinned in a severe bun, glasses on a chain around her neck. She sweeps the floor with her gaze, inspecting for invisible dirt or slacking employees.

Kass sidles over to my station, mouth close to my ear. "She's in a mood," she whispers. "Think it's the muffins. She did two extra trays, which means she's expecting a madhouse."

I wash up at the small sink, scrubbing my hands longer than hygiene requires, then get the drip going for the openers. I measure the grounds, pack the basket, pour the first water. The ritual helps crowd out the memory of yesterday. We work in tandem to Kass's ongoing monologue. She is already mid-story about her niece in Auckland, who sent a photo of her new kitten in a teacup. I nod, make noises at the right intervals, and keep my hands busy behind the counter.

My chest tightens whenever the door swings open, which happens twenty-six times before noon. I count every one. Each time, my hand hovers near the grinder lever, an automatic reflex. I watch for scars, for certain postures, for the way a man holds his phone in the palm—a tell, a signal, a sign. I know Todd's walk, his smell, his angle of approach. I know it all, but paranoia is a poor substitute for certainty.

The morning stretches. The crash of pans, the scald of steam, and the hum of the mini fridge all blur together. I lose track of the hours. I only know it's lunch because Fred arrives and orders his usual: a pot of Earl Grey, a variety of the daily finger sandwiches, and a scone with jam.

"Yer not yourself today," he says, his tone only half playful. "You should take a walk and get fresh air. Do ya some good."

I make a noise, a smile mostly teeth, and retreat to the safety of the espresso machine.

By half-past two, children high on festival fizz shriek like birds of prey, weaving around the tables as their parents struggle to order. Kass basks in it. She gives every kid a wink, every tourist a theatrical "Welcome to Werneth!" as if she's the mayor. She even gets a laugh from Miss Sue, which is worth its own headline.

But I can't relax. The busier it gets, the easier it is for someone to slip through unnoticed. I see every face twice, sometimes three times, looking for the bone structure, the jaw, the thick neck. Even when it's women, I check anyway. Todd could be in drag, or a wig, or—hell, who knows? That's how it works. You think you're being paranoid, and the world proves you right.

The whole town is out—children on shoulders, dogs in costumes, old women wrapped in shawls. They're all angling for the best spot, the front row, the unimpeded view. And I am just another face in the window, counting the seconds until something happens. Because something always does.

I catch a face in the glass that makes my heart stop. Not just the rhythm, but the whole world; time jerks sideways, and all I can hear is blood. The man is standing on the sidewalk, arms folded. He's not tall, not imposing. Dark hair, cheap sunglasses, a blue windbreaker zipped to the chin. Could be anyone. Or could be him. There is no better hiding place than a crowd.

I duck my head, fake a spill with the milk jug, use the commotion to recalibrate. When I sneak another look, he's gone. Just a gap in the crowd, quickly filled by mothers and strollers. I scan the cafe, check every table, every shadow. Nothing.

I fumble for my phone, thumb already hovering over the emergency contact. I don't think about whether it's overreacting. I don't care.

He picks up on the second ring. "Kade," he says, voice dry as splinters.

"It's me," I whisper. "I think he's here."

A pause—just long enough to register that he's recalibrating, shifting into federal mode. "Where?"

"I'm at work. He was across the street. Blue jacket, jeans." I try to keep my voice flat, but it sounds like I'm reciting a hostage note.

Kade doesn't ask if I'm sure. He never does, which is why I call him.

"Stay inside. I'm already logged into the traffic feeds," he says. I can hear the soft click of keys. "There's a street musician set up near the corner, partially blocking the view. But I'm not picking up any hits on your description."

"I ducked behind the counter as soon as I saw him. When I looked again, he was gone. But I'm telling you, it's him."

"I can be there in twelve minutes," he says. "Faster if I run the red lights."

"No," I say too quickly. "Don't. It's festival day. Crowds everywhere." The idea of him showing up, drawing more eyes to the place, fills me with a different kind of dread.

"That's good. Safety in numbers."

I let the silence hang. He's wrong. Crowds are only good if everyone in them wants you alive.

"I have someone checking not only flight manifests, but vessel manifests, too. There haven't been any hits on him, so I don't think it's him."

There's a brittle edge to his words, like he's repeating a mantra he doesn't believe. I close my eyes and nod, forgetting he can't see me. "Okay."

"Call me if you see him again. Or anyone who looks wrong. And Tara—"

"Yeah?"

"You're not overreacting." He hangs up without waiting for an answer.

I stay in the back until my hands stop shaking. It feels safe. Outside, I can hear the festival crowds. I imagine they are snaking along the sidewalk, pinched and jostling, no room to breathe. I used to like crowds. The idea of losing yourself in the press of bodies, of melting into anonymity. Now all I can see is how easy it would be for someone to slip through, to reach out, to grab.

I force myself to focus on the orders, hoping to keep the pace until closing. The bells jingle, and I look up. Kade is in the entryway. His eyes are on me, and nothing else. The room shrinks to just the two of us, the air between us alive with static. I think he's here because I called him, but there's unspoken communication in the way he crosses the café to the register quickly. I immediately know something is wrong. Very wrong.

Kade walks straight to the counter. His voice is pitched for a courtroom.

"We need to go. Now."

I don't move. Not at first. The old instincts kick in—fight, flight, freeze. I do all three at once. Knees lock. Pulse hammering in my neck. My hands clenched so tightly my nails dig into my skin.

Kade doesn't blink.

"Tara. Now."

I look at Kass, at the roomful of eyes on me—all the witnesses I could ever want, but none of them will stop whatever this is.

"Looks like it's important. Go. I'll cover," Kass says.

I wipe my hands on my apron, unfasten the strings, and hang it on its hook. My mouth is dry, and words are stuck behind my teeth. I reach for my purse.

"Is it—" I can't finish.

"Come quickly."

I step out from behind the counter. The world outside is noise and color—too bright, too full. Kade's hand hovers at my elbow, not touching. We step into the sunlight. The door closes behind us, and the crowd swallows us whole.

I want to ask where we're going. I want to know what's waiting for me on the other side of this. But all I can do is follow, one foot in front of the other.

CHAPTER 35

KADE

My government-issued sedan crawls forward. The crowd closes in on both sides—kids waving, faces painted, adults waving flags. One guy stumbles into the street, trips, and nearly face-plants into my bumper. Tara tenses so hard that the seatbelt digs into her collarbone.

At the roundabout, we hit a jam. Orange cones, temporary barriers, and a hundred people lining the curb with flags and homemade signs. A parade, today of all days. The line of cars inches forward—brake, slow roll again. The worst possible scenario.

"Hold on," I say, half to her, half to myself.

I take the next side street hard, tires skipping over the gutter. The road narrows, barely wide enough for a car and a half. I thread us through a corridor of parked vehicles and garbage bins, the parade noise echoing off the buildings. At the end of the block, I look back.

Nothing.

The engine roars when I gun it through the next intersection.

Tara finally speaks. "Is it him?"

I steal a glance at Tara and perform a quick assessment. Rigid. Hands clenched. Wide eyes, slight tremor in her jaw. Fear. Shock, maybe.

I debate how much to tell her. The truth is a tangled knot. It is a mess of threads that lead back to people I know and trust. I can't make sense of it yet. I haven't had time to think since Ryland's call. Only react. Tara deserves to know. At least some of it.

"Do you remember Deputy Bill Cooper? He's the one that—"

"Of course I remember him."

"He was killed." I stop there. Maybe I'll wait to see how much she wants to know.

Tara stares out the window, watching as Werneth fades into the distance. She's not saying anything. Better yet, she's not asking anything. She's processing the information, I imagine.

Maybe she wants to know, but is too afraid to ask.

Maybe I need her to know.

"How?"

Air passes deliberately through my lips. I don't answer right away. The question hangs for a minute.

"Shot. Until law enforcement can identify the perpetrator, I'm taking you to the safe house as a precautionary measure."

"You think it was him?"

"I don't have all the details yet. My goal is to get you to a secure location."

She nods, looking down at her hands. "Where are we going?"

"Safe house, up north. You'll like it. Sheep, grass, no people for miles."

She huffs a brittle laugh. "Sounds great."

I let the silence fester. Her breaths come in tight little gasps, like she's learning to breathe for the first time.

Getting out of town to the main road is taking longer than I want, but I'm zigzagging through backroads. It's protocol to obscure the route to the safe house. With Tara silent, I begin to process what happened in the span of the last thirty or forty-five minutes.

I was sitting at my desk, staring at the holes in Tara's files, when the phone lit up. The flashing red light pulsed like a warning beacon. Calls on the secure line aren't common, but they're not rare either. I lifted the receiver and entered my six-digit pin.

"Kade."

"Secure call from Director Ryland." The man's voice had a sharp edge that sliced through the handset.

My spine seized with a jolt. Every individual vertebra snapped into a rigid line. "Put him through."

There was a three-second delay, then the click and squawk of the encrypted line.

"Kade?"

"Sir."

No greeting on the other end. Just the click of a headset and Ryland's voice, dry as salted earth. "Cooper's dead."

There are a hundred ways to react. My body goes for the most primitive: jaw clamps, lungs forgetting the finer points of oxygen intake. A breath stalls in my throat. The news of any officer with the agency being killed in the line of duty is rare, but it hits me like a punch to the gut.

Bill Cooper. I think about the last time I saw him. Cooper had flown to headquarters, where I was stationed, and wanted to meet for lunch before I went TDY. He said he was planning on retiring next year. The last words he said in that bad Italian joint was: "The older I get, the more I care about these victims, you know?"

There was no time to linger on the questions that ran through my head or the ache in my chest. It wasn't the time to tell Ryland I've kept in touch with Cooper since I left the States. Much less, I was the one who sent him to check on Todd Bennett.

"When?" The syllable was raw in my throat.

"Uh . . . I'm not clear on exactly when. Local PD called it in since he had his badge on, but they're being kept at arm's length. The service has taken over the investigation."

Ryland pauses but then talks more quickly.

"I'm waiting for more information, but I think we should assume it is the work of Bennett. Cooper was shot, execution style. His service weapon is missing."

An electric shiver raced across the back of my neck. Tiny hairs bristled to full alert. I'm the one who put Cooper in the line of fire. I press the phone harder to my ear. It's not like Ryland to jump to conclusions so quickly.

"Why do you think Bennett is involved?"

"Witnesses saw a man matching Bennett's description in the area. That's all I have, for now."

"Witnesses? I—"

"Look, I've told you everything I know." The anger in his rising voice was seeping through the phone. "Follow protocol. Get the asset to the safe house."

He was right. My problem was the asset. Tara. Here, breathing New Zealand air and trusting me to keep her safe. "I don't think Cooper would crack, even with a gun—"

"Kade! Follow the protocol. It's an order."

I felt heat flash behind my eyes. "Copy."

I removed the Glock from my holster, checked the action, and re-holstered it. I grabbed an extra box of ammunition and started the mental checklist that had gotten me through twenty-three years of near-misses.

Every second felt like an eternity slipping through my fingers. I had to alert the safe house, let him know I was on my way. I lifted the receiver again, entered my pin, and punched in the safe house number. The rings stacked up—one, two, three—before Stony picked up.

"Site 23."

"It's Kade. I'm en route—"

"Ryland already called it in. We're on lockdown as of twenty minutes ago."

"He called you direct?"

"Affirmative. Said to prep for immediate guest arrival."

The words sink in like a stone through pond water. Ryland went around me.

Stony coughed a smoker's gritty cough. "ETA?"

"As soon as I secure the asset. What else did he say?"

"Only that it's a credible threat, and we may have an active in play."

I nearly clip a delivery van, swerve hard. I squeeze the bridge of my nose as questions swirl. Why would Ryland call the safe house himself? That isn't protocol. Directors are never involved at the asset level. They mostly just want to be kept informed as the situation develops.

Ryland is a professional. He's probably concerned about losing an asset while he's in charge. After all, he's nearing retirement, just like me. No one wants to go out with a stain on their record.

The world around me blurs as my thoughts drift, but the jarring reality crashes back when a shadow darts onto the road.

My heart leaps into my throat, and instinct takes over. My foot slams the brake—a violent force that sends the car skidding, tires screeching in protest. The rear end fishtails, swerving left, then right. My adrenaline spikes so high I feel dizzy. The car jerks to a halt. My gaze snaps to Tara. Her eyes are wide, pupils dilated with shock, her hands clutching the seatbelt. I look back at the road and see a dog crossing to the shoulder of the other side.

"Damn it!" I slam my hand down hard on the steering wheel. "Sorry about that."

I release the brake tentatively, feeling the car shudder as it inches forward in a tentative crawl. We gain momentum as I press the gas. Urgency propels us onward. We need to reach the safe house. We need to get there now. We've only just reached the outskirts of town.

Tara doesn't say a word—not for the first six kilometers, or the next ten. I keep the doors locked, windows up, every sense on a hair trigger. My hands grip the wheel at ten and two.

I note a silver Subaru taking the same turns, but it peels away at the dairy, so I let it go. We put twenty more kilometers between us and the center of town before I ease up on the gas.

"Do you trust me?"

She absorbs the question before she answers. Not a good sign.

"Yes, I trust you."

"It's important that you do, Tara. I only have your best interest. But I need to know that if I tell you to move, you don't hesitate. You move."

Tara nods slightly, still looking out the window. It doesn't give me any comfort. My phone dings with a text message.

Ryland

ASSET SECURE?

All caps. That's not his style. I don't answer. It's not because I'm driving. It's because something isn't sitting right.

"What happens next?" Tara's voice is so soft that I almost don't hear it.

"We survive."

I hope it is true.

CHAPTER 36

TARA

The blindfold Kade claimed was protocol was one of those eye masks from a long-haul flight. He told me to put it on when we were outside of town, on a two-lane highway. The inside has a thin layer of something pretending to be memory foam.

We are still driving. Each swerve and deceleration maps into my skin—leather on polyester, friction building heat in the dark. I let my head rest against the window, catching vibrations as Kade punches the accelerator, then feathers it at stop signs or blind bends.

Every few minutes, I run my thumb along the seam of the seatbelt, testing the tension. It bites into my collarbone. The air in the car is dry and recycled. We ride in silence for what feels like an hour. Maybe less, maybe more. Deprived of sight, time has a way of melting into itself.

"How much further?"

Kade takes three breaths before answering. "Not much. But we have to take the long way. Standard protocol."

I let the phrase hang in the air.

"You realize it's overkill, right?"

He doesn't answer. Just shifts in his seat, the creak of the leather his only reply.

We take a hard left. There's no turn indicator, just the momentum. I brace with both hands, catching a spike of panic before it settles. I don't ask again. Instead, I try to build a map in my head: the first stretch, flat and fast, must have been highway. Then city surface roads, too many stops, the faint rise and fall of hills under the wheels. Somewhere rural, maybe. Then a narrowing, a sharper rhythm of turns, engine working harder against gravel or loose stone. We coast, the crunch of tire on driveway unmistakable.

Kade kills the engine. The sudden absence of noise is a violence of its own.

He waits, letting the silence grow legs.

"You can take the mask off now."

I snap it off my head and toss it onto the dash. I blink rapidly, letting my eyes adjust to the brightness. A house sits on a bluff, its roofline hunched like a broken shoulder. No lights show, not even from the security strip above the door. I spot the camera lens glinting, a tiny green LED winking in the porch eave.

Kade leads me from the car. I can feel the tension in his palm, the electric possibility that he might switch from guide to jailer in a split second.

A man doesn't so much greet us as occupy the doorway, arms crossed. He wears a flannel shirt and jeans stiff with old paint. He looks like the kind of man who washes his hands with sandpaper and doesn't trust central heating.

"'Bout time he says, eyes flicking over Kade before landing on me. "You must be the asset."

The word trips me. Not "her," not "Tara," but "asset," as if I am a lost shipment or an expense line in a ledger. The bottom of my jaw tenses, but Stony isn't watching for a reaction.

He holds the door with one hand, gestures us to come in with the other.

Inside, the temperature is kept at a precise twenty-three Celsius. Every surface is clean. The scent is pine and bleach, with a faint undernote of stale cigarettes. The farmhouse kitchen is frozen in time. The only sign of habitation is a smattering of dirty dishes piled by the sink.

Stony closes the door, resets the five locks, then gestures to a seat.

"Protocol says we keep you in the open, one room, for observation. But I don't like protocol. You can move around, long as you don't touch the comms."

I can still feel the imprint of the blindfold on my face. Even with the sun still shining outside, the world seems too dark. I look for a clock, but there isn't one. I close my eyes, counting the seconds until I wake up somewhere else.

"Stony," he says, by way of introduction. He sizes me up, then turns to Kade. "You want tea, or the rundown first?"

"Rundown."

Stony nods. "Upstairs is clear. No sightlines from the road. Back fence is electrified, but you won't notice unless you try to piss on it." He grins. "I recommend you don't."

Kade doesn't smile. I pick at the cuff of my shirt, digging out a loose thread.

Stony continues. "Satellite phones are in the basement. Food's basic. Bedding's clean." He turns back to me. "You'll be safe here. As safe as anyone can be."

I meet his gaze, not blinking.

"You can rest, or you can talk. Up to you. My job's to keep you breathing, not comfortable."

Kade leans against the far wall, still and silent.

Stony turns to him. "I'll let Ryland know custody has been transferred."

At the mention of Ryland's name, something shifts in Kade's expression. I don't know how to read him.

"Will you stay?" I ask, more plea than question. There's a nervous energy about him that seems almost too controlled. I can't put my finger on it, but Stony sets off alarms in my mind.

Kade shakes his head. "No, you'll be under Stony's care now."

Stony gives him a look, somewhere between mockery and commiseration.

"She's in good hands. You can bugger off now, mate."

Kade hesitates, then nods.

Stony coughs, loud enough to break the moment. "You want to see yourself out?"

"I'm just going to do a quick perimeter check before I head out."

"Suit yourself."

Kade strides across the room. The front door shuts behind him. He doesn't utter a goodbye, leaving an emptiness in the air, and me standing there, uncertain of when, or if, I'll see him again. I cross my arms and rub them to comfort myself. I feel utterly alone.

Stony shows me the kitchen first, all Formica and cold tile. "You eat, you clean."

He explains the perimeter, the alarm system, the schedule for meals. I listen, but my mind maps escape routes, improvising weapons from household objects. The hallway is long and bare, the sort of chill that lives under paint and inside the bones of old wood. Stony leads the way, his boots leaving ghost-prints in fine dust on the floor.

Stony opens a closet and raps his knuckles on the shelves. "Emergency water, blanket, candles. If you get cold, layer up. Power cuts happen, but the woodstove never fails. I'll show you later how to keep it stoked."

I nod, as if I plan to be here long enough to learn.

When Stony shows the bath, he says, "Don't flush unless you must. Septic's ancient and backs up when it rains." He leans in, voice low, as if confiding a secret. "That's most of the year."

I see a wet line of mold on the tiles, creeping toward the drain. The mirror is so old that it clouds every reflection.

He walks on, narrating the tour in clipped, functional beats.

"Laundry is attaway. If you want to open a window, ask first."

At the far end of the hall, he stops in front of a wall, runs a finger under the molding, and clicks something hidden. The wall slides sideways with a whine, revealing a narrow space lined with steel panels.

The safe room.

He ducks inside, pats the single steel bench bolted to the floor. "In case of emergency," he says, his voice echoing in the box. The walls are unpainted, raw metal. "You sit here, you keep quiet, you wait. Reinforced, negative pressure."

As if I know what that means. He shows me the locking mechanism.

"Twist left, pull in, then slam. Nobody's getting through unless they got a backhoe." He grins, showing off a row of tobacco-stained teeth. "You'll only need this if things get noisy. Hope they don't."

Stony's steps echo back down the hallway, more measured now. "Bedroom's this way. You have a bag?"

"No time," I say.

"There're clothes in the bedroom. Stuff others have left behind and some stuff the service requisitioned for situations like this. Help yourself."

We enter a narrow room painted gray-blue, with a single bed, a desk, and nothing else. The mattress is covered in a rough wool blanket, Army surplus by the feel and the green-black color. I sit on it, testing the give. The springs groan like a wounded animal.

Stony gestures at the corner.

"You get the good room."

He waits, as if I might argue. When I don't, he nods.

"Settle in. I'll bring food in a bit."

Stony lingers in the hall.

"You hungry, or want to sleep first?"

"Not hungry." It's not a total lie.

He shrugs and walks off.

I lie back on the bed, counting the cracks in the ceiling. When I lose count, I start again. The house groans and sighs, as if settling deeper into the earth. I wonder if this is what safety feels like: alone, watched, waiting for a door to open or a wall to slide away.

I think about the word "asset," and how easily it could be turned into "liability."

I hear a door open somewhere, light and sharp, not the clumsy stomp of Stony. A shadow flickers under the door. Then it opens quietly. I don't register it until Kade is inside.

His eyes are blazing. He shuts the door behind him. "We need to move. Now."

My heart stumbles. I stand.

"I just got off the phone with Cooper," he whispers. "He's not dead. Someone wants us to believe he is."

The words buzz in my skull, a swarm of hornets. "I—"

He clamps his hand over my mouth. "Quiet. He could be listening."

I fall in behind him because I'm grateful to leave. He leads me out. His breath is ragged, every step a calculated risk. My shoulder brushes the wall. We creep toward the living room. We turn the corner and pause. Kade presses me to the wall, barely breathing. Over his shoulder, I see movement —a flannel sleeve, the shadow of Stony crossing into the kitchen.

We wait. Time pools in the space between heartbeats.

Kade mouths, "Quickly."

I nod.

We move as one, his grip never slackening. He eases the door open. The cold hits me like a punch as I step onto the porch. I have no idea what I'm running from or where I'm running to. All that matters is that Kade needs me to run. And in this chaos, I place my unwavering trust in him—and I hope I'm right.

CHAPTER 37

KADE

O n the lawn, I check over my shoulder. No movement, but that's meaningless. With Stony, you never see him until it's too late. We hit the porch at a run without closing the door. I've got a grip on Tara's wrist, guiding her down the steps, every sense braced for movement, sound, heat, the prickle that signals danger in the brain. We're halfway to the car when there's a deliberate noise.

I look back.

Stony. His right hand dangles just shy of his belt, the way men do when the real weapon isn't a gun but the certainty that they'll use it. His eyes flick from me to Tara and back, settling somewhere in the middle.

Assessment.

Calculation.

"Kade." No inflection. No warmth. Just the name, stripped down to its syllables.

I pull Tara behind me, angling my body between Stony and the car.

"We're leaving." I'm not asking permission.

"You got a courier order from Ryland I didn't see?"

"Ryland says we move her. Now." I'm improvising.

Stony's head tilts, micro-angle, like a hawk regarding a nestling. "Funny. My feed says she don't go nowhere. Custody of the asset transferred, brother. That means I'm responsible. That means she goes back inside until I get the all-clear, just like everyone else."

Tara's arm is a live wire in my grip. I tighten my hold, just enough to say: Stay. Trust me. Or at least, don't trust him.

"We're not going back in."

Stony steps from the porch, slowly rolling his neck. The cracks echo. He's never needed a gun to kill anyone. He uses his hands, then calls it "de-escalation." He holds his ground six feet away, but I know I can close the gap faster than he can.

"Don't make this ugly, Wes. You got options. You hand her over, you walk. We'll call this a misunderstanding."

Don't do it, Stony. I don't know if Stony is involved in whatever is going on. I don't want to draw my service weapon on a fellow officer, but I will if it means protecting Tara.

He takes a single step.

"Move!" I push Tara toward the car.

Stony moves before I finish the word. I lunge toward him, covering the distance in three strides. He aims a kick at my knee—textbook perfect. I pivot. He misses. My right hand comes up, fist clenched tight. I catch him in the nose. It doesn't stop him. He absorbs the hit and swings a fist at my temple. It lands, and his academy ring makes contact, causing a bloom of stars in the corner of my vision.

My head snaps right. I drive a fist into his solar plexus. He grunts, grabs at my wrist, tries to torque it. I go limp, letting the momentum swing me behind him. Elbow to the back of his head, then another—this time I hear bone meet bone.

He's slower now, but not out. He pivots, tries a bear hug, and for a second, I feel the breath leave my lungs. His arms are steel cables. My right hand finds his thumb, and I wrench it backward. The pop is wet and final. He lets go.

I step back, gasping. Stony's hand reaches under his shirt, a flat black .45 already coming up.

I instinctively react—arm sweep, aim for the wrist, pray that muscle memory is still intact. The gun discharges once—a sharp, metallic thunder. The round goes wide, punching a hole into some distant tree. Tara screams. It's a short, torn sound, like she's never used her voice before.

Stony's finger is still on the trigger, but I'm inside his reach. I ram my forehead into his nose. Cartilage crumbles, blood jets onto both of us. He reels. I grab the gun, break it out of his grip. I bring the butt down on his temple. He goes down like a tree, stiff and slow, folding at the knees before collapsing onto his side.

"Get in the car!" I scream at Tara.

Stony's gun is now in my grip, arms slightly bent at the elbow to absorb recoil. The barrel is trained on him. He's not moving. Blood seeps from Stony's head, a dark red ribbon into the grass. His eyes roll, tracking nothing. I bend down, place two fingers on his neck. He isn't dead. I stare down, count the seconds. He doesn't get back up.

I keep the gun fixed on Stony as I walk backward to the car. My hands tremble, adrenaline humming under my skin. I spit out the blood pooling in my mouth.

Tara's not in the car.

I walk toward the back, keeping Stony in my sight. I don't want to kill him, but if he moves toward Tara, I will. At the back of the car, I see her. She sits crouched, her head against the trunk, face white. I reach for her, but she moves away—a reflex. I stand there, arms up.

"Are you hurt?" I ask.

She shakes her head, once.

"We need to go."

"What the hell is going on? What was that about? Is he dead?"

I catch my breath and tuck Stony's gun into my waistband. "We'll talk in the car, but we need to move. Now."

I walk around and open the passenger door. I stand behind it, so she doesn't feel any more threatened than she already does. Both hands are hooked over the top so she can see them.

My back is to Stony, but I've got an advantage over him if he comes to.

"My job is to protect you, Tara. Please, let me do my job. We have to go."

Tara eyes me with caution before she slow-walks toward me. She eases into the car. I fly down the gravel drive in reverse, checking the windshield for any movement. Stony's still out— limbs splayed like he fell from a tree.

Tara hugs herself, trembling. The silence is total except for her rapid breathing. We crest the hill. I punch the gas, tires spinning. The safe house shrinks in the rearview, then disappears.

No words. Not yet. The drive is a wall of unspoken things. We don't speak until the trees thin and the lights of the road flick on in the dusk. My hands are slick with sweat. Every few seconds, I wipe my palm on my thigh, but it doesn't go away.

Every mile buys us another minute of life, another breath. I don't know where I'm going. My head pounds from the blow I took. I touch my temple and wince from the pain. There's blood on my fingers. I wipe it on my pants.

"You're hurt," Tara says softly.

"I'm okay. There are napkins in the glovebox. Can you hand me one?"

She does, and I thank her. I press the napkin to my temple, ignoring the pain. My vision blurs for a second, then the road comes back into focus. I wait for my blood to coagulate and stop the bleeding. It's not much. I've had worse. I can't make sense of why Ryland would lie about Cooper. I never told him I had lunch with Cooper before I left the States. I never told Ryland I'd promised Cooper I'd keep him updated on Tara.

Why would Ryland lie about something that's easily verifiable? Unless he's keeping me busy with the asset because something bigger is at play—something he doesn't want me to know.

Tara breaks the silence first. "What the hell was that?" She's not screaming. Her voice is even, brittle, like glassware loaded in a shaking truck.

I keep my eyes on the road, scan the mirrors. "I don't know. And that's an honest answer."

"You said it was safe."

I check the rearview again, expecting headlights, sirens, the whole circus.

"It's been burned. I don't know by whom, and I don't know how."

She turns and fixes me with a look I can feel through my throbbing skull.

The turnoff appears suddenly, unmarked gravel branching from the asphalt. I take it at speed, sending a plume of dust behind us. The car bucks over the ruts, every jolt a reminder that we're running on borrowed time.

"Are you trying to kill us?"

"No. I'm trying to keep you alive, but they will."

"Who? Who is 'they'?"

I can't tell her that I think Ryland might be involved. I can't tell her Bennett might be here. I can only confirm what she already knows: that Stony is bleeding on the front lawn of the safe house. I jerk the wheel again, and we're back on asphalt.

Her voice cuts again, closer this time. "I need to know what you're doing. You said you'd keep me safe."

"You're alive, aren't you?"

She looks away, out at the farmland, the dying daylight tracing every ditch and weed. "That's not enough."

We hit the next crossroads. I kill the headlights, let the momentum carry us until I'm sure we're alone. Tara's jaw is clenched, her hands balling in her lap. My knuckles are raw, one split and leaking onto the gearshift.

The phone vibrates in my pocket. I don't check it. Every call is a liability now, every text a landmine waiting to detonate. I keep driving, lefts and rights at random.

Tara stares straight ahead. "You fought him. Why did you fight him?"

"He tried to stop us."

"But he's with the same program you are, right?"

I grip the wheel tighter. The pain sharpens my focus. "He is."

She takes that in, silent for a few miles. The only sound is the hum of tires and my ragged breathing.

I scan the horizon. There are no lights, no towns, just dark shapes of mountains and the glitter of stars above.

Tara shudders, arms crossing her chest. She looks like a kid lost at an airport, waiting for someone to claim her. "I don't know if I can keep running."

I want to tell her she can. That she must. That the only way out is forward, even when the ground is gone beneath her. "You'll be fine."

She shakes her head. "You keep saying that, but none of this is fine."

I take the next turn at random. A wave of dizziness washes over me, and I grip the steering wheel tighter.

The wipers kick on. It's raining now, a fine mist growing into streaks, blurring the glass.

Tara leans her head against the window, eyes closing, lashes wet. "I just want to know if I should be afraid of you, too."

I watch her for a second, a wet line streaking her cheek.

"You don't have to be." It's the closest thing to a promise I can offer.

She sighs. "I'm not so sure."

The phone vibrates again, a message waiting in the ether. I leave it unread.

We drive until the tank is nearly empty, then keep going. The system will catch up eventually. They always do. But for now, there's just the road and the rain. I run through it all in my head and come up with a theory: If I'm right, Cooper is the only one I can trust.

Ahead is a sign for the Little Wanganui Hotel. It promises RV spots, cabins, and a full-service pub. It's the off-season; the place should be nearly deserted—perfect for the solitude I need to unravel this tangled mess.

Instead of parking in the lot out front, I drive around to the back and kill the engine.

I turn to Tara. "I know you're confused, and you want answers. I don't have answers. I don't know if Todd is in New Zealand. I don't know who burned the safe house. I need time to sort through everything and figure out what's really going on. I need you to trust me. And only me."

"As if I have another option." Tara steps out of the car.

We make our way inside the pub. Tara chooses a tall table near the bar, which gives a clear view of all the entrances and exits.

I thrust cash into Tara's hand, instructing her to grab me a soda. I don't want one, but I need her to stay busy so I can make a call.

I slip into the dimly lit corridor beside the pub, positioning myself where I can watch Tara, the table, and the exits all at once. My grip tightens around the flip phone. My eyes are locked on Tara as I hit redial.

Cooper answers on the first ring.

"Yeah."

"It's me. The safe house is compromised. I'm moving with the asset."

"Don't give me any more details. I'm better off not knowing."

Tara's leaning against the bar, her shoulders tense and wary. She's talking to the bartender, but I'm not concerned.

"Someone's pulling Ryland's strings, and I've got a strong suspicion who it is."

"Bennett?"

"Yeah."

Cooper releases a sharp, audible gasp. "Are you absolutely sure about Ryland? He's been known to stray, but this is a serious accusation."

"He's the only one with override authority. Stony is as straight as they come. He wouldn't act without a direct command from Ryland. Look, is there anything else I should know about this case? Anything that didn't make it into the sanitized version?"

A snort.

"You read the file. You know as much as I do. Woman's been running even before I got her. Makes you wonder what kind of asshole sticks with a grudge that long."

"He's more persistent than most."

"He's a sick bastard, but he knows the system. Most of his threats don't even cross the legal line. But if you ask me, it's only a matter of time. Do you have a strategy?"

"The agency has the car's location. I can't be sure whether Ryland's feeding Bennett the intel or if he's planning to handle it personally. Either way, I'm going to be prepared."

"The only safe way forward is through the fire. You don't stop to count the bodies. Keep that girl safe."

My mind is turning fast, assembling the puzzle. Each piece snaps into place perfectly. Doubt claws at the edges, hissing that my theory teeters on an unstable foundation. I need confirmation—solid proof—to silence the doubt.

But that can only come from walking through the fire.

CHAPTER 38

TARA

The first step to surviving a long night is realizing it never ends. It just waits. I know that now. I think Kade has always known this.

I count the people: four, not including the bartender. I count their drinks, their glances, the way they pivot toward and away from the exits. Even now, I imagine the bartender memorizing our faces, rehearsing them for some future retelling: "They sat in the corner, two Americans, both wound tight enough to pop."

The chair is slick with a hundred years of spilled beer and the sweat of people who were just passing through. I sit where Kade told me to, back to the wall, nothing behind me but a stretch of wallpaper patched with yellowing tape. He's in my periphery, his body haloed by the soft gloom, phone to ear. Little beads of blood dot his head. He clutches the phone against his ear, the skin on his knuckles raw. He speaks so low that I can't hear him. His eyes stay fixed on me, always on me, as if my death certificate might issue itself the moment he looks away.

The light inside the pub at the Little Wanganui Hotel is anemic—a dim white that exaggerates every surface. A dartboard hangs askew in the corner, punctured and scabbed. The only sound is the drone of rugby on a wall-mounted TV, volume mercifully low.

At the far end, a man in a blue sweater sits with trembling hands around the glass he's been nursing since before I walked in. At a distant table, a couple with brown hair parted the same way whisper. The last is a woman with fiery red hair, sits checking her phone. Every few minutes, she checks the door like she's waiting for someone. A date, maybe.

There's a television above the bar showing rugby with the sound muted. The bartender is a handsome, jolly man with a smile that could charm anybody. He polishes glasses from behind the bar. Every so often, he glances at me and smiles, the way you smile at an animal you think might bite.

Kade's soda sits in front of me, untouched. I stare at the condensation, counting the beads as they crawl down the glass. I wonder how long I can keep still, how long before my nervous system rebels and I shatter the silence with some involuntary scream.

A movement in Kade's direction catches my eye. He pockets the phone, traces a slow arc of the room with his eyes, then comes to the table. The set of his jaw says nothing good happened in that call. He doesn't bother sitting, just braces both hands on the tabletop as though he's intentionally leaving fingerprints.

I watch as Kade's eyes flick to the doors, then to the bartender, and finally settle just above my head. He reaches for his drink, takes a single sip, then sets it back exactly where it was. He's still got blood on his knuckles, barely visible in the dim lighting. I know it's there. Worse, I know how it got there.

I want to ask what happens next, but I don't. There's a script here, and my lines have all been redacted.

"We're leaving," he says. Not a suggestion.

Okay, I'm wrong about the fingerprints.

"Already?" I ask because there's nothing else to say.

He doesn't answer.

Kade's hand hovers a centimeter from my shoulder as I pull my arms through the sleeves of my jacket. The bartender is waiting for the next order, mouth open. Kade nods, polite, then gestures me toward the hallway to the restrooms. The layout here is classic: a corridor, a vending machine buzzing faintly, doors to the toilets on one side and an exit at the end.

He steers me down the hall, his hand gentle at the small of my back. We pass the vending machine, and I feel the air grow colder. Kade checks his watch, then looks up at the CCTV bubble on the ceiling. We step outside, and he walks faster now, gripping my elbow with a force that says: don't argue.

At the end of the lot is a row of cabins, maybe ten feet apart, each with a single bulb burning above the door. We stop in the cut between the hotel and the first cabin. Kade positions himself so that he has a line of sight in both directions. He pulls me into the shadows.

"Listen." His voice is flat, a new voice, not the one from the café or the conference room. "There's no point running. Whoever's on us, they're trained. They'll find us." He scans as he talks, hands never still.

"Then what?" I whisper.

"We wait until they come to us. Confront the enemy head-on. If it's who I think it is, they have our location. It's just a matter of time."

He fishes a knife from the band around his ankle, pulls the blade from the sheath, then offers it hilt-first. "If you pull this, you use it. Understand? You don't threaten. You don't posture. You don't negotiate. You commit."

I take it, trying to keep my hand from shaking.

"Don't aim for the heart. Go for the soft stuff— throat, belly, groin. If you hesitate, you're dead."

"I don't—"

"I'm going to hide you, but you must stay put. No matter what you hear or see, you stay quiet."

The words pin me, each one a steel rivet.

"What if you don't— What if you can't—"

His eyes snap to mine. "It's my job to keep you safe. I am good at my job, remember?"

"Okay." My teeth are chattering, but I don't feel the cold.

He touches my shoulder, not gently, not cruelly, just enough to press the moment into me. "This is what I do. You and me, we make it out. That's all that matters."

I nod. I watch as he pulls a phone from his pocket and flips open the old-style device.

"If anything happens to me, call the last number I dialed. It will connect you to Bill Cooper. He's the only one I trust. You can trust him, too."

Kade walks me to a dark spot under an overhang, wedging me between the side of the laundry shed and the ice machine.

"Keep your back to the wall. Stay small. Stay quiet."

I nod. I want to puke, but there's nothing in me. He watches me for another second, then shifts, glances around.

"Ready?"

"Never," I reply.

He almost smiles.

"Good answer."

I crouch in the very spot Kade put me. I sweep away cigarette butts and petrified candy wrappers. The ground is gravel, and tiny pebbles are embedded in my palm. I pull my knees to my chest, the knife held tight.

Blood rushes through my ears. It feels like the whole world can hear my pulse. But only me. The air is cold enough that my breath is visible. I suck in small sips, so the fog doesn't give me away. The ice machine reeks of chemicals and mold.

Stay small, stay quiet. Kade's words have become my new mantra.

From here, I watch Kade circle to his car and open the trunk. He pulls out a camouflage bag—all zippers and Velcro. He slips a military-style vest over his shirt, cinches the straps. He pulls his handgun, releases the magazine, looks at it, and quickly taps it twice before pushing it back in. He chambers a round, ready for action, then returns the gun to his side holster. He rummages in his trunk, finds another magazine, and drops it into a front pocket on his vest. Then another. He trades his shoes for black boots, laces them in seconds, not even looking down.

He glances back once, catches my eye, and nods. Then he's gone, melting into the night. I count every second. Every blink of the blue LED on the ice machine. The knife feels heavier now, the handle sticky from my sweat. I grip my hand tighter around it, anchoring myself to the thought: If it comes to me, I will do it. I will.

Time slows. Or maybe it accelerates. I refuse to look at the clock on the blue phone in my pocket. I lose track of Kade. I lose track of myself. No movement, just the distant cough of an engine.

In the back of my head, I start to build a story: This is how it ends. Not with a scream or a shot, but with waiting. With the knowledge that somewhere out there, a man wants me dead— and there's nothing in the world I can do to stop him.

I clench the blade tighter. I am not a victim. I am not a body to be tagged and bagged. I am a weapon.

The ice machine rattles, dumping a load of cubes into the bin. My body jerks violently. I shiver, count to twenty. *Stay small, stay quiet.*

A door slams—not close, but not far. I hold my breath. Another door, softer. Then footsteps, slow and measured, crunching over gravel. I press myself deeper into the shadow, blade up, just like Kade showed me. My heart is so loud, I'm sure they hear it.

The footsteps pause, right outside my line of sight. I can't see who it is. I don't dare look. If anyone looks back here, if anyone rounds the corner or thinks to check the alcove, I am finished. I am evidence.

Another step. A wet, heavy cough, like someone clearing dust from their lungs. I grip the knife, close my eyes. I try to think of nothing. The footsteps fade. The silence returns, thicker now, pressed against me like a weighted blanket.

I blink, try to reset, but my vision swims. My legs are numb, my back hurts, and the handle of the knife has left an imprint in my palm. I want to move, but Kade said to stay. So I stay. I wait. I try to believe in the promise that he will keep me alive. I want to believe it's true, but I know better. Promises are the first casualties.

Maybe he will.

Maybe he won't.

Either way, I'm ready to get this over with.

CHAPTER 39

KADE

The light on the laundry shed's soffit flickers erratically, sputtering like it's on its last breath. Its glow casts shadows across an area trampled down over the years by tourists staying in the nearby cabins. I stand in the shadow of a tree. Branches scratch overhead with the wind, brittle and eager to snap. My head throbs, a low, insistent pain. I touch the wound and draw back my hand. No blood. Sweat soaks the inside of my collar. I press myself tighter to the tree, ribs stuttering against the bark.

My phone vibrates. Once. Twice. A thin, persistent whine against my thigh. I let it go, pulse tripping over itself. Again, more insistent. The screen glows through my pants like a warning light. I fish it out carefully, keeping my body angled away from the parking lot.

Maddie's name appears on the screen. The phone stops. Starts again. Three rings in rapid succession. She's not going to stop. A flicker across the street, a glint of metal in the dusk. I flatten my body and let the phone ring out. I regulate my breathing. I focus on the area where Tara is. No movement. Good girl.

I think about Ryland, the way he always said protocol was just another word for common sense. But then he'd break it, just to see if anyone noticed.

I thumb open the phone. Three missed calls. One text.

MADDIE

URGENT INTEL. Call me back. NOW.

I scan the area. No sign of anyone. I dial, and Maddie answers before the first ring finishes.

"Kade. Oh my god, I thought you were—" She stops short of finishing. Her breathing is too loud, too close to the microphone. "Never mind. Listen, Ryland is . . . he's . . ." Her voice fractures.

I whisper sternly into the phone. "You have sixty seconds."

She has a tell: when she's hiding something, she talks quickly, stringing the vowels out and chewing the consonants, like she's racing to outrun her own lie.

"When I was in Auckland," the words tumble out, vowels slurred and nervous, "I dated a guy from immigrat—"

"I don't have time for this. Do you have intel or not?"

She barrels on, ignoring me. "The logs, my guy, he sent them to me. Every American passport to hit the system. Bennett's here."

The bottom falls out of my stomach.

"Bullshit. There's a flag on him. I would've known."

"That's what I thought, too. I checked the list. A name popped . . ." She hesitates, unsure how much to tell me. I let the silence fester.

"Lawrence Hyde. He came in on a charter flight from Sydney."

Lawrence Hyde. My head is pounding. I can't think. "Lawrence Hyde? What's the connection?"

"Lawrence Hyde is the name Ryland uses for Todd Bennett, a code name, of sorts," Maddie explains. "That's why the name popped. My guy sent me the photo taken at immigration. I'm telling you, Kade, it's him. It's Todd Bennett."

The throbbing in my head intensifies, now a pounding.

"I never wanted to do this, Kade, I swear." Maddie's breathing is ragged now.

"Do what exactly?" I hiss.

She hesitates. I recognize that pause. She's weighing her words.

"Spit it out."

Near the building, something moves. I freeze. A shadow leaks out from the service door. It's the bartender taking out a bag of trash.

"Ryland asked me to keep tabs on you and Tara. I'm the one who changed Tara's address in the system. Ryland would send me an encrypted message, name the file 'Lawrence Hyde.' I'd read them and remove them before the backups could record them." Maddie's voice rises with panic. "I was only sending him harmless information, I swear. He lied to me. Why would he lie?" Her voice quivers, as if she's afraid to say it out loud.

I bite back the urge to scream.

"There's more." Maddie clears her throat.

"Go."

"The guy at the bookstore? I'm pretty sure that was Todd, based on when he arrived in the country. I think Todd's on his way to your location."

"How does he know my location?"

"Ryland called me from the safe house after he found Stony. I linked him to the agency tracker on your car."

Hearing Stony's name fills me with guilt. I never meant to hurt anyone.

"Is Stony okay?"

"You roughed him up, but he'll survive."

"Don't tell Ryland we talked. Keep doing whatever he asks, but keep me informed."

"I never wanted—" She sobs. "I'm sorry. I just . . . it's just that . . . he said he'd help me move into a field position. I mean, he *is* the director—"

"It doesn't matter right now."

Static on the line, then a sharp intake of breath.

"Why would—"

"I gotta go." I end the call and stare at the phone in the sudden, gut-wrenching silence.

The air tastes like a mouthful of iron. I spit into the dirt. My lungs burn. My mind is a hornet's nest. I drop the phone in my pocket and secure my hand on my gun. Quickly, I run through the bullet points in my head. *Shit. If Bennett's here, he'll be close. Ryland would never let him out of sight, given their history.*

My hands won't stop shaking, not from fear, but adrenaline. I flex my fingers until the knuckles pop. *Bennett.* A shudder ripples through me. The man's a ghost. A wraith conjured from the darkest recesses of my past.

Ryland's plan. How could I have missed it? Especially after the hell we endured in Afghanistan—me, Ryland, and Bennett. Our bond forged in fire and lies. When Ryland called, saying he needed my help in New Zealand, I didn't hesitate. I assumed Ryland needed me on the asset because he knows I can handle Bennett. My mind races back to Bennett's psych report. The man described there is a stranger. A shadow of the soldier I knew in Afghanistan.

I force myself to focus, channeling the adrenaline into razor-sharp clarity. Tara's safety is my priority now. I steady my breathing the way I was trained to do in combat.

Think, Kade. What's the plan?

I glance over to the laundry shed, carefully stepping around a gnarled tree. The ice machine, old and rusted, stands in the corner, its hum barely audible. I squint, trying to see past the shadows. Tara is perfectly still. Perfectly quiet. Perfectly in danger. I take a deep breath, square my shoulders, and feel the weight of responsibility settle in. Tara is my asset, and I can't let anything happen to her. I am ready to protect her, no matter what it takes.

CHAPTER 40

TARA

There's a moment when everything goes silent, a true, suffocating blankness. My legs ache to be stretched out, but I keep them firmly against my chest. Every nerve in my body flickers at full wattage. My fingers are locked around the knife. The world stinks of old cigarettes and the ever-present stench of fear.

I think of every time I've hidden in my life: my bedroom, closets, the shower. My eyes were shut so tight I saw stars. I don't dare shut my eyes now. Todd once asked me if I wanted to see death coming. I answered no. I've since learned that isn't true. I do want to see death coming. I am a fighter, and if I see it coming, maybe I can stop it. Stop him. Like I said, I don't dare shut my eyes.

The footsteps are soft at first, nothing more than the suggestion of a human presence. Then I hear him. The same Southern drawl, as if he's on a front porch sipping sweet tea with his grandma.

"Kaaa-thrynnn."

Todd. He's here. Singing my name. Not loud, but enough to crawl under my skin.

I freeze, every muscle crystallizing. My hands tremble so badly I worry the blade will clatter to the gravel. I wrap my second hand around it, arms wrapped around my knees, the knife in front. I press my lips to my knuckles and try to slow my breathing, but all it does is make the panic rise.

There's another sound. A crunch, a ripple. Kade. His gun is raised.

"Hands where I can see them, Bennett."

Todd Bennett. Since coming to New Zealand, I haven't said his name. Never dared to summon that ghost.

Todd steps closer. I see the edge of his blue jacket first, then the oval of his face, glinting in the sodium glow of the light. I see the full head of gray hair, eyes that might seem kind, but aren't. Not tonight. Not ever.

"Well, if it ain't Sergeant Kade." Todd pivots with a slow, rotten smile spreading across his face. It's like he's enjoying the moment rather than staring down the barrel of a gun. "Or should I say, Deputy U.S. Marshal Kade? Didn't think you'd slum it this close to the polar cap. Never took you for a cold-weather guy."

I clamp my jaw to keep from making noise. My lungs constrict around the air, refusing to let go. He's twenty feet away, head tilting, scanning. He knows I'm close. Acid and bile climb up the back of my throat. I taste it in my mouth.

Kade keeps the gun on him.

"Stop where you are, Bennett."

"Is that an order, sir?" Todd's voice is honey and broken glass. He's relishing this, the standoff, the audience, the script he's written in his head a hundred times. "Last I checked, I wasn't under your command," he adds with a smirk.

For a heartbeat, I'm outside my own body. I see them as if through glass, two men in a parking lot, one holding a pistol, the other revealing truth. Both locked in a dance older than language.

"Tell me where she is, Kade. Then walk away. Be smart. Like Ryland."

I should run. I know this. But my body is encased in concrete. My brain is running too many calculations at once. If I run, Todd will chase. If I stay, maybe Kade will keep him away. If I scream, maybe someone will come, but then again, maybe no one will.

"I have one job to do, and that is to protect her. Even if you were my brother, and you're not, I'd still do my job."

"Your *job*? Were you doing your *job* in Afghanistan when Ryland shot Thurmond? I think not, my friend." He steps back, eyes locked on Kade's. "You can shoot me if you want. But it won't fix anything. You let me take the fall for Ryland. How do you live with that?"

Kade's eyes narrow.

Todd licks his lips. "You were never the hero, Wes. None of us were. Except Ryland. A chest full of medals to prove it. But at least I admit it."

"You're not here for her!" Kade shouts. "Not really. You're here for Ryland."

Todd laughs, a hollow, deep sound.

"Ryland's the reason I'm here at all. I negotiated this with him. He gives me my girl, and his debt's paid. You weren't innocent. You let him frame me. So, your debt, too, my friend, could be paid if you just hand her over to me."

Ryland's the reason Todd is here? My mind reels. It can't be true. I can't trust what Todd is saying. This is another one of his mind games.

"Ryland's not the one holding a gun on you, Bennett. Whatever happened back then, this is on you now."

I clasp a hand over my mouth to keep from making a noise. Kade's not denying it. It's true. What Todd is saying is true. It can't be. My heart is squeezed with the iron fist of betrayal.

Todd looks at Kade.

"You and Ryland both owe me. And now it's time to pay the piper. Tell me where she's at and step aside. Handle the paperwork like Ryland's good boy, and he'll sign off on it." Todd scoffs, then adds, "How's it feel, being his dog on a new leash, anyway?"

"Clever, Todd. Very clever. Why would Ryland go along with that?"

"He didn't have to. He could've been stripped of his medals. Lost his career. Probably lost his family when they put him in jail."

"On your knees, or I will shoot." Kade's voice thunders with the resolve of a man who will not hesitate.

"Oh, but you want to." Todd takes a step forward. "Because you know that when Ryland shows up, I'll get my girl back anyway."

My stomach churns at Todd's reference to me as *his girl*. He once told me, *"You are mine and I don't share."* I thought he was delusional, but I think he really believes it.

"You're insane," Kade's voice is cold as the night.

Todd shrugs.

The world blurs at the edges, watching two men locked in hatred and history, frozen by the lens of my fear. It's at this moment that I realize: I'm not a survivor. I'm a witness. My mind claws through the details.

Sergeant Kade.

Ryland.

Todd took the fall for Ryland.

Debts. Is this about Kade's Afghanistan story? Has Kade known Todd all this time?

I remember the coin Kade pressed into my hand, the warmth of his fingers closing around mine.

Was it comfort or warning?

I look at Kade now, really look, and for the first time, I see the sadness in him. A kind of exhaustion, not just of the body but of the soul. He wants this over. Not just tonight, but all of it.

Kade's jaw tics. "You take one step, and I'll drop you."

Todd grins wider, teeth bared. He raises his hands in mock surrender. "Relax. We're just talkin'. Kathryn, sweetheart. Come out, come out, wherever you are." He uses the same Southern drawl I found charming the first time I met him. It makes me sick.

Kade steps toward Todd. "This can end badly or peaceably. Get on your knees, interlace your hands behind your head."

"You didn't tell her that you knew me, did you?" Todd shrugs again, like Kade just asked him to take his plate to the sink after dinner.

I want to run so badly I can feel the flight in my calves, but I'm paralyzed. By Todd. By Kade. By Ryland. *How? How could this have happened?*

Todd arches his neck and shouts. "It's not your fault, Kathryn! You deserve to know, sweetheart. You think they're protecting you? They're not. Come home with me, Kathryn, where you belong."

"Don't listen to him." Kade's jaw tightens. His eyes flick in my direction for the briefest second. I see it there: not just calculation, but something like an apology. Maybe regret. Maybe fear.

"Is that where she is?" Todd turns toward me. "She's over there?"

A thousand tiny ants crawl on my skin. I grip the knife tightly, knuckles white. If he finds me, I will be ready.

"Eyes on me, Todd!"

Headlights bounce, painting the darkness with light. A car engine sounds. Tires crunch gravel, then slide. A car door opens but doesn't shut. Movement at the far end of the lot. Kade and Todd both snap their heads in the same direction. I can't see what's coming.

Ryland. There's no mistaking the silhouette: the lean frame, the ramrod posture, the military neatness of every gesture. For a second, I think he's a mirage, but the glint off the gun in his hand is real. He folds his hands behind his back and stops less than ten feet from Todd.

"Bennett," he says casually.

Todd grins, all teeth.

"Ryland. I'm glad to see you. Can you talk sense into Kade? You said you had him handled."

"Sure. Kade, kill 'em." Ryland's voice is like a file against stone.

"You facilitated this?" Kade's tone rises at the end. He's as surprised as I am.

Ryland turns to Kade, eyes narrowing. "How else do you think he got in without you knowing? The asset is your responsibility. Protect her. End this, Kade. Now!"

"*You* set *me* up to take *him* out because he was threatening *you*?"

"Not your place to ask," Ryland snaps back with authority.

Todd balls his fists at his sides. "You son of a bitch! You told me Kade wouldn't be an issue." His voice is primal, thick.

Ryland's head swivels between Kade and Todd.

"Do it, Kade. Do your job."

Todd charges straight at Ryland, arms swinging.

A gun goes off. A deafening crack. I watch the gun flick up in Ryland's hand. Todd slams into him. They land on the gravel with a sound I will carry forever. The gun skitters across the gravel as the two men grapple. Kade lunges, kicking it further out of reach. I don't see where it lands.

Ryland shoves Todd off. Rising to his feet, he adjusts his cuffs, as if the whole confrontation was a minor inconvenience.

Todd collapses onto his back, one hand clutching the growing crimson stain on his chest. His strength is fading, but he still claws at Ryland, refusing to relent.

"Finish it." Ryland's voice is devoid of emotion. "He's done."

Kade hesitates, eyes flickering between Todd's broken form and Ryland's cold steel gaze.

Todd weakly slithers toward Ryland, face wild, animalistic. Strangled sounds escape his throat.

Kade circles, gun tracking.

"It's over, Bennett."

Todd bares his teeth. For a moment, I see the boy he must have been, the one who wanted to be a hero, a soldier, but never got the chance because Ryland stole it from him.

Ryland tosses his head from side to side. "Finish the job, Kade."

There's no grace in the ugly choreography of violence.

I don't move. I sit in silence. I don't know if I will run or if I will stay.

All I know is, it's not over.

Chapter 41

Kade

My hands are steady, but only because I'm trained, over and over, in sand and jungle and the drywall labyrinths of urban combat. My posture is rigid, the barrel of the gun tracking with my eyes. It's the only thing in the world not shaking.

Bennett lies there, body crumpled. His blood spreads into a black disk on his shirt. For a second, I think he'll make another move, but then his head rolls to the side, and he exhales a long, wet sigh.

There's blood on Ryland's face, another splash on the collar of his suit. He brushes grit off his pant leg. He squares his shoulders, all business now. He inspects his jacket, tries and fails to wipe off a blood stain on his cuff.

I should have known better than to trust Ryland from the moment he assigned me to Wildfire. Should have seen the trap he was laying, the strings he was pulling. But he played me. I let him convince me that taking on this case was my duty, my chance at redemption, as if anything could wash away the sins of our past.

Ryland's eyes meet mine. They are glassy, opal-colored, and perfectly dry. Mine are not. I can feel tears threatening to spill over. The throbbing in my head intensified the moment the gunshot pierced the air. It feels like it's going to explode.

"Standard protocol. You had every right to shoot Bennett. Should've done it as soon as you saw him."

Bennett makes a noise, a small whimper, then a cough. He rolls halfway onto his side, hands pressed to the wound. There's a tremor in his legs, the involuntary dance of a man whose body refuses to quit. He looks at me, and for a moment, the old Private Bennett is there: the brother in arms, the man who looked up to me as his sergeant, who once fixed a jammed M9 with nothing but a bottle opener. Then it's gone, replaced by the rage that made him what he is tonight.

Ryland walks a slow circle, surveying the carnage. He kneels beside Todd, checks the pulse at his neck, then stands again.

"He's still alive." He says it with the disappointment of a child denied his favorite toy. "Finish it. I'll sign off on it."

I say nothing. I can't. The silence returns, thicker now. My vision blurs at the edges. I taste bile at the back of my throat.

"You used Maddie."

Ryland faces me, head cocked.

"I needed eyes and ears, and she wants a promotion. What difference does it make?"

I swallow, trying to steady my breathing, but it's like drawing air through a broken reed. "Why are you doing this?"

Ryland's gaze sharpens. "You want a reason? Because Bennett was going to keep coming. Do you know how many times I've had to do him favors, bail him out so he wouldn't tell what really happened in Afghanistan? He would've just as easily killed you, then gone after Quinn or whatever her name is. He's a liability to you and me."

I shake my head once. "You."

Ryland scoffs. "What?"

I gesture at Todd's body. "He was a liability to *you*. He never asked me for a single favor because I'm not the one who killed Thurmond."

His eyes turn cold. For a moment, I see the old Ryland, the one from Afghanistan, who could order a dozen men into the meat grinder and not flinch.

"This is what the job is. Just this, over and over." He waves his forefinger around Todd's body.

Bennett groans again, softer now.

Ryland steps back, gives me a nod. "Finish it, or I will."

I can't move. I want to, but my feet are cemented to the ground. The only thing I feel is the gun, the way it's an extension of my hand, my will, my guilt.

Bennett's eyes meet mine, a plea. His eyes are telling me not to do it. The blood pools and spreads, slick and shiny.

The gravity of what Ryland is asking threads through every cell in my body. This was supposed to be protection. It was an execution. I look down at my hands. They don't shake. Maybe they should.

Ryland eyes Todd with the same look he once reserved for broken gear: a brief inventory, then a silent calculation of the cost to repair or replace.

"C'mon, Kade. You screwed up. You should've just left her with Stony. This is on you. Put the wounded dog out of its misery."

I'm horrified when I see Ryland kick Todd's defenseless body. He glances around, spots the pistol where I kicked it. I watch as he picks it up, wipes the grip, then slides it into his shoulder holster with a movement so smooth it barely disturbs the air. He keys a radio clipped to his belt and speaks in code.

"Target is down. Send a crew to Little Wanganui Hotel, back by the cabins. Scene is hot. Repeat, scene is hot."

He lets go of the mic, his finger lingering for a half-beat before clipping it back. Ryland watches me, arms crossed, waiting for me to step up and do the right thing—*his* right thing. I kneel beside Bennett. His eyes flick up, see me, and a thin line of saliva leaks from the corner of his mouth.

"You always were . . . soft." The words catch on the edge of Bennett's ruined throat.

Ryland circles around me. "Don't make this personal."

I feel the weight of the gun in my hand. The weight of every decision that brought me here. The weight of Tara, and the fear that this was never about protecting her. It was about Ryland settling the score with Todd.

"This isn't what you said my assignment would be." I look at Ryland.

Ryland smiles. "It never is. You know that."

"What about the asset?"

Ryland's smile is all teeth. "She's your asset, Kade. Your problem. Get her out of the line of fire, or don't. Makes no difference to me."

My eyes flick back to Bennett. I remember the first time I shot a man. It was supposed to be clean, clinical, over before I had a chance to think. But it's never that simple. The act lingers, threads itself through every minute of your life that comes after.

I clench my jaw. I will not be the instrument of his version of the story. Ryland used me. Used Bennett. Worse, he used Tara Quinn.

I push off from the blood-wet gravel. When I get to my feet, I see Ryland's gun is now in his hand, down by his side. Instinctively, I train my own gun on him. Or Todd, depending on a flick of the wrist. I see Bennett's right leg spasming, the way a dying animal tries to flee. For a brief, delusional moment, I think Ryland will let him die on his own terms. But then I see the set of his jaw, the way his hand hesitates.

"The cleanup crew is ten out. End him," Ryland demands.

His gun is pointed at Todd now. If I don't shoot, he will. "Don't do it. Step away from him," I bark, and my body moves before my mind does. I lunge forward, gun raised, half-hopeful I'll miss, half-sure I won't.

I grip the gun, feel the tendons in my arm scream. My chest is a tight box full of broken glass.

Ryland gives me a look that could freeze helium. "Don't be a child, Kade. This is non-negotiable."

He steps closer to Bennett, looming over him. I catch a flicker of movement at the edge of my vision, it's the bartender, hunched in the doorway of the hotel, pretending not to watch but failing.

"What's the plan? You gonna kill me and him, too?" I nod toward the bartender.

Ryland looks over his shoulder, then back at Todd and finally, directly at me. "After."

"After what?" I already know the answer, but I'm trying to distract him.

"After I kill him."

Ryland fires, and in the same instant, so do I.

The world explodes sideways. The noise is a crack of thunder, echoing off the timber. A molten spike tears through my body, spins me ninety degrees. I see a red halo blooming from Ryland's right temple just before I crash into the mud.

The bartender yells something, but the sound doesn't reach me. I taste metal, hot and thick. The pain is immense, but distant, like static from a radio in the next room. I try to push myself up, but the left side of my body won't respond. My breath comes in wet, ragged hitches.

Both men are still. The only evidence of the struggle is the pooling blood seeping out, black on black, impossible to tell whose is whose. The raw evidence of every bad decision I've ever made. I want to say something, some benediction or last rite. I try to speak, but all that comes out is a cough and a splatter of blood.

Sirens are approaching, faint at first. Maybe it's just the ringing in my ears. Someone will have to write the report.

I close my eyes and let the pain take me. For a moment, there's nothing but Tara's face, alive and terrified, but safe.

In the end, nobody gets what they want.

CHAPTER 42

TARA

The gun smoke stings my nostrils. My eyes blur with tears. I stop the video recording on my phone with a tap, then slide it into my pocket. I rise from behind the ice machine, clutching the knife in my trembling hand. Three forms lie crumpled and still. I can't tell who's dead and who's wounded, not from here.

Slowly, I emerge from my hiding spot. I peek past the ice machine. The service door hangs open, swaying slightly. The bartender must have run inside, fleeing to safety.

Forcing my spine straight, I step out. I walk, measured and deliberate, toward Todd. He looks weak lying there. Pathetic. Harmless. I know better.

His eyes snap open as I approach. He finds me instantly, like he always did. Even now, even ruined, his stare is a needle threading through the old holes he pierced into my soul. His lips twist into a gruesome smile, that smug, arrogant smile.

"I knew you'd come," he whispers.

That's the last straw. My vision pulses red.

White-hot rage detonates inside me. I plunge the knife into his chest with a force beyond me. I barely register the resistance of skin, muscle, and bone. His body jolts. Blood sprays up, stippling my chin and shirt. I rip the knife free. The sound of steel against flesh and bone is so raw, I gag. The metallic stink of blood blooms, coating my tongue. The knife goes in again. And again. The third time is easy, the fourth easier still. Every stab pulls something poisonous out of me, replacing it with something Todd took from me long ago.

Todd's blood paints my hands, my arms. I can't stop. Won't stop. I need to be sure he's gone, that he can never hurt me or anyone again.

"Tara," Kade's wheezy voice cracks through my mania like a whip. I freeze, the knife poised for another strike.

Clarity returns in a nauseating rush.

Oh God! What have I done?

I step back, the knife falling from my hand with a clatter against the gravel. My hands are coated in blood. The trembling won't stop. I drop to my knees and look at what I've done, at the ruin I've made of Todd's chest. Todd's face is slack, drained of life. Todd Bennett is dead. Gone for good. Gone in a way that defies resurrection.

Hot tears rain down my face, unstoppable. They carve lines through the blood splatter.

Kade coughs, then manages, "You have to go. Now." He hisses as pain hits him.

I look up. I see a bright light. Not red or blue. White. The beam pins us like insects. I raise a bloody hand to shield my eyes and squint into the light.

"Don't trust anyone. Except . . ." His mouth goes slack, eyes rolling up for a second. "Cooper. Trust him. No one else."

A silhouette emerges into the light. Thin. Feminine. Maddie. Her face drops when she sees the carnage. She pauses, then bends down to check Ryland's pulse. She doesn't find one.

Kade lifts his head, teeth gritted against a wave of agony. "Get her out of here. Somewhere safe."

His head drops with a thud. I stare at him, frozen.

"Is he dead?"

Maddie reaches for me, her nails carving crescents into my arm.

"Tara. In the car. Now." Her eyes are locked on me, bright and ferocious.

I look at the knife, slick and red, lying on the ground. Maddie covers her hand with her sleeve and lifts it. She wipes it, clean-ish. Then she bends down and, with clinical detachment, curls Ryland's dead fingers around the handle.

I stare, open-mouthed. "That's—" I start, but my mouth stops working. I feel cracked open by another secret I must bury.

"Let's move." Maddie tugs my arm. My body follows. She calls over her shoulder, "I got 'er, Kade."

The wail of a siren splits the quiet. Maddie's pace quickens, and I struggle to keep in step with her. Her car is a battered Corolla that smells of sour coffee and wet dog. She pushes me into the passenger seat.

"Don't touch anything."

Maddie buckles me in. She guns it out of the lot, tires screeching. I look back through the window, see Kade's shape still slumped where I left him. I don't know if he's breathing. I don't know if he'll live. I don't know if I want him to.

We drive. My hands tremble in my lap, blood drying into a rusty crust. I try to wipe them on my pants, but it only makes the stain larger, more obvious.

Maddie slows as we pass an emergency vehicle coming from the opposite direction. The flashing lights blind me. I close my eyes. She reaches for her purse in the backseat. Dumps its contents.

"Here. Put your hands in here. Don't look at them." Maddie holds open the purse, and I slide my hands inside.

"Don't take them out until I say, okay?"

I nod.

Maddie keeps one eye on the rearview mirror.

"What the hell happened?"

"I have a . . ." I hesitate. The video. The blue phone in my pocket. Kade said to trust Cooper. He didn't say anything about Maddie. "Where are you taking me?"

"I'm taking you back to my place to get you cleaned up. Can you tell me what happened?"

I shake my head. *Ryland was working with Maddie . . . for her promotion.*

"Talk to me, Tara. Are you okay?"

I don't respond. Instead, I stare at the door handle and imagine flinging myself onto the asphalt. Then I remember the knife. She put Ryland's fingerprints on the blade.

I'm alive.

Dizzy.

Panicked.

"I killed him," I utter. I keep my hands buried in her purse, not daring to look at the blood drying on my skin.

She nods, not looking at me. "You finished it." She says it like she's talking about taking out the trash.

Nothing feels finished. For now, I am content to no longer have a reason to be afraid of the dark, or of the night, or of the things that live inside either one.

"Cooper's on his way from the States. He'll be here tomorrow."

My mind spins. *Cooper. Bill Cooper.*

"Where are we going?" My voice cracks.

"Auckland. I have a guy who owes me a favor. We can make it look like we never crossed the Cook Strait." She checks the rearview, then the dash. "Tonight's a long haul, but Cooper lands in about sixteen hours."

"What happens after?" I ask. "After Cooper gets here?"

"The U.S. Marshals will want to debrief you—probably Cooper himself, maybe someone else from the VPP. They'll want to know everything about tonight."

"I killed him." The words come out so quiet I'm not sure she hears.

Maddie's foot lifts from the gas. "You did what you had to do. After what Ryland did, they'll write you a medal. Or at least a pardon."

My skin prickles. "You put the knife in Ryland's hand."

"It's what Kade would've done if he'd been able. I just made it easier for the police to leave you out of it. Ryland's prints will be all over the handle."

I'm not sure of anything anymore—who's real, what's true, or what darkness waits beyond dawn. The only thing I know with unshakable certainty is that I trust Cooper. When he comes, I'll have to stick to Maddie's version, the one with Ryland as the villain and me as the accidental survivor. I wonder if he'll believe it.

"And you . . .," she glances over to her purse, the mess of me, ". . . need a change of clothes. I have a go bag in the trunk."

I want to ask why she has a go bag, but I realize it's probably standard operating procedure for every employee of the U.S. Marshal Service. I hunker lower in my seat and pull the purse tighter around my hands. I wish I could disappear inside it. Become a receipt, a smudged lipstick, a pack of gum that's lost its flavor.

My heart leaps into my throat as Maddie steers the car into a scenic overlook and cuts the engine. "Why are we stopping here?" I ask, my voice tight. The place is deserted, nothing but the black void of the cliff's edge beyond the guardrail.

"Stay here." Maddie cuts the engine and gets out.

I twist in my seat, and anxiously watch as she pops the trunk and rummages around. *Is she grabbing a weapon to finish me off and dump my body over the cliff?* My mind spins worst-case scenarios.

But then Maddie opens my door, a water bottle in one hand and a small duffel bag in the other. "Hold out your hands," she says softly.

I hesitate, then slowly extend my arms, the dried blood cracking along my knuckles. Maddie unscrews the cap and pours the water over my hands. It's cold, shockingly so, and I gasp as rivulets of pink water run down my wrists.

"Take off your shirt," she instructs. "Use it to clean your hands and your face. Change into the clothes in the bag, then we'll put your old clothes and my purse in."

Maddie walks back to the trunk. The efficiency is terrifying. Maddie never panics. She just adapts.

I do as I'm told, and bring the bag around to the back of the car. "Why are you helping me?"

"Because I promised Kade. And because you don't deserve what happened to you. No one does."

We get back on the road and I glance over at Maddie. Her eyes flick to the rearview mirror again, scanning the road behind us. The concern etched on her face does little to ease the dread in my gut. I don't want to ask, but I do. "You were working with Ryland."

Maddie flinches. "I never sold you out, Tara. I helped him with . . . tech stuff. That's it." Her gaze briefly meets mine before returning to the road. "I thought Ryland didn't trust Kade, and that I was helping to keep you safe."

The urge to believe her is as strong as the urge to punch her in the face. Todd's blood no longer crusts my fingernails, but it has seeped into every cell of my being. It is a stain that will never wash away. I crossed a line I can't uncross. I'm no longer a victim. I am what I feared most—a killer.

What Follows

By Kathryn Caraway

Tara Quinn has killed once. Now, she must decide how far she will go to protect other victims.

She escaped a sadistic stalker and a botched federal relocation abroad, but the blood on her hands refuses to fade. Now she's back in the U.S., scarred, hardened, and determined to turn her pain into purpose for other victims.

When a desperate plea for help exposes a predator exploiting her work to evade the law, Tara must unmask the stalker lurking in the shadows of her good intentions—or risk more blood on her hands. But this predator is more cunning and ruthless than the one she survived—and one wrong move could be her last.

Some wounds never heal. They sharpen into weapons.

A NOTE FROM THE AUTHOR

On the surface, I am like any other woman. I stay busy running errands, caring for my beloved dog, and cooking new recipes for dinner. Beneath the surface, I live with the weight of waiting—for a knock, a shadow, a death I won't see coming.

Writing *Unfollow Me*, my true crime memoir, meant I had to sift through difficult memories, confront pain, and shape my messy reality into a story that readers could follow. In doing that work, I learned how a well-chosen detail can pull a reader straight into a scene.

But something else happened: after sharing so much of myself, I felt a creative itch to explore what-ifs. Writing this fictional alternative ending to *Unfollow Me* allowed me to illustrate what life after a conviction might look like for a victim of stalking. There's a verdict, a sentence, and the assumption that justice closes the door. Nobody tells you that, on the other side of that door, I would feel locked in a world where fear, paranoia, and anxiety hum constantly.

Fiction allowed me the freedom to share the truth of that aftermath. I could bend timelines, invent characters, and push my imagination into places my real life could never go while still exploring the themes that matter to me—resilience, justice, survival. The truth will always be my foundation, but writing fiction after a memoir felt like stepping out of a cage and onto an open stage.

Today, I'm thankful to be in a safe, happy place—a place where I'm surrounded by love and support. I am grateful for the freedom to work on

THE UNFOLLOW ME PROJECT and to write books that shine the light on stalking. Every page feels like my small way of turning fear into understanding and to remind others that victims of stalking deserve empathy, safety, and a voice.

Kathryn Caraway

g goodreads.com/kathryn_caraway

♪ tiktok.com/@k_caraway

⊙ instagram.com/un.follow.me_kc

f facebook.com/authorkathryncaraway

𝕏 x.com/UnfollowMe_KC

@ threads.com/@un.follow.me_kc

Also by Kathryn Caraway

Unfollow Me

He Follows Me

What Follows